A Clean Break

Also by Keira Andrews

KEIRA ANDREWS

A CLEAN
BREAK

A Clean Break
Written and published by Keira Andrews

Copyright © 2015 by Keira Andrews
Print Edition

ISBN: 978-0-9938598-7-8

Cover by Dar Albert
Formatting by BB eBooks

Acknowledgments

Thanks to Anne-Marie, Becky, and Mary for their cheerleading and excellent beta work, and Lisa and Aimee for their Filipino expertise and friendship. Special thanks to Rachel for whipping this book into the shape it needed to be—and for doing it with love, as always. My gratitude again to the ex-Amish who have shared their stories and answered my many questions while writing this series, and to Heidi Cullinan for sharing her love for *A Forbidden Rumspringa* on Twitter and introducing Isaac and David to so many new readers.

Author's Note

The most surprising thing I learned while researching this series was how much variation exists in the Amish world. My settlement of Zebulon is fictional, but is based upon the practices of the Swartzentruber Amish, one of the most conservative subgroups of the Old Order. I discovered that even among the Swartzentrubers, each community has its own rules. Something that may be true of one Amish settlement might not be true of another.

PART ONE

CHAPTER One

THE WORLD WAS waking.

A bird chirping beyond the window was the only familiar sound David could pick out amid the hum of engines and the distant tolling of a bell. His stomach fluttered as he opened his eyes and realized it was still true—Isaac was with him in the plush guest bed in San Francisco. *San Francisco!*

From David's spot stretched out on his back, he could glimpse himself beyond Isaac in the mirrored closet doors, full length, and ever-so vain. In the reflection he could see Isaac's face, slack with lips parted as he breathed deeply on his side, the thick quilt-like blanket pulled high over his bare shoulders. David barely resisted the urge to caress Isaac's mussed sandy hair.

They'd started out in each other's arms, naked and damp from a quick shower. David wondered if he could draw Isaac near again without waking him. Probably not, and Isaac needed to rest. Still, he ghosted his hand over Isaac's head.

It hadn't been a dream. They'd really done it. They'd left Zebulon behind.

Here in Aaron's house, it was so deliciously warm. David had always woken after midnight in winters to stoke the wood-burning stove downstairs. He hated sleeping with socks, and he'd hopped around on the icy floors in the darkness, shoving more wood into the maw of the stove and welcoming the sparks that nipped his toes.

As more gray light squeezed between the slats of the blinds covering the window above the bed, David stared at a huge black and white photograph of the Golden Gate Bridge hanging over a sleek black dresser. The picture's silver frame gleamed.

The bed itself was what the English called queen sized, and the mattress felt as though it was five feet thick. David wasn't sure he'd ever experienced anything quite so comfortable. They didn't have any chairs or seats with cushioning in Zebulon, yet here even the headboard was padded.

Excitement thrummed in David with each beat of his heart. He was all the way in *California*! It was a place he'd seen in the movies on his secret trips to the drive-in. He wondered if they might visit the bridge, and he knew Isaac would want to go to the water. They'd actually made it to *the ocean*. After all his hopeless dreaming and despair, they'd really done it.

In the end he and Isaac had run with nothing more than the clothes on their backs. A hiss echoed in his mind, reminding him that he'd run away from more than the church. He'd left Mother and the girls alone. Sweet Mary, and Anna, and Sarah, and—

Stop! What's done is done.

For a minute, David could only concentrate on breathing in and out as the swell of panic receded. Beside him, Isaac murmured and stirred before settling back into sleep, still curled away on his side. David listened to the lullaby of Isaac's inhalations and exhalations.

On bus after bus from Minnesota to California, he and Isaac had sat with shoulders and knees pressed close, their fingers threaded together as the miles ticked by. Flat expanses had given way to hills and mountains, and then the desert. Never had David seen for himself just how vast the world truly was, and America was only a small part of it.

Time had lost meaning, and he imagined it might be what purgatory was like. They'd watched the land go by through dingy glass, only stopping in bus stations choked with exhaust and rumbling engines. In the darkness of long nights broken by only the harsh glare of the station lights, David had felt like they might never get to San Francisco. It all seemed like some kind of dream. But now they were here. It was *real*.

Isaac snorted and rolled toward him before falling quiet again, his lips still parted. With a smile, David folded his hands behind his head and watched. He wanted to trace the freckles that danced across Isaac's nose and the tops of his cheeks, and kiss the corners of his eyelids to feel the flutter of his pretty lashes. Rub against the stubble on his face as their lips met, and see the amber of Isaac's eyes as they opened.

David glanced at the electric clock with glowing red numbers on the table beside him. It was after seven, but they hadn't been sleeping long. As much as David wanted Isaac against him, to simply have the freedom to watch him sleep was more than he'd thought possible. The only other time they'd shared a bed, there was no time for rest.

Quick as a snakebite, the familiar guilt returned, images of that day spilling through his mind. *Scratchy sheets and yellow blankets at the Wildwood Inn, he and Isaac sweaty and sticky in their own world. The blinding white of the snow, and the crimson blood. The gray hospital, and—*

He squeezed his eyes shut. No matter what anyone might say, the accident was his fault. If he'd resisted the selfish need to sneak away with Isaac, his mother would never have been hurt. Even if he gave her all his savings for the hospital bill, how would she and the girls get by on their own?

It had been three days now. He tried to imagine what they were doing right that moment. Were they going on like usual with washing and cooking and cleaning? What if Mary or Anna needed help with the sticky latch on the icehouse door? What of the barn work, and the horses? Kaffi could be a handful early in the mornings when he was grumpy and stubborn.

David thought of the inadequate note he'd scrawled over a scrap of paper on the kitchen table.

Isaac and I are going into the world. I will write soon, and please tell his parents he will too. June Baker has money for you. Kaffi is there. I am sorry.

He knew Mother wouldn't understand his choice. He could write her a thousand letters, and it would never matter. He still heard the echo of her wail in church on Sunday before he and Isaac had run from Zebulon.

"Why does God punish me?"

It was the only time he could remember Mother showing such emotion, even when his brother and father died. To hear her dare question God's will still made him shiver.

She deserved an explanation, but David could never tell her the truth about loving Isaac. He was an abomination in the eyes of the Lord and the church. He thought of the English word he'd heard in the movies—gay. Mother could never understand it. That he'd rejected the plain life was already undoubtedly a heartbreak for his family. If he told them who he really was...

His chest tightened. They could never understand. It was unthinkable. He imagined it going one of two ways—either they would do everything to convince him to repent and live a good Amish life, or they would shun him. Even if he wasn't officially *Meidung* in Zebulon since he hadn't followed church, his family could shut him out all the same.

Beside him, Isaac mumbled and shifted before settling back into sleep with a little rattle that wasn't quite a snore. A line of drool spilled onto his pillow. David smiled to himself, again resisting the urge to hold Isaac close.

We're really here.

Watching Isaac, David shoved his thoughts deep inside. No matter how much he hated himself for abandoning Mother and the girls, he'd had to leave. He had no doubt he was going to hell, since without joining the church heaven was far out of reach. Never mind his multitude of other sins. But it was the only path he could take.

For so long he'd tried to be a good Amish man. But when it came time to give his vow to God and join the church, he'd faced the truth. On his knees in front of Bishop Yoder and all of Zebulon, David had said the only thing he could: *no.* To say yes would have been a betrayal not only of his heart and honor, but of Isaac.

And he would not betray his Isaac. Watching him, David again resisted the urge to pull him near and kiss him awake so he could see Isaac's smile. After the accident, David had caused such misery when Isaac deserved only joy.

Even before they'd become lovers, working side by side each day had given David a new sense of peace. Even a new appreciation for carpentry. Isaac had been the one to show him what true happiness and companionship was. Exhilaration rushed through him at the thought that soon they'd work together again. He didn't know how or where, but they'd make it. They'd build a life with new tools, piece by piece.

As he stretched his arms over his head, David wondered if Aaron was awake yet. The house felt still, so he didn't think so. The bus hadn't arrived until one-thirty in the morning, but Aaron had still picked them up at the station. Isaac and his brother had hugged each other for a long time by the car in the cold rain.

The city had seemed ghostly in the small hours, almost empty but for the lights peppering the glass and concrete. David had sat in the back of the car, craning his neck to see the tall shadows of buildings looming beyond the fog. He could hardly believe this place was real. It was a far cry from the little towns of Northern Minnesota.

They hadn't spoken much on the drive to Aaron's home—a townhouse, he'd called it—in a place in the city called Bernal Heights. There was so much to say, and David supposed they hadn't known just where to start. It was still hard to imagine that Aaron was welcoming them with open arms even knowing the truth about their sin.

As the guest room brightened inch by inch, David wondered what it would be like to see his own brother again. For a minute, he let himself imagine that Joshua had only been lost to the world like Aaron. He could still hear the last words Joshua had said when he climbed out their bedroom window that night with a wink and a smile.

"Don't wait up."

David hadn't, and he told himself it wouldn't have made any difference—that even if he'd crept to Mother and Father's room to whisper the truth, Joshua and those poor girls would have already been dead, caught in the current of the Ragman River. He told himself he hadn't failed his brother with his misplaced loyalty and cowardice.

He wished he had a picture of Joshua to remember him by. It had been more than seven years, and Joshua's sharp smile was growing soft around the edges in David's mind. Would the memory of his mother and sisters fade too?

With another long look at Isaac, David tiptoed over the smooth wooden floor to the tall mirrors. He hadn't shaved in days, and he rubbed a hand over his rough cheeks. He supposed he could grow a full beard if he wanted. A mustache, even. There would be no Amish beard hanging off the bottom of his chin now that he'd refused baptism. Or he could simply shave every day as he'd always done.

The choice was his, and he smiled faintly at the notion. His light blue eyes had been red-rimmed the last time he'd looked in a mirror—dirty with a jagged crack in the corner—in a bus station bathroom in Reno. David blinked at his reflection now. He was pale, and his dark brown hair was sticking up after going to sleep with it wet. He patted it down uselessly. It was growing over his ears in the Amish style, but now he was free to cut it as short as he liked. Maybe he could go to a real barbershop.

His gaze swept down the reflection of his body. Although he'd seen his face many times in the bathroom mirror at June's, he'd never looked at himself without clothes on. It gave him a strange little thrill as he traced a finger over his chest, and the dark hair scattered there over his reddish nipples.

There was more hair leading down from his belly to his cock, which was half hard as usual when he woke up. He pulled down his foreskin lightly to look at the head, and a tingle shot up his spine. After a few tugs, he continued his exploration.

More hair sprinkled his thighs, and when he turned his back to the mirror and peeked over his shoulder, he was pleased to see his rear was round and tight, and overall he was muscular and lean. To be admiring his own body was sinfully vain, and strictly against the Amish rules, of course. But there was no one to stop or shame him here. Not about mirrors or pride or *anything*.

Now that he could do everything, David wasn't sure what to do first. He watched Isaac in the reflection again, smiling to himself as Isaac smacked his lips and sprawled onto his back. Every time David had woken on the bus, Isaac had been peering out the window with his forehead against the glass. David wished they could've taken one of Isaac's beloved trains to California, but the bus had been easier.

He'd tucked away the names of all the places they'd rolled through on their way—Fargo, Bismarck, Miles City, Butte, Rexburg, Idaho Falls, Salt Lake City, Battle Mountain, Sacramento, and a dozen more little towns and outposts. He wanted to go back and see them all one day. He wanted to see everything.

"Go see the world."

David's chest tightened at the memory of June driving them to Grand Forks that night. She hadn't asked a single question, and had smiled so brightly, supporting him without judgment as she had since they'd met. He'd always thanked God that something good had come out of that terrible day.

Racing over the field to Father's side, the corn stalks slapping against him. Gripping Kaffi with his thighs as they thundered through the trees to June's. The sun-baked wood of June's porch under him as he struggled to breathe, her calm voice talking to whoever answered nine-one-one, her hand solid on David's shoulder.

He wasn't sure now how his later visits to June had gone from sipping lemonade to setting up a workshop there and borrowing her truck to taste the English world. He'd tamped down his curiosity for years, especially after Joshua. But bit by bit, something inside him had loosened the more times he visited June. She'd never pushed or judged.

And now here he was, more miles from home than he'd dreamed possible. In the mirror, he peered at June's purple suitcase on the floor. He'd had a small collection of English clothes at his secret workshop at June's farm that they'd changed into before leaving.

They'd left their hats behind at church when they ran, but inside the suitcase were their plain clothes. Clothes their mothers had made. Clothes they would never wear again unless they went back. David looked at himself, naked and free. No. They could never go back.

As the Greyhound had pulled up in the bitter January wind, June had held him close and said she loved him. He'd never heard his parents say that to him or any of his siblings in all his years. It just wasn't their way to talk of such things. He knew Mother did love him, but to hear it from June had made him warm inside even as snow drove into their eyes.

He blinked at his reflection. He kept waiting to find himself alone in his bed in Zebulon—his mother and sisters buzzing around downstairs, lighting the lanterns. They were two hours ahead in Minnesota, and right now he'd be in the barn at his worktable, and one of the girls would have brought a snack soon—apple bread or sugar cookies.

Would old Eli Helmuth help with the men's work around the place? Would he marry Mother and take care of the girls? How would they have enough money? Would they have everything they needed? David had to ask Aaron for a pen and paper to write them. Although when he imagined what he would say, his mind went blank.

He heard a muffled sound that was oddly familiar, and after a moment he realized it was water through pipes. Through a door beside the mirrored closets was the bathroom. In the tub there was a silver shower head you could lift in your hand and move all around while the water flowed endlessly like a waterfall. No heating up rainwater in the barn anymore, or tripping to the outhouse in the darkness.

Smiling, David listened to the distant rush of water and thought of mornings in the house back in Red Hills, when Joshua was young and happy. When *rumspringa* was just a faraway notion, and their family whole.

As the only two boys, he and Joshua had slept in narrow beds in the smallest room. The pipes in the wall were by David's head, and each morning—even before the rooster crowed—he woke to the rush of water as their parents began the day. Joshua would remain burrowed under the quilt for as long as possible, able to sleep even if a herd of cows had broken their fence and thundered by.

After they'd moved to Zebulon and their world changed to one of outhouses and lugging buckets of water into a tub in the kitchen, for months David had missed the rush of water in the mornings. Eventually he'd stopped thinking of it. It was like anything, he supposed. With enough time, it would be forgotten.

Before long the staircase creaked with footsteps, and David pulled on jeans and a T-shirt. He'd have to start wearing some kind of underwear if he was going to wear pants with zippers every day.

After another long look at Isaac, he closed the bedroom door quietly behind him and paused on the landing. He could hear someone downstairs in the kitchen, and the smell of fresh coffee already wafted up. It was silent on the floor above where Aaron and his wife slept. Jen had been working overnight at the hospital, and David wasn't sure if she'd come home yet.

He took a step, and jolted to a stop. *I didn't say my prayers.* Morning prayers were such an automatic part of his routine in Zebulon—sliding to his knees by his bed before he was barely awake. Now he stood stock still at the top of the stairs, not sure which way to turn.

Would God even listen now that David had turned his back on the church? On the Lord Himself? And more than that, he'd just woken next to his lover. Though he knew he should beg forgiveness for their sins, he couldn't. He wouldn't truly repent in his heart, and he would sin again—gladly—before the day was out. So what was the point?

Yet it felt wrong not to pray at all. With a glance around, David dropped quickly to his knees on the landing. Closing his eyes, he prayed for guidance, and the welfare of Mother, the girls, Isaac, and Isaac's family. He hoped that in these things, God would still be listening.

David was careful to be quiet on the stairs, the wood polished beneath his bare feet. The sun was up now, although the day was gray and wet. He peeked through the long window beside the door, and saw little more than fog. Steps led down to the street, and the red tail lights of a car glowed in the murk.

The main floor of the narrow townhouse had the same pale hardwood throughout, and the furniture was light as well, with green and purple cushions here and there. Tall windows made up one side of the living room, with an enormous television mounted on the wall nearby.

Most of the room was dominated by a lush wrap-around couch he thought was called a sectional, made in a pale beige. It had matching footrests he knew were ottomans. Then the space flowed into the dining room. David ran his fingers over the wide table, which was made of what he knew English people would call reclaimed wood. Pine, perhaps?

"It's rustic."

David jerked, turning to find Aaron on the other side of the white counter that separated the dining room from the kitchen. He smiled nervously, his heart skipping. "I like it."

He knew Aaron had told Isaac he didn't care that he was gay, and that David was welcome. But it was still hard to believe. Did Aaron *truly* not mind that David was sinning with his brother? As he tried desperately to think of something else to say, he wished he'd woken Isaac after all.

"Thanks. We wanted to mix up the modern look a bit. You could probably make something like it no problem." He held up his mug. "Coffee?"

"Yes. Thank you." David joined him in the kitchen, gazing at the stainless steel appliances and sleek white cupboards. Watery green tiles covered the wall by the wide sink beneath a window offering a view of a narrow garden and wooden deck with a round table and four chairs piled on each other. He touched the tiles tentatively. Glass, he thought.

Aaron chuckled as he poured the coffee. "This is probably the vainest kitchen you've ever seen, right?"

"Yes," David answered. "But I like it." He took the mug from Aaron and tried not to stare. Last night it had been dark and late, and he'd been too tired to pay much attention. But now he examined Aaron in the light of day.

David vaguely remembered him from years ago in Red Hills, but he wouldn't have recognized Aaron if not for the twinkle in his smile that was so reminiscent of Isaac. Aaron was blond and taller than he remembered—probably six-two; a bit bigger than David—and he looked so...*English*. He wore gray pants with a buttoned-up shirt and *pink* tie that matched little checks on his socks. His belt buckle gleamed around his slim waist.

David had to say something. "Um, how did you make the coffee so fast?"

"It's on a timer. Here, I'll show you." Aaron nodded toward a machine on the counter where he put the glass pot back into its slot. "See these buttons? You can set it to start brewing for whatever time you want. It's great to wake up and have it ready."

"I guess I'm used to Mother getting up early to make it. I have no idea how to do anything in the kitchen. I've seen things in movies, but..."

Aaron smiled easily. "Yeah, there's quite a learning curve. But you'll get the hang of it. Oh, did you want to try it with milk or sugar? I still just drink it black."

"No—this is fine." David took a sip, sighing as he swallowed the bitter liquid. He was struck by how light and happy Aaron seemed now. After following church, Aaron had been so somber. He heard Joshua's voice echo in his mind. *"If I end up as miserable as Aaron Byler, run me over with the plow."* How Joshua had laughed at David's scandalized expression.

"I thought you'd both be fast asleep most of the morning after that journey. I have to go into work until lunch, but I got a sub for my classes this afternoon and tomorrow."

"I don't know why I woke up." He gulped his coffee. *Aaron knows there's only one bed in there.*

But Aaron went on like everything was normal. "Are you hungry? Help yourself to anything." He opened a wood box on the counter. "There are bagels and bread in here, and that's the toaster. Do you know how to use it? It's plugged in already, so you just need to put the bread in the slots and press this knob down." He mimed the motion.

"Looks easy enough. I know a bit, I guess. I used a fridge at my friend June's."

"I spoke to her the other night after she took you to the bus station. I'm so glad she was able to help you guys. You can give her a call if you want. I did email her this morning to let her know you made it safe and sound."

For some reason, David hesitated. It would be wonderful to hear June's voice, but the thought of speaking to anyone close to Zebulon made his pulse race. "I will soon. I just want to settle in first."

"Take all the time you need. Believe me, I know this is a tough transition." Aaron sipped his coffee. "So, you like movies?"

"Uh-huh. There's a drive-in near Zebulon I'd go to sometimes. I took Isaac once." David ran his hand over the shiny stone counter, his ears burning as he remembered how that night had ended.

Isaac was beneath him on the ground, David fitting between his legs as if it was exactly how it was supposed to be. The wet heat of Isaac's generous kisses burned, and his fingers were tight in David's hair, his whisper hot.

"Yes."

Aaron grinned. "I'll show you how to use Netflix, and you can watch all the movies you want. If you have any questions about anything, just ask. I know how overwhelming it can be at first." He glanced at the clock on the microwave. "Jen came home a while ago. She'll sleep until the afternoon, but don't worry about noise. That's the great thing about having a townhouse. Besides, I swear she could sleep through a nuclear war. Doctors get so used to staying up during residency that if they get the chance they're out like a light."

"Okay. Thanks." He wasn't sure what residency was, and he couldn't help but marvel a bit that Aaron's wife was actually a doctor. Not only did she go to work, but at all hours as well. He wondered if it bothered Aaron, but he supposed it must not. When he tried to imagine Mother or his sisters working anywhere but at home, he failed completely.

"Isaac's still asleep?"

His cheeks hot, David stared at his mug. "Uh-huh. He didn't rest much on the way here."

"You don't have to be embarrassed. You and Isaac sleeping together doesn't bother me at all. Or Jen. I promise."

David risked a glance at Aaron's face. "But how does it not bother you? I know Isaac's your brother, but you barely even know me, and he and I are…and it's…"

"What?" Aaron leaned a hip against the counter, his voice calm. "What is it?"

David tried in vain to think of the right word, but all he could come up with was, "Wrong."

"Does it feel wrong?" Aaron sipped his coffee as if he'd just asked about the weather.

"No." Heart thumping, David stared at his bare toes on the pale wood. "I know it's a sin, but I can't help myself."

"I don't think it's a sin at all." Aaron laughed sharply. "And I think the Bible's nonsense that men use to keep people under their thumbs."

Blinking, David opened his mouth and closed it again, half expected a lightning bolt to strike them down right there in the kitchen. *Nonsense?*

"Sorry—I didn't mean to upset you." Aaron smiled ruefully. "I know you and Isaac are believers, and that's totally okay. Jen believes in God too. So don't let me make you feel uncomfortable."

David tried to find the words. "What do you mean?"

"I don't believe in God. I did growing up, of course. It never occurred to me that it was even a possibility not to."

"I…" David opened and closed his mouth like a fish. "How can you not believe in God?"

"I just don't," Aaron said, as if it was nothing. "It was a process. I went to other churches here and there after I left Red Hills. I did a lot of reading. A lot of soul searching, I guess. Eventually I realized religion doesn't make sense to me. The notion that there's an omniscient being up there controlling our lives and passing judgment? I don't believe it."

"But…" David's head spun. "I guess I've never considered it. I've thought about the Amish church, and the things about it that don't make sense. But to think that there's no God at all…" He shivered, gripping the ceramic mug. It was impossible. Even though he knew he was going to hell, the idea that God might not actually exist made him feel horribly wrong all over.

"Hey, it's okay." Aaron squeezed David's shoulder. "Everyone has to make their own journey with their faith, or lack thereof. I'm not trying to convince you. It's a personal thing, and there's plenty of time for you and Isaac to explore your beliefs." He winced. "I sound like a self-help book. Sorry. And this is a heavy conversation to be having on only one cup of coffee after the bus ride you just had."

"I don't mind." David forced himself to breathe again. "I suppose I've never known anyone who didn't believe." He couldn't help but feel saddened by Aaron's lack of faith.

"We can talk about it later. Or not—no pressure." Aaron splashed more coffee into his mug and blew out a long breath. "And I didn't want to get into it until you guys were rested, but can you tell me what happened? Isaac had said you wouldn't leave Zebulon, but obviously something changed."

David traced the rim of his mug. "I was afraid. I knew I had to stay and look after my family. It was selfish to leave, but when it came down to it, I couldn't do it. I couldn't live without Isaac. And even if he didn't want me anymore, I couldn't marry some poor girl I'd never be a real husband to."

Acid bubbled in David's gut as he imagined what kind, quiet Grace would think of him running away to the world. Granted he'd only driven her home from the singing twice—they hadn't even been going steady by Amish standards, let alone been close to marriage. But she'd liked him for ages, and he'd used that.

I never should have gotten her hopes up. He'd known deep down he was fooling himself. He let himself think that once he made that vow to God and his community everything would somehow fall into place, like an English magic trick. If he'd gone through with it, he'd have only made them both miserable.

"It's not selfish, David. You wouldn't be doing anyone any favors in the long run. Trust me. I thought I could do it too. If the plain life isn't what you want in your heart, all the prayers in the world won't change it." Aaron smiled faintly. "I thought if I could just get it out of my system and join the church, God would help me fit in. That He would bring me peace. It doesn't work like that."

"You've never regretted leaving?"

Aaron sighed. "Only that it meant being cut off from my family. I'm not going to lie—it's hard. Since I'd joined the church before I left, I'm shunned. If anyone found out my sister Abigail in Red Hills still writes me, she'd be in serious trouble. Abigail keeps it a secret from her husband. Our sister Hannah is there too, but she wouldn't break the rules."

"My sister Emma is still there. I should write to her. Although she's so much older she might as well be a stranger."

"Is she the eldest?"

David nodded. "After her, I think there was a baby that didn't make it. I don't really know, but there was almost five years before Joshua came. That's not the usual way. But I never asked. Emma has half a dozen children of her own now."

"I wish I could know Abigail's kids. I feel a little like I do from her letters." Aaron swallowed thickly. "I hated leaving my brothers and sisters. Isaac especially. He was always…we were close. I can't tell you what it means to see him again. When he called, I couldn't believe I was hearing his voice. So grown up now."

"I've never been so far away from my mother and sisters. I wish there was a way I could still talk to them."

"You can't be excommunicated if you didn't join the church. If no one knows you're gay, it should be fine to write. Even visit if they'll have you. Of course you know you'll get guilt tripped into going back for good. Your mother will tell you the only way to heaven is to be Amish. If you write, that's all you're likely to get in return: pleas to go home."

"My sister Anna would write more, though. I know she would. Mary…" He winced.

"What?"

"Even if Mary doesn't know the whole truth, I'm not sure she'll forgive me for taking Isaac away. She's had her heart set on him for ages." He scrubbed a hand over his face. "I'm a terrible brother."

"But you love him, don't you?"

Again, there was no judgment in Aaron's gaze. How odd it was to talk so plainly with him about feelings. But David said the words. "More than anything."

Aaron smiled. "Then that's all that matters. Gay or straight, love is the same. Straight means men and women together. There are so many different words here—it was almost like learning English all over again." He got a faraway look in his eyes. "I used to switch back and forth between German and English so easily. My German's pretty rusty now. I wonder what word they'd use instead of gay. Not that the Amish would ever really talk about it."

David shook his head. "You say it out loud so easily. I can when I'm alone, or I'm with Isaac. When I can forget it's a sin. But you act like it's nothing at all. And I think the word they'd use is abomination." *Heathen. Unclean. Deceiver.*

Aaron grimaced. "Undoubtedly. But it isn't an abomination. It's the way you were born. There's nothing wrong with being gay. I know you and Isaac probably don't believe that yet, but you will. And there are plenty of Christians who don't think it's a sin either."

For a moment, David could only stare at Aaron. "Christians? But…how?"

"The Bible can be interpreted in so many ways. There are religious people who aren't homophobic."

David contemplated the word. *Homophobic.* "It *truly* doesn't bother you? That we're…" He waved his hand.

Aaron chuckled. "Not even a little. I'm glad you're here, David. You don't have to hide your feelings now. You don't have to hide who you are."

David gulped his coffee for fear he might cry otherwise. He took a deep breath. "I don't know what to say. I have some money saved, but I need to make sure my Mother gets most of it. Everything else I'll give to you, and—"

"No you won't. At least not until you and Isaac are settled and you figure out what you want to do. There's no rush. Jen and I agreed." Aaron smiled softly. "I always hoped one of the kids would find me. I thought it would be Ephraim, though. Isaac always followed the rules so quietly and diligently."

"Until he met me. I don't want to impose."

"I made sure we had a couple of spare rooms when we bought this house, just in case. We want to have kids one day, but even if I never saw my brothers or sisters again, I needed to be sure they had a place here. We're glad you're here, okay? Please don't worry about money right now. Jen and I have enough. Her parents practically paid our entire mortgage as a wedding present."

"Wow."

Aaron laughed fondly. "Jen says they were so happy she was finally getting married they were probably willing to pay me too."

David smiled. "She sounds nice."

"The best." Aaron drained his mug. "Okay, I've gotta run. I'll see you soon. In the meantime, make yourself at home."

Not sure what else to do, David walked with Aaron to the front door and watched him put on his shiny leather shoes and zip up his coat. He waved and stood at the front window, watching Aaron back his car out of the driveway onto the steep road before zooming away into the lingering fog.

The house was still again, and David imagined Isaac upstairs still fast asleep and peaceful. He rolled around the word in his mind as though it was brand new.

Home.

CHAPTER *Two*

I SAAC GASPED AS he bolted up in bed. "David?"

David tossed aside the sweatshirt he'd been unfolding and crawled onto the mattress, his jeans hanging open and his feet and chest bare after another blissfully hot shower. "I'm here. Shh, it's all right, *Eechel.*" He wasn't sure why he'd started calling Isaac *acorn*, but somehow the name just fit. "Did you have a bad dream?"

"No, but..." Isaac pushed away the covers and threw himself into David's arms, his fingers digging in.

They knelt in the middle of the bed, and David smoothed his palm over Isaac's back. "You're safe."

"For a second I didn't know where I was." Isaac took a stuttering breath.

"We're here in San Francisco." David sighed as he felt the softness of Isaac's lips on his throat, and the tickle of his stubble. He kissed Isaac's head before sitting back on his heels. "We made it."

Isaac glanced around the guest room, and a smile flitted across his lips. "We did. I can hardly believe it's real." He looked down at himself. "I'm *naked*," he whispered.

"That you are." David leered playfully.

Laughing, Isaac swatted his shoulder. "And we actually *slept* together. I was so tired I hardly had time to enjoy it."

"It feels like a dream."

Isaac nodded. Biting his lip, he stretched back on the pillows, tugging David forward to straddle his hips. David ran his hands up Isaac's sides. Sometimes he thought he could be happy forever just being close with Isaac like this. Not even because of sex—just feeling the warmth of his body and seeing the curve of his smile.

"I can't believe I'm waking up with you." Isaac caressed David's bare chest. "That I can touch you, and no one will mind." He frowned. "At least I don't think anyone will mind."

"They won't. Not here." David raised one of Isaac's hands and kissed his palm.

"You don't think it's… We're not being disrespectful, are we?" Isaac waved a hand between them. "Doing this in my brother's home? I know he said it doesn't bother them, but how can that be true?"

David brushed back Isaac's hair from his forehead. "I suppose we have to trust that he's being honest. It doesn't seem like he's lying, does it?"

"No. It's been years, but I still know him. He wouldn't lie. I guess it's just hard to believe. To not have to sneak around and hide feels strange. Wrong. I used to daydream about having our own bed, but I never thought we really would."

David threaded their fingers together. "In this room it's only the two of us. No matter what happens out there, I don't want us to be afraid here. I want us to be free. With ourselves. With each other. Deal?"

Nodding, Isaac drew David down for a kiss. "Deal."

David rolled his hips, grinding against Isaac's groin. His jeans were just rough enough to send delightful tingles through him.

Isaac groaned, but then pushed himself up on an elbow. "Wait—what time is it? Aaron must be wondering where I am."

"Almost noon, but it's all right. He had to go to work for the morning. He'll be home soon."

"Noon!" Isaac bolted up and tried to shift David off. "I haven't slept this late in…ever. I need to—" His brow creased, and he stopped fidgeting. "Well, I guess I don't need to do anything, actually."

"Not today at least. It's odd, isn't it? But in a nice way."

Isaac smiled and relaxed back against the pillows again. "I can't believe we really left. I wonder…" He shook his head. "No. I don't want to think about them. Not right now." He ran his hands over David's thighs. "I don't want to think about anything."

"I think I can help." Smiling slyly, he shifted back and spread Isaac's legs wide, pushing his knees apart so he could bend and nuzzle at Isaac's cock and balls.

With a soft moan, Isaac lifted his hips. "Yes, please," he murmured. "It's been too long."

David loved the feel of Isaac's shaft growing in his mouth, filling him as he sucked up and down with one hand wrapped around the base. He inhaled through his nose, his spit dripping down messily. When he pulled off and licked toward Isaac's hole, fingers grasped at his damp hair.

"*David.* I missed you so much. Your mouth…" Isaac whimpered.

Still teasing Isaac's balls, David lifted his hand blindly to Isaac's lips. Isaac opened for him, getting David's fingers slick with spit, his tongue swirling over and between. When David inched a wet finger inside Isaac's ass, he started sucking his cock again, looking up through his eyelashes.

What a sight it was. He loved how Isaac met his gaze, his amber eyes dark and wild, his lips parted and skin flushed all the way down his chest. David had thought he'd never have this again, and he savored the sensations—the clench of Isaac's ass around his finger, and the little whines from Isaac's throat.

Isaac stroked David's hair, his fingers gentle and his eyelids fluttering. David swallowed Isaac's shaft, imagining he could feel the pounding of Isaac's heart on his tongue.

"Oh, David. You make me feel so good."

David's nostrils flared and he breathed in the heady musk. It made him so hard just to taste and smell Isaac, his lips stretched over Isaac's thick cock. A sense of power flowed through him. Isaac was splayed out—so trusting and vulnerable—and David wanted to keep him safe always. They may be sinners, but Isaac was still a gift from God.

He crooked his finger and felt around for just the right swollen spot inside Isaac.

"I'm not—" Isaac gasped. "I'm going to—"

Humming, David sucked harder, swallowing each salty spurt that filled his mouth, wanting every drop of Isaac he could have. He milked him gently, and Isaac panted, mumbling David's name. When David pulled off with a wet *pop* and sat on his heels, Isaac smiled in a daze.

"Can we wake up this way every day?"

David chuckled. "Sounds good to me." He was painfully hard in his open jeans against the zipper. He freed himself, groaning as he wrapped his hand around his straining cock.

"Let me." Isaac reached for him, still splayed against the pillows with bent legs wide.

"I'm almost there." Tingles shot up David's spine as he jerked himself, his eyes locked on Isaac. "Is it okay if I…I want to come on you," he confessed. "Is that weird?"

Shivering, Isaac shook his head and spread his arms as well.

One hand still on his cock, David pushed forward onto his knees, bracing himself against the padded headboard with his other hand. Isaac nodded, his gaze locked with David's.

"I want it all over me, David. I want to be sticky and yours—all yours. I'm…" He paused and blurted, "I'm going to lick it up and—"

Gasping, David's release rushed through him, splashing onto Isaac's chest and belly. David worked himself until he was too sensitive for any more. With a shaky hand, he swiped up his seed and fed it to Isaac, who sucked it greedily from his finger, his lips red and shining.

David settled over Isaac, kissing him languidly and tasting himself there. It was so *dirty*, and it made him hot all over. "So good," he murmured.

Isaac smiled. "You're going to have to have another shower."

"We can have all the showers we want now." David grinned. "Instant hot water."

"Good thing we both fit in there, huh?" Then his expression grew serious, and he held David's face in his hands. "I thought I'd lost you forever."

"I'm all yours," David whispered, kissing him again.

He pulled the covers back up and sank into Isaac's arms. For the first time in their lives, there was no place else they had to be.

THE FAINT SMELL of grease had David's stomach rumbling as he and Isaac made their way downstairs.

"Wait." Isaac paused halfway down the staircase. He whispered, "Is it rude to go barefoot in an English house? My socks are smelly, but I can put them on."

"I think it's fine. I was barefoot this morning, and Aaron didn't say anything." Their shoes were by the front door on a rack, and although David had seen people in movies often wear shoes in the house, that didn't seem to be the way Jen and Aaron did things.

"Okay." Isaac ran his hand over his T-shirt and straightened his hair. "Do I look all right?"

David's spare jeans were loose on Isaac, but the white shirt fit well enough. "You look great, and your brother doesn't care what you're wearing. Come on." He gave Isaac a nudge.

Aaron grinned as they came into the kitchen. "Hey! Sleep well?" He pulled Isaac into a hug. "I hope you don't mind if I hug you a lot for the first little while. After all those years of stoic-ness and hiding emotion, I've become a big hugger."

Isaac's voice was muffled in Aaron's shoulder. "I don't mind."

Aaron stepped back and ruffled Isaac's hair. "I'll give you a reprieve for now."

David laughed softly. "I guess it's something to get used to, hugging people." The Amish adults he knew tended to be stoic indeed.

"You hug me," Isaac said before blanching. "I mean…"

"Well, I'd hope you two are well past the handshake stage." Aaron laughed. "But yeah, the English are definitely *waaay* more demonstrative than you're used to. Just wait until you meet Jen." He hugged Isaac again playfully. "I'm just so happy you're here. I can't resist!"

David watched them with a smile, although a pang of longing for Joshua washed through him.

When Isaac stepped back, he touched Aaron's shiny tie. "It's so…"

Aaron grinned. "Pink? Extremely vain, I know. My shrink once said he's surprised I don't drape myself in a rainbow of silk every day given how I grew up."

"Your what?" Isaac frowned.

"Psychiatrists are doctors who deal with the brain, and years ago people called them head shrinkers. We just call them shrinks now. They ask a lot of questions to try and figure out what you're thinking, and how you're feeling. They get to the bottom of your issues. Shrink them down, I guess."

"You have to go to a doctor? Are you sick?" Isaac's voice rose.

"No, no. I'm fine." Aaron raised his hands. "I promise. A lot of English people go to therapy. It's just to talk stuff out and try to make sense of your life. Jen has great benefits with the hospital, and it's covered for us on her plan. So I figure I might as well take advantage."

"So you get therapy with…benefits?" Isaac glanced at David, a furrow between his brows.

"It's a perk people get at their jobs. Extra stuff as well as their salary," David said. "It helps pay for health care and that kind of thing. Right?" He asked Aaron.

"Right." Aaron squeezed Isaac's arm. "I'm sorry—I was just telling David this morning that it took me quite a while to get used to all the English words we never learned. I'll try and slow down, and if you're confused about anything just ask, okay?" He picked up a paper bag from the counter. "Now here's an English name I bet you remember."

Isaac bounced on his toes. "Is that McDonald's?"

"Yep. I got you and David Big Macs. I figured you probably had the Golden Arches on your way down, but I remember it was your favorite."

"We didn't, actually. I wasn't very hungry." Isaac's stomach growled loudly, and he laughed. "I sure am now."

Aaron arranged the food on the part of the counter jutting out before the dining room, and walked around to the other side so he was facing the kitchen. "Come on, have a seat and dig in."

There were four stools, and David left a spot between him and Aaron for Isaac. When Isaac bit into a fry, he groaned. "Oh, I missed this."

David ate a few fries, savoring the salty crispiness. "Me too."

For a while they ate in companionable silence, and David smiled as Isaac licked the burger sauce that dripped onto his fingers.

"I'm going to eat Big Macs every day," Isaac said.

Aaron smirked. "There's a movie I'll have to show you that might make you rethink that idea."

David slurped his Coke. Soda made him think of the drive-in and his workshop at June's. Now he could have soda anytime. For breakfast, even. "I guess we'd get tired of them after a while."

"But until you do? Big Macs whenever you want." Aaron popped a fry in his mouth. "The world is your oyster. Speaking of which, we'll go for seafood down at the wharf one night. And there's an amazing Indian pizza place a few blocks away. Although I suppose you should try traditional Italian pizza first so you can compare. Oh, and you have to try Mexican food of course." He sighed contentedly. "There's so much food you've never tasted."

"I had Taco Bell once, but I didn't like it much," David said. "It tasted fine, but my stomach wasn't too keen on it."

Aaron laughed. "Don't worry, real Mexican food won't give you the runs. Although it'll be an adjustment, all the spices and flavors in food here compared to what our mothers cooked."

"Not that I don't like Amish cooking," David hastily added as he thought of the hours Mother and his sisters spent in the kitchen.

"I've never found a chicken pot pie that could compare," Aaron said.

Isaac dipped a fry into ketchup. "I never thought about it much, that there's different food out here. After you left—" He stopped.

But Aaron smiled. "Go on. You can say anything, Isaac."

"I tried to imagine where you were, and what you were doing, but I couldn't." He glanced up. "But you look almost just like I remember."

"Minus the Amish beard hanging off my chin." Aaron grimaced. "That was not a great look for me."

"I mean before you followed church. You don't have bangs, though."

"Nope. And I think my hairline's starting to recede now that I'm pushing thirty, but Jen says it's all in my head."

"You're happy, though," Isaac said. "Like when we were kids. That's how I remembered you."

David tried to imagine Joshua as a man. He'd always seemed so grownup in David's eyes, but they'd both been boys. He sat quietly and finished his last fries even though his belly was stretched already.

Aaron smiled sadly. "I'm glad to hear that. I know the way I left was sudden. I wanted to say goodbye, but I was too scared. I didn't want to fight with Mom and Dad, or let them convince me to stay even though I knew I had to leave. It's strange to think of them as 'Mother and Father.' So formal, even for the Amish. I guess it's a good thing I left before the move to Zebulon. Sounds like a lot of things changed after that."

"Yes." David shifted on his stool and toyed with his crumpled Big Mac wrapper. "After what Joshua did… After he and the girls died, everything changed."

"No more rumspringa—not even the mention of it." Isaac tapped his box of fries and the last few slid out. "But even Mervin secretly had a piece of English technology, and he almost always followed the rules. A Touch, it was called. We watched a movie on it and listened to music." He sighed. "We were best friends our whole lives."

"It's hard to leave people behind," Aaron said quietly.

David thought of Mervin that day in the barn, and the disgust creasing his face.

"I'd already lost him anyway." Isaac paused. "He…he found out about me and David. He didn't understand. Could barely even look at me after that, let alone talk to me. But at least he kept it a secret."

What if Mervin had told them now? David forced the thought away. There was no sense in worrying about it.

"I'm sorry, Isaac." Aaron looped his arm over Isaac's shoulders. "That must have been awful." He shook his head. "God, how I wanted to take you with me, but you were way too young, and for all I knew you'd be happy as an Amish man once you were grown. But I hated leaving you. Running away in the night with a piece of paper the only thing to leave behind."

"You left more than that." Isaac pulled the folding pocketknife from his jeans.

Aaron's eyebrows shot up. "I can't believe you still have that!" He took it from Isaac and traced the simple edges.

"I carry it with me most of the time. I still love to carve things. And now I've learned so much about carpentry from David."

"He's a natural, that's for sure." David nudged Isaac's knee with his own as warmth bloomed in his chest. Soon they'd be building things together again.

Aaron blinked rapidly as he handed the knife back, and his voice was thick. "I'm glad to hear it. I can't tell you how much it means to have you here. Both of you."

Isaac's lip trembled. "I knew you'd help me. Us."

"We're so grateful to you and your wife," David added awkwardly, emotion suddenly dense in the air.

"I can't wait to meet her." Isaac wiped at the corner of his eye and sucked the last of his soda through his straw loudly.

Aaron chuckled. "Just remember she's not like the women you know. She says exactly what's on her mind, and she definitely does not do everything her husband tells her—not by a long shot. But I wouldn't have it any other way. Have you guys seen the pictures?" Aaron jerked his thumb toward the living room. "Come on."

David had already looked that morning, but he followed. On a low table along one wall, there were at least a dozen photos in glass and metal frames. In one, Aaron wore a black suit and held hands with a woman in a long white dress that hugged her slim body. Her arms were bare and the neckline dipped right down to the top of her breasts. They were on a low bridge in a garden with trees and flowers everywhere.

"That was our wedding day. There's a whole album of us in every conceivable pose all over that park." Aaron pointed to another photo where he and Jen stood surrounded by other people. "These are Jen's parents. Her bridesmaids are all in purple, and her best friend Clark's in the purple suit—he was the maid of honor. It would usually be a woman, but Jen insisted. He's gay too."

David examined the man in the purple suit. He looked almost like a girl, with glossy lips and sparkles on his tie. Another actual gay person. It was comforting somehow.

"English weddings are way fancier than Amish ones, as you can see. No celery for the centerpieces."

Isaac peered at the photo. "Jen's very pretty." He quickly added, "Not that it matters."

"It's okay, you can say she's pretty." Aaron grinned. "I'd add that she's smokin' hot as well. This pic's my favorite." He pointed to one where Jen smiled back at the camera while Aaron walked a few steps ahead, holding her hand.

Jen's teeth were gleaming white, contrasting with her tan skin and black hair knotted on her head with two curls hanging down. Jewels shone in her ears and around her neck, and the dress looked like it would be so soft to touch. She was laughing. David couldn't tell how old she was, but he assumed around Aaron's age.

Isaac asked, "Is she…Chinese?"

David had wondered as well, but didn't know a polite way to ask. He realized he'd hardly met anyone in his entire life who hadn't been like him.

"Filipino. The Philippines are islands in the Pacific, near Malaysia. I know that probably doesn't mean much to you guys. I hardly knew anything when I left Red Hills. But I learned, and so can you."

Isaac stared at the pictures. "Do a lot of English get married to people who aren't...the same?"

"Sure," Aaron answered. "It happens all the time now. You'll be amazed how many people here aren't white. I know it must seem weird to you."

"No." Isaac smiled. "Just different. But I'm different too." His tender gaze met David's.

David smiled and wondered if Aaron really wouldn't mind if he held Isaac's hand or touched his arm in front of him. But he kept his hands to himself anyway.

"We're all different, which is exactly what the Amish are afraid of. They definitely don't want women outside the home. I can't imagine what Mom and Dad would think of Jen. She works more than I do, and she makes a hell of a lot more money than a new teacher."

David blinked. Although he'd heard June and people in movies use the word *hell* casually, it was still jarring to hear it come so easily from Aaron.

Aaron sighed, gazing at his wedding photos. "No matter which Amish community and how different the *Ordnung*, the goal is always to make everyone and everything fit into little boxes. I could never squeeze in."

"And the boxes are all measured right down to the quarter inch, just like our boots, and hats, and buggies, and every last thing," David said. The freedom the English enjoyed seemed impossible.

Aaron laughed ruefully. "I sure don't miss that. It was so strange at first, buying clothes and trying to figure out what size I was. Not having to worry about hems or brims being exactly a certain length or width. Not having to wear galluses anymore." He tapped his leather belt. "Much better than suspenders in my book. Most pants just stay up on their own. I'll take you guys shopping tomorrow and you can try on a bunch of clothes. See what you like."

See what I like. While David had jeans and casual shirts, there was so much else out there.

"I don't have any money, though." Isaac bit his lip. "David has some, but—"

"Stop." Aaron held up his hand. "I already went through this with David. I don't want either of you to worry about money right now. All you need to concentrate on is getting used to the world. It's a lot to take in. Let me take care of everything else. When I left Red Hills, I only had a couple hundred dollars saved up. I was lucky to come across people who were amazingly generous to a total stranger. You're my brother, and David's your boyfriend. I'll take care of everything for you, okay?"

Boyfriend. David liked the sound of it as he rolled the word over in his mind.

Isaac swallowed hard. "Thank you. I'll get a job as soon as I can, and—"

"Isaac." Aaron took hold of his shoulders and peered at him seriously. "Don't worry. First we need to get your birth certificates so you and David can get social security numbers."

David blinked. It hadn't even crossed his mind.

"What's that?" Isaac asked.

"It's a government thing," Aaron answered. "You can't legally work without it. There's a lawyer in Ohio who helped me get my birth certificate. He's ex-Amish, so he knows how to deal with the community. Since we were born at home, Mom and Dad never filed birth certificates for us. At least they didn't for me, and I don't think they would have for you. David, do you know if you have one?"

He shook his head. "I doubt it."

"The lawyer will get affidavits from people in Red Hills who can testify about your births. Isaac, Abigail can sign one for you, and I'm sure there will be enough people who'll help. Hannah might as well. David, we can ask your sister Emma."

Isaac's brows drew together. "An affi...what?"

"It's like an official statement." Aaron waved his hand. "Don't worry about the details now. I can go over the paperwork with you once we start the ball rolling. Then we can get your passports, and you can learn to drive and get your licenses if you want. But at least in the city you don't need to drive. I'll show you how transit works. Don't worry about all that stuff right now. It's your first day."

Isaac sighed. "It feels like there's so much I don't know. David's been going to movies and reading books for a couple of years. Before I went to work with him I'd barely been off the farm. Father said…" He took a sharp breath. "Oh. I need to write them. I should have done that right away today. Do you think…" He shook his head. "Never mind."

"What?" Aaron and David asked in unison.

Isaac stared at his feet for a moment before addressing his brother. "Do you think it would upset them more if I told them I'm with you?"

Aaron yanked at the knot in his tie, smiling tightly. "Probably. You should just tell them you're safe. I can ask Abigail what Mother says in her next letter. For now it might be better to keep it vague." He pulled his tie over his head and rolled it tightly.

Isaac and David shared a glance. "I didn't mean to upset you," Isaac said quietly.

"You didn't." Aaron pressed his lips together. "I'm sorry. Usually I don't think about it much, but sometimes it's…" He rolled and unrolled his tie, his gaze on his hands. "Did they ever talk about me?"

"No," Isaac whispered.

"That's what I figured. I mean, I knew that. I did." Aaron hitched his shoulders. "I'd still make the same choice."

The thought that he might be erased from his family like answered sums on a blackboard made David's palms sweat.

Aaron waved his hand. "Okay, that's enough of my pity party. David, I don't know about you, but I bet Isaac's ready for dessert. Isaac, I got your favorite."

"Ice cream?" he asked hopefully.

"What else?" Aaron slung his arm over Isaac's shoulders. "I bought five different kinds, so you guys can have your pick."

Sitting at the counter again, David scooped his spoon into a bowl of something called pralines and cream. As the smooth sweetness filled his mouth, he tried to forget everything else. Aaron was right—it was only their first day. They'd figure it all out. He pressed his knee against Isaac's, and they shared a smile.

With eyes alight and a smear of ice cream on his mouth, Isaac glanced at where Aaron bent over the low freezer at the bottom of the fridge. Quick as a hummingbird, the kiss was soft and perfect, and David licked at the trace of chocolate left behind on his lips.

CHAPTER *Three*

"TURN RIGHT AT the corner?" David asked.

He jumped as a car honked, but it apparently wasn't directed at them, since the vehicle sped past. A dog barked nearby, and more cars roared down the street. He found himself looking around constantly, and he made sure Isaac walked on the inside of the sidewalk.

Isaac consulted the small square of yellow paper. "Yes. Then it should be on our left." He gazed up as they passed a four-story apartment building. "There are so many people here."

Nodding, David sidestepped a woman with a baby carriage. It was the middle of the afternoon, but they'd passed quite a few other people in the three blocks from Aaron's house. The fog had lifted, and although it was cloudy with a chilly wind, it felt practically tropical compared to what they'd left behind in Minnesota. With a pang of guilt, he thought of the snow that would need to be shoveled without him.

Isaac pointed to the green hill that dominated the landscape. "We should go up there one day. Bet you can see for miles."

"I bet." There were trees and a metal tower atop the hill. Squinting, David thought he could see a few people and perhaps dogs running to and fro. He moved to take off his hat to scratch an itch on his scalp, and realized he was grabbing at air.

"I think that's the store up there," Isaac said. "It says up the hill and past the green house." He shook his head. "I never thought I'd see *green* houses! Everything is so…"

"Not plain?" David supplied as he eyed a colorful painting on the side of a brick wall. He wasn't sure what the zig-zaggy symbols were supposed to mean. It was art, he guessed.

The Sky-Vu drive-in near Zebulon had seemed so worldly to him even though it was only a screen in a field with a little concrete snack bar. The hardware store and main street in Warren had seemed bustling. But just walking a few blocks in San Francisco was like being on another planet.

Isaac bumped his shoulder against David's. "It's exciting, isn't it?"

David nodded, trying to ignore the tendril of worry that coiled deep within him. It *was* exciting, although sweat dampened his brow even in the brisk wind. "I wonder why Aaron called it a bodega?" The word felt strange on his tongue.

"He said it was like the corner store. Whatever that means." Isaac laughed wryly. "Aside from being a store on the corner. Not that we had any of those in Zebulon." He spun in a slow circle as he walked. "Here there's just…so *much*. So much everything."

"Uh-huh." Whether the buildings were squat homes, narrow town-houses, small apartments or stores, they all had one thing in common—they were squeezed together on the streets. Once in a while a tree would appear, but for the most part the buildings were squished as if they'd been pressed in a vise. He breathed deeply. "The air smells different here. Wetter. Almost like…salt?"

"Yes. It must be the water nearby." Isaac grinned. "I can't wait to see it—the ocean. I want—" He broke off, his stride faltering as he stared at something ahead.

"What?" David followed Isaac's gaze, and his heart skipped a beat. "Oh."

Talking and laughing, two men approached, their hands clasped between them. They passed by an old woman sweeping the steps of her blue house, and she didn't even look at them.

Striding through the world, the men were oblivious to anyone else. One had a mustache, and they both looked older than Aaron. David couldn't stop staring at how their fingers were threaded together tightly, their arms swaying as they strolled along.

"Wow," Isaac whispered.

They'd stopped in their tracks, and as the men approached, David realized he and Isaac were staring. He nudged Isaac and started walking again, his head down and cheeks flaming. A mess of emotion coursed through him—shock, embarrassment, envy, and even fear.

Fortunately the men didn't seem to notice Isaac and David's attention, and as they passed by, they chattered on. David couldn't help but stop to look over his shoulder after them, and Isaac did the same. The men walked by more people as they went, and not one gave them a second glance.

Was it really okay to hold hands right on the street in front of *everyone*? It was hard to believe, even after what he'd just seen. Isaac's hands were stuffed into the pockets of his too-big blue jacket he'd borrowed from Aaron. He scuffed the toe of his black boot on the concrete as he watched the men, who grew distant as the street stretched up a hill.

"Can you believe that? They were just…in front of everyone!" Isaac still whispered.

"And no one seemed to mind. I never thought I'd see anything like that."

"Can you imagine what they'd say in Zebulon?" Isaac asked.

David surely could, and the shiver that ran through him was icy. He nodded, and then walked on toward the yellow awning on the corner. "Come on, we're almost there." He wanted to hold Isaac's hand, but he didn't have the nerve yet. As they went up the hill, his thighs burned pleasantly. After so long on buses, it was nice to be moving again.

White plastic buckets filled with fresh flowers lined the sidewalk and wooden crates outside the store. David skimmed a finger over a daisy petal, unable to resist. A bell rung as they pulled open the glass door to the market. It was small, and like the buildings, everything was squeezed together on the shelves, using every available inch.

"*Hola.*" The older woman behind the counter was plump, and her dark hair was graying. On a little television set, she was watching some kind of show where people wore a lot of makeup and spoke what sounded like Spanish.

He and Isaac smiled at her and explored a narrow aisle. The cans and boxes were bright reds, blues, and greens. At the back of the store was a counter selling something called a burrito, which David thought he might have had at Taco Bell—although the smell of beef and cheese and onions here promised a tastier meal.

"There's the bread," Isaac said, coming around the end of the aisle to the side of the store with fresh food in refrigerated cases, and plastic bins filled with varieties of rolls. Isaac glanced at the yellow paper. "He said it's called a baguette."

"Long and thin, right?" David eyed the bins. "I don't see anything like that. Oh wait—there, sticking out of that basket."

The woman at the counter rang up their purchase, one eye still on the TV, and smiled as she passed Isaac the change. The baguette was in a paper bag, but since it stuck out so much, David held it to his chest to make sure the bread didn't tip out.

Outside, they turned right and retraced their steps toward the townhouse, going downhill this time. Beside him, Isaac laughed. "What?" David asked, already smiling even though he had no idea what had tickled Isaac.

"Is it silly to feel proud that we just went out by ourselves in the city and did our task?"

"Don't speak too soon—we aren't back yet. We could still get lost. Or attacked by hoodlums. They have gangs in the city." David dramatically clutched the baguette to his chest. "I've heard they love French bread."

"Maybe that's why Aaron sent us. Sure, he *said* he just forgot to buy it on his way home, but really he was too afraid to go himself."

David tried not to smile. "We'll be lucky if we make it back alive." Ahead, four elderly men smoked cigarettes on the sidewalk, huddled together by a coffee shop. "Look—gang members," he whispered.

"Aren't they too old to be in a gang?" Isaac murmured.

David put on a tone like ones he'd heard police officers use in movies. "It's the city. Once you're in a gang, you never get out."

Shoulders shaking, Isaac made his face serious and hissed, "Should we run?"

"Absolutely." David took off like a shot with Isaac on his heels.

As they raced past the old men, David inhaled a whisper of smoke before it was gone. All the anxiety of the noise and cars disappeared as his legs pumped. They dashed all the way back to the townhouse, their laughter trailing in the wind.

"IS THAT AARON Byler's famous spaghetti with meat sauce I smell?"

Twisting her long black curls into a ponytail, Jen shuffled into the kitchen in plaid pajama bottoms, a green shirt with no sleeves and thin straps, and fuzzy blue slippers on her feet. She went up on tiptoes and kissed Aaron lightly before turning.

"Let me guess." She pointed. "You're Isaac. It's all in the eyes."

Isaac got off the stool and extended his hand. "Hello."

With a smile, Jen pulled him into a hug. "No handshakes in this house for family." She frowned as she leaned back. "Uh, unless it makes you uncomfortable. Sorry, I have boundary issues sometimes. Probably why I married a patient."

"*Former* patient," Aaron noted, giving her hip a playful pat on his way to the pantry.

"Hugs are okay," Isaac said, smiling shyly.

David waited uncertainly by the counter. Was she going to hug him too?

Jen turned to him. "Don't think you can avoid the hugs just because you're not blood related. But again, I can be wildly inappropriate at times."

David awkwardly opened his arms. He could feel her small breasts against his chest through the thin cotton, and her bare arms were tight around him. Aside from June at the bus station, he couldn't remember the last time he'd hugged anyone but Isaac or his little sisters. Jen was short like Mary, only reaching his shoulder. "Thank you for letting us stay," he said.

She stepped back. "It's a pleasure to have you. I mean it." She went to the fridge and pulled out a tall carton, lifting it to her mouth before freezing. "I guess I should start using a glass."

"I've only been saying that for years," Aaron muttered as he stirred the sauce.

At the cupboard, Jen pulled out a glass and filled it with milk. "It's true, he has. It's a bad habit I picked up in med school."

Isaac was staring at her chest with a frown. "What does that mean?" he blurted.

Jen glanced down at her shirt, which read *Frak me*. "Yeah, I guess BSG isn't too big in Zebulon. Frak is the profanity of the future. There's this show—*Battlestar Galactica*—and it takes place in space hundreds of years from now. We have the old DVDs if you guys want to watch. Anyway, to get around the censors, the characters said frak instead of fuck, but it means the same thing. Fuck me."

David stared before forcing his gaze to the floor. June was English, but he couldn't imagine her saying something so…*crude*. Granted it was the way he and Isaac spoke sometimes when they were alone together, but to talk like that in the *kitchen*? Around other people?

Isaac opened and closed his mouth, his eyes wide. "Oh."

David's mind raced. Should he respond? What was the right thing to say? He couldn't imagine any women he knew saying something that bold so very casually—not even Anna. Perhaps it was common in Filipino women? But no, he'd seen white women swear in movies.

"Jen, you're shocking them with your foul mouth." Aaron laughed from the stove. "I warned you guys. Don't worry, you'll get used to it."

David cleared his throat. "But when you say that, it's not...literal, right? I've heard people say that in movies when they're frustrated about something."

"Exactly!" Jen said. "It's a lamentation. Well, more like an expression of frustration. It's not about sex."

Sex! Again she said it like it was nothing, and didn't seem embarrassed at all. David shifted from foot to foot, willing himself not to blush. Isaac's ears were red, and he tugged at a loose thread at the cuff of the sleeve of his hoodie.

"Lamentation—nice one." Aaron whispered loudly, "She went to Stanford, so she likes to use big words when she's not cussing."

Jen grinned. "You bet I do." She waved at the stools. "Sit, sit. Let's supervise Aaron."

David sat with Isaac on the left and Jen to the right. "So far it all looks good."

"And smells good," Isaac added.

"Excellent job supervising, boys." Jen swigged her milk. "Strong work." She patted David's back.

He tried not to flinch at the casual touch. She had a blustery confidence he hadn't seen in a woman before, and she watched her husband cooking without a shred of embarrassment. Mother would be mortified. When Jen gave him a smile, he realized he was staring, and whipped his gaze back to Aaron.

"You'll prepare your masterpiece this weekend?" Aaron added more salt to the pot.

"Toast with peanut butter?" Jen answered. "That's right. I make it in both smooth and crunchy. I know—it's impressive. Or there's always my famous call to Giovanni's. Or Little Nepal." She groaned. "I could murder some lamb curry right now. Hurry up with dinner, beloved."

"By the way, I'm going grocery shopping tomorrow." Aaron's expression turned grave. "Brace yourself, but I'm bringing home fruit and vegetables."

Jen made a hissing sound. "I thought we talked about that."

"We did, *Doctor* Paculba. You know what they say about an apple a day."

David wasn't sure what they said, but he didn't ask. There were a few moments of silence while they watched Aaron stirring the contents of the huge pot. It smelled of beef, tomatoes, garlic, and herbs David couldn't place. His stomach growled.

Isaac smiled nervously at Jen. "I hope we weren't too noisy while you were sleeping." After a moment his expression grew horrified. "I mean— not because of—we—uh—we weren't, um," he stammered.

The memory of the heft of Isaac's cock in his mouth filled David's mind, and his throat went dry. He couldn't even dare to look up from his hands where he kept them folded on the counter, his fingers laced together so tightly it hurt. But as Jen laughed, he risked a glance.

She winked at Isaac. "It's okay. I know what you meant."

"We have got to work on your poker faces," Aaron added with a chuckle.

Jen waved dismissively. "But seriously, you could have had the sur-round sound on full blast and I wouldn't have heard a thing up there. It was a long-ass night. Multi-car MVA, and—" She grimaced. "Sorry, that's ER speak. Motor vehicle accident."

David tensed. *Blood in the snow. White bone jutting out of Mother's leg.*

Isaac asked quietly, "Were the people all right?"

"A few of them. One DOA—dead on arrival—and another three in surgery."

David tried to push the memories away. Isaac touched his thigh hesitantly, and David gripped his hand. *Isaac's here with me. I didn't lose him. I'll keep him safe.*

"I'm sorry—did I say something to upset you?" Jen asked with a frown.

"No." David cleared his throat. "My mother and sister got hit by a car in their buggy in December."

Red sauce splashed the stove top as Aaron dropped the wooden spoon and whirled around. "They did? Are they okay? Abigail didn't mention it. But come to think of it, she hasn't written in a while since she's busy with the new baby. What happened?"

David hesitated, his body almost vibrating as he tried to find the words. It was as though he could hear the sirens right there in the kitchen.

Isaac spoke up. "Snow came all of a sudden, and the car didn't see them in time. Mary got thrown, but she landed in a snowbank and she was mostly okay. It was a miracle they said. But David's mother broke her leg very badly. We weren't sure at first if... But she had surgery and she's healing now. She's in a wheelchair, but she should walk again soon."

Aaron clenched his jaw. "Maybe if Zebulon would use orange triangles on buggies, it wouldn't have happened. It's ridiculous. Other Amish use them, but Swartzentrubers have to be so damn stubborn."

"I don't know if it would have made a difference in that weather, but I don't understand it either," Isaac said.

Jen touched David's shoulder lightly. "I'm sorry that happened. It must have made it even harder to leave."

Head down, David nodded.

"I'm sure Eli Helmuth is over there every day," Isaac added quickly. "They'll probably be married soon, and then you don't have to worry."

The thought of not worrying made David want to laugh humorlessly, and he pressed his lips together. He couldn't imagine the day would ever come.

"Your father died a few years ago, right?" Aaron asked. The sauce bubbled, and he picked up the spoon again. "I was sorry to hear it. I know how hard it must have been for you, being the only man left in your family. Especially after Joshua..."

David blew out a long breath. "I really tried. I wanted to stay for them, but I just couldn't." *I failed them. Failed Father.*

"There's never a good time to leave. Trust me." Aaron smiled softly. "But I'm so glad you did. Both of you. A lot of people are really happy in the plain life, but some of us just aren't made for it."

"You know what I think we need with dinner?" Jen asked with a slap on the counter. "Wine." She hopped off her stool. "Bordeaux always goes well with your sauce, right, babe?"

Aaron chuckled. "It does, but we'd better go easy on them. You guys don't have to drink anything if you don't want to."

Jen held up her hands. "Right. Don't let me peer pressure you. You probably don't know what that means. Let me rephrase: don't let me pressure you into doing anything you're not comfortable with. And Isaac, you're only eighteen, but I think a glass of wine at home is okay."

David smiled. "I don't think a glass will hurt." He raised an eyebrow at Isaac.

"Sure." Isaac shrugged. "Jen's a doctor, after all."

"*Exactly*. Doctor's orders." She whispered loudly to Aaron, "I like them already. They listen to me."

Laughing, Aaron said, "*Bahaef dich.*"

"Hey!" Hands on her hips, Jen glared at him, although she was still smiling. "No secret Amish German. Uh, not that I want to stifle your heritage. But no making rude comments about me. I demand all rude comments be in English so I can respond appropriately."

"I just said to behave yourself. And does that mean your family will stop speaking Tagalog in front of me?" Aaron asked. "That's what a lot of people from the Philippines speak," he added to Isaac and David.

Jen raised an eyebrow. "Touché."

Isaac whispered, "Huh?"

David could only shrug.

"It means…good point. Basically that the other person is right," Aaron said.

"I think it's a strong statement to say that you were *right*. We need more debate before we make a determination. Let me get the wine. Wine will help." Jen went through a door just off the kitchen and down into what appeared to be a cellar.

David had slipped in and out of German and English so easily his whole life. It was always German at home and church, and English at school and everywhere else. He hadn't even thought about the fact that he would likely lose the German out in the world. He felt a strange hollowness in his chest.

Soon Aaron heaped spaghetti and sauce onto plates, and David stood by one of the middle chairs at the dining table, with Isaac across from him.

"Sit, sit!" Jen said as she pulled the cork out of a bottle of wine by the counter.

David and Isaac looked at each other, hesitating. David realized with a sinking sensation that after his belated morning prayer, he hadn't said his silent prayer at breakfast or lunch. He bowed his head now to recite the Lord's prayer in his mind, speeding through the familiar words. He looked up to see Isaac finish a moment later.

Jen hovered by the table with the wine in one hand and a basket of bread in the other. Her smile was apologetic. "Sorry. Didn't mean to interrupt. My family only really says grace on the holidays, so I'm not used to it. But you can pray out loud if you want. We don't mind. We want you to be at home here."

"It's always silent when they pray at meals," Aaron said as he brought two plates of steaming spaghetti to the table. He smiled ruefully. "Wow, I haven't thought about that in a long time."

They. Aaron had spent the first nineteen years of his life Amish, but in ten years gone it had ceased to be an *us*. As David pulled out his chair, he wondered if he'd feel that way too. He supposed it was inevitable. He could see the sadness on Isaac's face as they took their seats, and he extended his leg under the table to rub his bare foot briefly against Isaac's.

Isaac smiled softly, and then cleared his throat. "These chairs are nice. So comfy."

Indeed, the dining chairs were padded with a thick material. David had never built any with cushioned seats. He knew it was silly considering the scope of his sins, but he'd felt a little better creating furniture in his secret workshop at June's that was still plain.

Jen poured wine into their glasses before taking a seat at the end of the table with Aaron at the other. David sipped his wine. It was very strong, and he wasn't sure he liked it. He took a bite of the crusty baguette, which Aaron had sliced and baked. Now *that*, he liked. He couldn't stifle his groan as he chewed the butter-soaked bread. "Is this what the English call garlic bread?"

"Yep." Aaron plucked a piece from the basket. "Delicious, huh? Garlic butter is one of humanity's greatest inventions."

"It's my new favorite thing." Isaac took a vigorous bite. "I can't believe you cooked all this," he mumbled.

Aaron laughed. "Well, the salad's from a bag, and the spaghetti and garlic bread are pretty easy. And thank you for getting the bread." To Jen he added, "They survived their first foray into the city alone. Although apparently they had to outrun a marauding gang of baguette thieves."

Jen whistled. "Close one, huh? Gotta keep those baguettes under wraps." She swirled the wine in her glass. "I feel like there's a 'is that a baguette in your pocket, or are you just happy to see me?' joke in there, but I'll refrain."

Aaron laughed. "Masterful restraint, darling. As always."

David smiled as Jen blew Aaron a kiss across the table. They seemed so *free* in a way he'd never witnessed before. So open and warm. He'd never seen Mother and Father even touch affectionately, although he knew they must have done more in private considering they'd had so many children.

As he ate, David found the wine went down more smoothly. He savored the beef sauce and listened to Jen tell a story about a patient who went crazy on the full moon, although he wasn't sure what the moon had to do with it. Isaac looked a little confused as well, and they smiled at each other.

"Oh my God, you guys are going to give me a cavity. But in the best possible way." Jen drained the wine bottle into her glass. "Hold on, more wine is needed, yes? Yes. Who was I kidding only bringing up one bottle?" She pushed back her chair, and her slippers slapped on the wood floor.

"A cavity?" Isaac whispered.

"She means you're sweet," Aaron answered. "The way you two look at each other, it's…"

David tensed as his mind completed the sentence. *Wrong. Abhorrent. An abomination before the Lord.*

"Wonderful," Aaron finished. "You have no idea how happy it makes me that you found each other. Being gay and alone in an Amish community would be…" He shuddered. "I can't imagine the loneliness."

David and Isaac's eyes met. David reached for his wine, gulping what was left. He spoke without meaning to. "It was a little easier before anything happened. Like how you don't really know what you're missing if you've never had something. But once you have…"

His despair in the weeks after the accident had been like a hard object lodged in his chest, choking him with each breath. The ghost of it lingered, constricting his lungs even now as he remembered.

Isaac's warm fingers grasped his across the table, and David was able to breathe again. The certainty that they'd made the right choice—the only choice—settled over him like warm honey. He glanced at Aaron, who only smiled kindly. But after a moment, Isaac let go of David's hand.

"I really hope you'll both be comfortable to be yourselves here." Aaron speared a piece of lettuce, but didn't eat it. "I know you had it even worse in Zebulon than it ever was in Red Hills. Swartzentruber rules are so strict. I feel like even though I grew up Amish, there are some things I can't understand about your experience. I'm trying, though. But tell me if I'm getting stuff wrong, or if I'm not being helpful. I don't want to pressure either of you."

"You're not," Isaac said. "Not at all."

"I don't know what we'd do without you," David added. "There's so much I don't know."

Aaron patted his arm. "You'll learn. And I should tell you there are a lot of stereotypes about the Amish here in the world. Most people think it's quaint, or *cute*, and that we're all the same. They've seen things on TV, and they think that's what it's really like in every Amish community. There are a lot of misconceptions." He laughed. "I sound ready to give a lecture on the subject."

"You are a teacher, after all," said Isaac.

"Never fear—I have returned from the trenches with provisions." Jen swept into the dining room with a new bottle of wine and the corkscrew.

Isaac picked up his fork again. "So, you two met at the hospital, right?" Isaac asked.

"That's right." Jen poured more wine for everyone. "Aaron got his bike wheel caught in a sewer grate and took a header onto the pavement. Paramedics brought him in with a nasty gash on his forehead, and a distal radius fracture."

"Broken wrist," Aaron translated.

"Did you like him right away?" Isaac sipped his wine with a grimace.

"Well, I thought he was cute." Jen winked at Aaron. "Obviously. I mean, look at that face."

Aaron was certainly handsome, with his bright smile and the little cleft in his chin. Was it wrong to acknowledge that Isaac's brother was attractive? Did it make David disloyal to Isaac somehow, even if he had no interest in any other man? He had another swig of wine, the gentle burn calming his mind.

"But she figured I was just a kid. This was...wow, six years ago now. I was twenty-three, and in my second year of college. It took a while to get my GED and figure out what I wanted to do. Math was my best subject since numbers are the same no matter where you grew up. Not that we learned more than the basics as kids, but it gave me a start. I heard math teachers are in higher demand these days, and I thought I could be good at it."

"And he is. Those kids love Mr. B." Jen spun spaghetti onto her fork using a big spoon as a base, smiling proudly. "I think it's because he knows how hard it can be to learn new things."

David picked up his spoon from his place mat and copied her motions. He'd wondered what the spoon was for, and had hoped there was more ice cream coming. The spaghetti formed a neat circle when he spun it, with only one strand hanging down. He felt foolishly pleased.

Aaron shrugged, but a smile played on his lips. "Anyway, back to the hospital. There I was in the ER, which was packed. I was on a stretcher beside an agitated old man who kept trying to get up and leave. The nurses were so fed up with him, but then this doctor comes along and sits with him. My first thought was that she was beautiful. I mean, look at that face."

With his stomach full now, David sat back and sipped his wine, listening contentedly. Under the table, he and Isaac idly rubbed their feet together. Isaac smiled, keeping his gaze on his brother.

Aaron went on. "I was listening to her talk to this poor old man, and she was so patient. It was chaos all around us, but she was like the eye of a storm. Totally calm. In turn, that calmed him down. She didn't raise her voice once, and by the time he agreed to treatment, I knew I had to know everything there was about Dr. Paculba. Not that she made it easy."

Jen laughed as she pushed back her chair a few inches to cross her legs. She was still wearing her pajamas and *Frak me* shirt, and she dabbed at a splash of wine on the green cotton. "In my defense, I wasn't in the habit of picking up dates at work. I wasn't really in the habit of picking up many dates at all, much to my parents' chagrin. Once I got the cast on his wrist and discharged him, he would not stop asking for my number. Finally I wrote it on his cast, and told him he could call once it was off."

"I thought that bone would never heal." Aaron scowled.

Isaac laughed. "So you called her right after it did?"

"Yep. She was all, 'Who is this? What do you want?' I reminded her that she said I could call, and she agreed to meet me for coffee."

David swirled his wine the way Jen and Aaron had. He wasn't sure what it did, but it seemed like the wine tasted better and better with each sip. "Then what happened?"

"I met him at a coffee shop by the wharf," Jen answered. "I set an alarm on my phone so I could fake a page from the hospital, because I couldn't imagine I'd have anything to talk about with this kid. I was thirty, and according to my mom, I should have been looking for a husband. Little did I know I'd found him. When the alarm pinged, I shut my phone off."

"What was it about him?" David asked.

She ran her finger around the rim of her glass thoughtfully. "He'd been through so much. He was the oldest twenty-three-year-old I'd ever met. He wasn't hanging at the frat house playing beer pong, you know?"

David was pretty sure he knew what a frat was, but beer pong was a mystery. Still, he nodded.

"I couldn't imagine leaving my whole family and everything I knew behind to start over. Just to get into college was a huge accomplishment considering he stopped school in the eighth grade. And I knew what it was like to grow up in a weird religion." She made a face. "I shouldn't say weird, sorry."

Isaac shifted in his chair. "I guess it must seem strange to English people even if it doesn't to us. Although sometimes it does to us too. I don't know how to feel about it."

David could well imagine how *weird* it all must seem to outsiders. As a child, any questions of *why* were answered by quoting the Ordnung, or a simple: *Because it's our way.* He'd once asked Father why God cared about the width of their hat brims, and had persisted until Father gave him a lash with the buggy whip. He'd never questioned out loud at home again.

Jen said, "No, that was disrespectful, and I'm sorry. We respect everyone's beliefs—or non-beliefs—in this house."

"It's okay." Isaac sat back. "What religion are you?"

"Funny story: While ninety-nine-point-nine percent of Filipinos are

Catholic, my family's Seventh-day Adventist. Missionaries went over back in the day, and my forebearers were convinced."

David pondered it. "I've never heard of that church. It's Christian?"

"Yep." Jen swallowed more wine. "Started in Michigan in the eighteen hundreds. In a nutshell, they observe Sabbath on Saturday, which was the original seventh day, and believe that the second coming of Jesus is going to happen any minute now. As such, we should be living clean and avoiding all those worldly temptations." She smirked as she lifted her glass. "Booze, for example."

"I take it you're not following the church anymore," David said.

"Nope. I went to an Adventist school until college, and I couldn't wait to move away from home and start *living*. I still believe in God, but not all the trappings made up by men."

Excitement rippled through David at the idea of still believing in God without being weighed down by the rules. *Trappings.* He mulled the word over in his mind.

Jen sighed. "Don't get me wrong—I love my family, and I grew up very happy. Adventists are good people. The church certainly isn't as controlling as the Amish, and even though they didn't want us to go to movies or parties, we still had a normal life." She winced. "Not that you guys aren't normal. I should stop talking now."

David huffed out a sudden laugh. "It's all right. When you think about it, it's not very normal to live like it's still two hundred years ago. What's wrong with everything God's done in the last two centuries?"

"An excellent question," Aaron said. "I think the answer is that there's absolutely nothing wrong with the modern world."

"Your parents still talked to you when you stopped going to church?" Isaac asked Jen.

"Oh yeah. They were disappointed, but it happens a lot. It's not really a big deal. Not like it is with the Amish. Adventists still live here in the real world, so it's not such a culture shock. I was a little sheltered, but college took care of that quickly." She whistled softly. "Spring break in Mexico. Innocence shattered within twelve hours."

David thought of a movie he'd seen at the drive-in about students on spring break. He'd sat there in June's pickup watching the screen with wonder, confusion, and half an erection.

"Anyway, back to our epic romance," said Aaron. "The coffee date lasted about seven hours. We walked down to the water, and ended up going for dinner. Then she really did get paged by the hospital, but she kissed me before running off." He grinned. "I didn't even want to brush my teeth that night because I imagined I could still feel her on my lips. I did, though, for the record. We got together again for lunch the next day, and here we are."

"It was that easy?" Isaac asked.

Jen and Aaron laughed loudly, and Jen answered, "Not always. But when you know you've found the right person, it's worth the work."

Isaac and David shared a look, and David lifted his glass the way people did in movies. "To the right person."

They all drank to that.

CHAPTER Four

A S DAVID WALKED into their room, Isaac was by the mirrored closet doors, and he scrambled, his head down while he yanked the sheet off the bed and wrapped it around his waist.

David froze in the doorway. "Should I have knocked?" He hadn't shared a room since Joshua, and it hadn't even occurred to him—especially given that he and Isaac had done a lot more than see each other undressed.

"No, of course not. Come in. It's your room too." Isaac didn't look at him.

David shut the door behind him, but didn't move any closer. "Are you sure? If you want privacy, I can…"

"Why would I want privacy from you? It's not like you haven't seen me naked before." Isaac laughed nervously.

"Then what's wrong?" Perhaps he shouldn't have had so much wine, because he couldn't figure out what Isaac would be upset about. He wanted to take Isaac in his arms and make whatever it was better, but hesitated.

"I thought you'd be downstairs longer."

"June wasn't home, so I left her a message." How strange and wonderful that he'd heard her voice and spoken to her machine from thousands of miles away. Still, David had secretly been relieved when she hadn't answered. She'd surely gone to see his mother by now, and he dreaded the news of Mother's reaction.

"That's too bad. I'm sure you'll reach her tomorrow." Isaac was still tense, gripping the sheet.

The wooden blinds were closed, and the lamps on the little tables beside the bed cast a warm glow that reminded David of the kerosene lamps from home, especially with the white paint on the walls. But Isaac's face was in shadow.

David skirted the bed. "Did I do something?"

Isaac sighed. "Of course not. It's the mirrors."

"Oh." Was he afraid or ashamed to see his body? David hoped not, because Isaac was beautiful. "Do you want to cover them like we did at the motel?" Forcing away thoughts of how that day ended, David squinted at the ceiling. "Maybe we could hang up a spare sheet? I'm sure Aaron will—"

"It's not that." With a sheepish expression, Isaac finally met David's gaze. "I was looking at myself. It's stupid. And vain."

Exhaling in a rush, David stepped closer and rubbed Isaac's arm. "Don't be embarrassed. We're supposed to be free in here, remember? It's not stupid, and it's not against the rules anymore. I did the same thing this morning."

Isaac's eyebrows shot up. "You did? Where was I?"

"Fast asleep and drooling." David grinned.

"You should have woken me." He nudged David's shoulder.

Inching forward, David reached around and ran his fingers down Isaac's spine. "You're awake now." The sweet buzz of the wine hummed through him. "We're going to be so hungover in the morning, but I don't care. I don't care about anything else tonight. Just being here with you."

Isaac kissed him. "Me either. What's that mean? Hungover?"

"It's what English people call it when they've had too much to drink the night before."

Isaac's skin had the same rosy flush as David's, and his eyes were bright. "I didn't really like the taste, but I feel nice." He rolled his head back and forth. "A little drunk I think. I've never been drunk before."

"Me either." David nodded to the mirror a few feet away. "Tell me—did you like what you saw?"

Isaac shrugged, his gaze skittering away. "I look okay, I guess."

"Better than *okay*, my Isaac." David tugged on the sheet at Isaac's waist. "Look again."

With a deep breath, Isaac faced the mirrors. David moved behind him to run his palms over Isaac's shoulders and down his arms. David was a little taller and bigger, and Isaac leaned against him. They looked good together. He thought of Aaron and Jen's wedding photos, and wondered if he and Isaac would ever have pictures like that. It made him warm and peaceful to think of it, while still being dressed when Isaac was bare in front of him sent a rush of blood to his cock.

"You should like how you look," he murmured, tracing his fingers over Isaac's belly and the trail of dark hair. "I could stare at you all day and never get bored."

Isaac licked his lips, shivering a little as his cock twitched.

"Do you see what I see?" David caressed Isaac's chest. He felt as though the wine had slicked his tongue, and it was wonderfully liberating. "So handsome." His fingers danced over a nipple and down Isaac's quivering stomach. "Beautiful, and so much stronger than you think."

Isaac shuddered while David touched him all over. As David's excitement grew, he watched Isaac get harder in the mirror, his cock red and straining. Goose bumps spread over David's body, his hair standing up as if electricity flowed through them the way it did the house. He couldn't tear his eyes away from the mirror.

"Take your clothes off." Isaac spoke quietly, his gaze locked with David's in their reflection.

David didn't want to stop his exploration of Isaac's body, but he peeled his T-shirt over his head and tossed it aside. Isaac took a step to the left, watching David closely in the mirror.

With each new bit of flesh he bared, David watched Isaac's face following along avidly. Isaac's Adam's apple bobbed when David kicked off his jeans and stood naked, his cock jutting out.

"Is that better?" Now that David was exposed, his desire hummed even louder.

"Yes," Isaac breathed as he reached back and stroked David's hip and thigh. "I can't believe this is real. That it's *allowed*."

David sighed at Isaac's touch, more goose bumps rippling over his skin. Outside, a vehicle roared up the hill, and they both jumped before giggling in a way David couldn't remember doing since he was a boy. He wrapped his arms around Isaac's stomach and kissed the top of his spine. He felt so *loose*.

Isaac swayed back against him and glanced to the window. "No one can see in, right? It really is just us?"

"Just us," David echoed. "So tell me—now do you see what I see?" He caressed Isaac's body. He felt so *warm* and joyful.

"This is me," Isaac murmured.

David skimmed over the light hair on Isaac's thighs before tracing along his shaft and down to his heavy balls. He whispered in Isaac's ear, "Be proud." He didn't care if it was a sin—more than anything he wanted Isaac to feel about himself the way David felt about him. Isaac deserved it.

They were both winter pale aside from the flush of wine and lust in their cheeks, and their bodies almost merged already in the glass. They looked *good* together. As though they fit the way they were meant to. A horn honked distantly, but here in this room with only each other and their reflection, they were safe.

"And I see you." Isaac met David's gaze in the mirror as he reached out, his fingers squeaking on the glass. "*Us.* I never thought I'd have this again. I thought you were lost to me. That I'd have to leave without you."

Clammy fear at how differently things could have gone constricted David's lungs. "I don't ever want to be without you again." He buried his face against Isaac's neck, pushing away the memories of the desperate loneliness and sorrow that had filled him the past months.

"You'll never have to, my David." Isaac ran his hands over David's arms where they encircled him.

Exhaling a long breath, David relaxed his grip and suckled at the tender skin behind Isaac's ear.

Isaac moaned, and then laughed softly. "You know, at first I was so afraid of you."

Startled, David raised his head. "What do you mean?"

"Mmm, don't stop." Isaac tilted his head to the right, baring the other side of his neck.

"All right. But tell me why." David mouthed at Isaac's skin, watching him in the mirror. They were both still partly hard, although not as straining as they had been. The desire flowed through him languidly. There was no rush tonight. They were safe here.

"Why do you think?" Isaac smiled, his fingers still tracing over David's hands and arms around him. "I wanted you. Not that I really knew it—at least not that I'd admit. You were so mysterious, David Lantz. Always keeping to yourself. That first day of work, I thought I might pee my pants. That would have made quite an impression."

David chuckled. "Quite." He pressed slow, wet kisses along Isaac's neck to his shoulder, and back again. "It wouldn't have mattered. I still would've fallen in love with you."

Isaac shuddered. "Really?" he whispered.

"Yes." David met Isaac's gaze in the reflection. "You're good and kind. Smart and loving. I'd thought so from watching you, but once I knew you for myself…"

"What?" Isaac waited, his lips parted and his breath coming quick.

"You were all the things I'd imagined, but so much more. Hard working and generous. Such a dreamer, and *oh* how I wanted to dream. I knew I could trust you. When we're together it feels like anything is possible."

Isaac jerked around and took David's face in his hands, kissing him hard. David opened his mouth, moaning as Isaac's tongue thrust inside. They stumbled back against one of the mirrored doors, which wavered with a rattle. David braced his palms on the cool glass, unwilling to break their kiss. In that moment he didn't care if they broke the mirror instead.

But Isaac tore his mouth away. "I love you." His eyes were darker, and his lips shone. "You showed me so much—that there really could be more than the life I knew. That there *was*. You showed me who I am. Who I can be. That night, when we went to the drive-in? You gave me hope that I didn't even know was possible. Thank you."

"It's me who should thank you. You're the reason we're here. The reason we're free." David rubbed his cheek against Isaac's hair, his body on fire as they pressed together with Isaac's thigh between his. The past didn't matter. He knew without a doubt that with Isaac by his side, he could be *happy*.

Isaac's voice was barely a whisper. "I need you inside me."

His nostrils flaring, David nodded at the mirrors. "Do you want to?" he asked boldly before he could think better of it.

Isaac shivered. "Yes." His voice was hoarse. "Show me."

"We don't have...we need..." David glanced around the room. "Maybe in the bathroom there's something..."

"I don't care. Just do it." Isaac snatched David's hand and sucked on his fingers.

The warm rasp of Isaac's tongue sent sparks up David's spine, and he closed his eyes, rutting his hips against Isaac's. "Wait. There's lotion—" He gasped, his cock throbbing as Isaac sucked his fingers harder.

It took all his willpower to break away, but David lurched the few steps to the bathroom and snatched the bottle from the counter. It was plastic and had a pump at the top, and he splashed the pale yellow cream onto his palm.

David's breath caught in his throat when he returned. Isaac was leaning over with his legs parted, his forehead against the mirror and his hands behind him, spreading himself open. He looked so *wanton*, and David tingled all over. He felt almost outside his body while he slicked his fingers. There was too much lotion, and he slathered the rest over his cock, giving himself a few firm tugs while Isaac waited, trembling.

Wrapping one arm around Isaac's chest, David drew him back so he wouldn't hit his head. Sure enough, when he pressed the first finger inside, Isaac jerked, biting back a gasp as David inched him open.

"I love your hands," he muttered. "Love watching you work with wood. With me."

"You're so tight after all this time, Eechel. Let me in," David whispered, biting Isaac's earlobe gently.

When David pushed the head of his cock inside Isaac, he shook with the effort of restraining himself from plunging all the way in. Isaac leaned over to brace his left hand on the wall beside the closet, his other palm flat on the trembling mirrored door. They were both breathing hard, and Isaac licked at the sweat dampening his upper lip as David filled him. Isaac felt so tight and *perfect*.

When Isaac winced, David froze. "Too much?" He started to pull away.

"No—don't stop." Isaac bore down. "It feels…" He groaned, his eyes rolling back.

David tried to brush against that spot again, and each time he did, Isaac vibrated, the tension draining from him as he took David deeper. David wished he could control himself better, but being in Isaac felt so good. The sound of their flesh slapping together echoed in the room along with their grunts.

"Yes," David muttered. "Isaac…"

Movement behind them caught his eye, and his heart skipped. But he realized it was only their shadows, stretching up one wall to the ceiling. In the electric light they didn't waver the way they would in a lantern.

David rocked forward and back in a jerky rhythm, holding Isaac's hip with one hand, his other arm still locked around Isaac's chest. Their skin was damp where it met. Vehicles still growled outside every so often, but they felt miles away. Isaac's little cries filled David's ears, and he couldn't look away from the sight of them straining together, slick and panting.

When they'd been together in the barn, it had smelled like manure and sawdust, but here there was only the pure scent of Isaac's sweat and the lingering mint of the green soap in the shower. David inhaled deeply.

"I should be ashamed," Isaac muttered, gasping.

David's heart sank and his hips jerked to a stop. *No!*

But Isaac spoke again, his fingers streaking the glass and his breath fogging it.

"But I'm not. We make our own choices now." Isaac pushed back on David's cock and started fucking himself. "We—" He cried out, quivering. "We make the rules."

David slammed into him now. There were no words as he watched Isaac take him. Isaac's cock bounced, so hard and ready that David knew it wouldn't be long.

The mirror shook as Isaac spread his legs farther apart. "I love how it feels to have you inside me." He squeezed around David's cock.

The buzz of pleasure in David's body became a deafening roar that swept through him without warning. It wasn't the first time David had come inside him, but seeing not just Isaac but *himself* as they joined together made him feel as though he'd peeled back his own skin. His mouth was open, his face an even darker red, and his hair wild. He barely recognized himself.

He met Isaac's gaze again, and Isaac smiled. "*Schee,*" he murmured as he squeezed around David again.

But it was Isaac who was the pretty one, flushed all over and reaching back for David's thigh, his cock leaking. David lowered his arm from around Isaac's chest, running his hand all the way down Isaac's trembling belly. Isaac's gaze followed David's movement. When David wrapped his hand around Isaac's shaft and stroked him, Isaac cried out—little nothing words that were like music to David as he watched him near the edge.

"Oh, oh—uh. Oh." He sucked in a breath, shaking. "*Ngh.*" Then as he came, David's name graced his lips.

Shaking in David's arms, Isaac splattered the mirror. They watched the mess drip toward the floor as they caught their breath, David softening inside Isaac and panting against his head. He closed his eyes for a moment, caressing Isaac's belly.

"David?"

The seriousness of Isaac's tone made him snap back to attention. "Yes?"

"Do you know how English people clean mirrors?"

With a deep laugh, David kissed the side of his head, tasting the salt of Isaac's sweat at his temple. "I guess we'd better find out."

Isaac swiped his finger across the sticky mirror. "This is us," he murmured.

David lifted Isaac's hand to his mouth to lick his finger clean.

CHAPTER Five

"FIRST THINGS FIRST. Boxers or briefs?" Aaron held up a package. "Or boxer briefs?"

David rubbed his eyes. The florescent lights in the huge Target store were unrelenting, and even though he'd followed Jen's instructions on water and ibuprofen before bed, his head felt like a block of ironwood. He tried to focus. "Uh…what do you wear?"

Aaron opened the package. "I went with boxers first. They're like shorts. See?" He unfolded the plaid material. "Now I wear the boxer briefs. We can get a few packages of each for you both and you can give them all a whirl. Sound good?"

David glanced at Isaac, who seemed equally adrift and bleary eyed. "Sure," David said.

Aaron chuckled. "Did you guys have coffee before we left?"

They shook their heads miserably.

"Lucky for you there's a Starbucks in here. Look around, and I'll be back in a few. Just black for both of you?"

They nodded, and David stifled a yawn. "Usually we'd have done almost half a day's work by now." He gazed at the endless packages of underwear and socks hanging in plastic from metal racks. They stood in an aisle with tall shelves on both sides, and he could hardly believe there were this many varieties.

"I wonder what they're doing at home." Isaac wrapped his arms around himself. "Same things as ever, I guess. It feels so far away, doesn't it?" He blinked up at the ceiling. "It's so *bright* here. And there's music."

A woman sang about how they were going to hear her roar, and it was certainly accurate given the volume. David peered around, but couldn't tell where it was coming from. It seemed to be everywhere—just a part of the air. It scraped at his nerves like sandpaper. "Pretty different from our songs."

Isaac examined a package of socks. "It'll be odd, won't it? Not going to church or the singing next Sunday."

"Probably for the best given that I sound like a dying cat when I sing."

"You do not!" Isaac laughed. "Well, maybe a little."

"Mary once said that—" David stopped. He felt strangely disloyal talking about her with Isaac. "Never mind," he finished lamely. He reached for the nearest hanging package, which proclaimed in red capital letters:

NEW! 2X THE DURABILITY

"What do you think two x means?"

His shoulders slumped in his too-big clothes, Isaac ignored the question. "Do you think she's all right?"

David hung the socks back on the metal rod, poking it through the small hole in the plastic bag. He pushed it with his finger, making the package sway. "I don't know. I hope so. If not now, then soon."

"I'm sorry I hurt her."

He turned to look at Isaac. "You know it's not your fault. You never drove her home from the singings, or let her believe there could be a future." *Not the way I did with Grace.* "It's not your fault she liked you. There's nothing for you to be sorry for."

Isaac shook his head. "I don't even know why she did. I barely talked to her."

A memory of Mary and Anna's quiet voices from the kitchen echoed in his mind, and he smiled softly. "She thought you were shy."

He'd been sitting stiffly in Father's rocking chair, feeling like an imposter as he tried to focus on a letter in *Die Botschaft* from a farmer in

Pennsylvania who'd cured his cows' tick infestation with apple cider vinegar. Mother had been upstairs with the younger girls.

"Mary, you need to forget about Isaac Byler. He's never even hinted that he wants to drive you home."

Mary sighed. *"I know, but he doesn't seem to have his eye on any of the other girls. He's shy, Anna."*

"Maybe you should just ask him, then."

"Anna!" Mary sounded suitably scandalized. "Girls don't ask out boys. Isaac's just...a gentleman. He's worth waiting for. Did you see him taking care of his little brother at the barn raising last week after Nathan hammered his thumb? He'll be a good father."

"And she thought you were a gentleman," David added. He didn't mention fatherhood. Mary was right—Isaac was wonderful with children. *But we'll never be fathers now.* He shoved that thought away with all the others he was avoiding.

Isaac ducked his head. "What about you? Do you think I'm a gentleman?"

"Most of the time." David raised an eyebrow suggestively.

Blushing, Isaac lowered his voice and stepped closer. "Tonight I'll show you—"

They jerked away from each other as a woman appeared at the end of the short aisle, pushing a shopping cart. She smiled absently.

"Excuse me, I just need to..." She pointed to the rack behind David.

"Of course. I'm sorry." His heart fluttering, David scurried out of the way. He and Isaac hadn't even been touching, but he felt sure she *knew.*

Isaac moved as well, and they both examined the packages of socks and underwear intently. Once the woman wheeled her cart around the corner and disappeared, David exhaled.

"David," Isaac whispered. "Look at this."

The package of the underwear called briefs—a value pack, which sounded like a good thing—proclaimed *NO RIDE UP*, whatever that meant, and featured a photo of a man's lower body.

And the man's very big bulge against the tight white cotton.

"How can they show a picture of…" Isaac waved a hand at the package. "*That?* Where everyone can see it?"

"It's normal to them." David couldn't help but enjoy looking at it. He gazed around. All the men on the packages had tanned skin and flat stomachs, their thighs muscular. "Briefs look…" *Sexy.*

"Snug?" Aaron said behind them. He held out their coffees. "We should buy some underwear first so you can try on pants."

David sipped his coffee, sighing as the hot bitterness flowed down his throat. Just smelling the familiar aroma made his headache fade. He watched Aaron plucking a variety of packages from the display. "We need to keep track of everything you're spending on us."

"I really don't want you to worry about that, but if it makes you more comfortable I'll file away the receipts," Aaron replied. "Nothing here is expensive, so you can try different styles and see what you like." With his arms full of underwear he nodded toward the end of the aisle. "Come on. Check out the men's section while I buy these."

They watched Aaron go, weaving easily around the tables and racks of clothing, where garments dangled from vain hangers that were forbidden in Zebulon. A new song about blowing a whistle blared, and David took in what seemed like an acre of choices. He hadn't been in a big store like this since he was a kid in Red Hills and they'd visited the Walmart once in a while.

Other shoppers milled around the store, confidently pushing their carts along the aisles. Target seemed to sell just about everything, from food to clothing to lawn mowers. It was certainly far grander than the highway grocery store near Zebulon.

Isaac glanced around uneasily. "How do you even know where to start? There's so much."

"I don't know." David looked down at the jeans and hoodie he was wearing. "June bought my English clothes for me." He drank more of his coffee, clutching the paper cup as though it was some kind of anchor. "Okay. We like T-shirts, right?" He pointed to a table covered in folded cotton.

As he caught their reflection in one of the long mirrors nearby, he thought about the night before in their room, and a thrill sparked through him like a flame to tinder. David couldn't wait to get back there. He wanted to hide away with Isaac for days.

But he couldn't, and as he poked through the dizzying sea of clothing—and this was only what to *wear*—his headache returned. His stomach churned as he remembered the letter he needed to write. On the bus ride he'd pushed it out of his mind with silent promises that he'd write Mother as soon as they arrived. But now it was his second day in San Francisco.

"How about this?" Isaac asked, holding up a pale blue shirt with buttons up the front. "Except for the buttons, I guess it's kind of Amish looking. I don't know if that's a good thing or a bad thing."

"I don't know either." David pushed a hanger aside on a rack of thin sweaters. He rubbed the material between his fingers. It didn't feel like wool. *What am I going to say to Mother? Will she even read it?* Running a hand through his hair, he sighed.

"Are you okay?" Isaac's eyebrows drew together.

"My head hurts. It's nothing."

But Isaac still frowned. "Tell me."

David didn't want to lie, and if anyone would understand, it was Isaac. He glanced around, even though with the music booming no one would hear him even if they wanted to. "I'm thinking about the letter I have to write. I should have done it yesterday."

Isaac fiddled with the arm of a sweatshirt. "Me too. I feel like, one minute everything's great and exciting, and the next I'm thinking about home, and my belly hurts." He glanced at a man nearby who was pawing through jackets, and then snagged David's hand. "We'll figure it all out."

Nodding, David squeezed Isaac's fingers. The more he thought about it, the more jittery he became, so he cleared his mind. *Later. It could all wait until later.*

"Underwear mission accomplished," Aaron announced as he suddenly appeared.

Isaac and David ripped their hands apart, and David shoved his into his jean pockets.

"Geez, if you guys are going to go around looking that guilty, people are going to think you're shoplifting. Stealing, I mean." Aaron gave them both an affectionate shake. "It's okay to hold hands. You can kiss each other too. This is San Francisco. I promise no one's going to care."

The thought of *kissing* Isaac in public seemed absolutely insane. "I…we…"

Aaron smiled. "I'm not saying you have to. Just that you don't need to be afraid Bishop Yoder will appear out of thin air to yell Bible passages at you." He clapped his hands. "So what did you pick out?"

"Um…" Isaac picked up a gray T-shirt. "This?"

Aaron chuckled. "Okay, that's a good start. You know you can wear colors now, though. Not if you don't want to, but don't be afraid to try."

"There's just so *much*," Isaac said.

"It's a little overwhelming, huh? I remember standing in a store like this for an hour like a lost duckling before I even touched anything. I might as well have been shopping on the moon. But a saleswoman took pity and helped me figure out my size. Isaac, you're probably a medium, and David a large, although it'll depend on the store and the brand."

"The sizes aren't the same everywhere?" Isaac asked, frowning.

"You'd think they would be, but not even close sometimes. Hey, Isaac—go grab a few of those jackets. If there's one thing you'll need in San Francisco, it's a jacket."

As Isaac scurried away, David looked through the T-shirts on the table, this time choosing a large in dark purple.

"This can be fun, you know." Aaron nudged his shoulder. "It's allowed."

"I know." David tried to smile. "It's just…"

"What?" Aaron tilted his head.

"Here I am having *fun*, and my mother and sisters are alone. It was my duty to provide for them. It *is* my duty. Your father's still alive, and Ephraim and Nathan can take care of the men's work if they had to. There are only so many quilts my mother can sell to English people who happen along."

Aaron shook his head. "I really wish Zebulon would do more business with the English. If they were allowed to go to the markets... Bishop Yoder is making it so much more difficult. Abigail says she hears some families in Zebulon are barely getting by."

David folded and refolded one of the T-shirts. "It's hard just having enough to eat sometimes. It's winter, and even though the girls canned in the fall, they won't have anything growing in the gardens for months. Never mind the hospital bills, even though the community is helping." Bile rose in his throat, and he swallowed hard.

"I understand how you must feel. I know you already left all the money you'd saved to give to your family. David, you've done all you can. The community won't let them suffer."

"But..." It was true, wasn't it? They'd be all right without him. They had to be.

"You're young, David. You're what, twenty-two? I know by Amish standards you're all grown up, and that you had to be the man when your father died. You've taken on so much responsibility. It's time to put yourself first for a change. You deserve it."

Deserve. David unfolded another T-shirt as his mind clattered around like buggy wheels. He'd failed to save his father's life that day in the fields, and he'd failed to protect Mother and Mary from being out on the snowy road. And hadn't he done so because he *had* put his own needs first? It had been his idea to go to the motel that day.

His throat was dry. "I'm not as selfless as you think."

"You don't have to be selfless. You're barely getting started. I want you to enjoy it. Experience new things. Explore the world. Explore who you *are*. There's so much to discover. Try not to worry so much. I know—it's easier said than done."

He nodded. "I'll try. Thank you."

Aaron clapped a hand on David's shoulder. "Remember that if there's one thing the Amish have going for them, it's that they take care of their own. Your family will be just fine."

While the English way of touching casually would still take getting used to, David soaked up the warmth of Aaron's hand. He had to pray that the community and the Lord would care for his family. He'd prayed that morning, and he'd plead for it every chance he had.

He watched Isaac looking through the coats intently, his tongue between his teeth. A swell of affection thickened David's throat, and his eyes prickled. He didn't deserve Isaac, but he'd be better. He'd earn it. He'd disappointed his family bitterly, but he wouldn't fail Isaac. Never. He'd keep Isaac safe and happy here in the world no matter what. As Isaac returned with his arms full, David concentrated on breathing evenly and smiling.

Aaron unzipped his jacket. "Do you guys like the shirt I'm wearing? It's called a Henley. It's basically a long-sleeved T-shirt. Goes well with jeans."

"Uh-huh. Whatever you think," Isaac said. He held up the jackets. "I got medium and large. A couple have hoods, and others don't. I think a hood would be good?"

"Yep. A hood is always a good idea. Why don't you go try on some underwear, and I'll bring you some other clothes. The dressing rooms are right there." Aaron handed over the plastic shopping bag. "There's a recycling can there for your coffee cups if you're done. The blue container."

A middle-aged man stood at a counter by the dressing rooms, folding an enormous stack of shirts. "Good morning. How many?"

"Uh." David glanced at Isaac. "There are two of us."

The man stopped in mid-fold and peered at them with a furrow between his brows. "I meant how many things are you trying on?"

"Oh. Hold on." David counted the jackets in Isaac's arms. "Eight."

"Four each, then?"

"Sure."

The man smiled quizzically. "Where are you boys from? I can't quite place it."

"Minnesota," Isaac answered.

David had a feeling it was their German accents the man was hearing. "We just moved here. We lived on a farm."

"My brother's getting more clothes for us. But we need to try on underwear first." Isaac pointed to the plastic bag. "He already bought it, though."

The man handed them plastic tags with the number four. "All right. Just go ahead and we'll work it all out." He waved an arm toward the hallway of dressing rooms with a bench at the end.

They reminded David of stalls in a barn, but obviously smaller. He and Isaac went all the way to the end, and David was sure he could feel the man's gaze on them. He wished they could share a room, but they didn't look big enough. He opened the shopping bag and examined the contents before giving Isaac the smaller sizes.

Isaac took the room on one side of the narrow hallway, and David the other. He could still hear the ever-present music, which he supposed was better than silence, since he felt incredibly self-conscious all of a sudden.

After hanging up his hoodie, David perched on the little stool in the corner and removed his sneakers. He peeled off his T-shirt and with a deep breath, stood and pulled down his jeans. The air felt cool against his cock and balls, and he was acutely aware of how many strangers there were just beyond the flimsy dressing rooms.

He grabbed the first package in the bag and ripped it open. They were briefs of different colors, and he chose the white ones. He wasn't sure if the size was right, since they felt tight as he pulled them up. They seemed to fit around the waist, but they squished everything else together, his privates bulging against the cotton even more than the man's in the picture.

"Isaac?" he whispered. "Have you tried any on?"

"Boxers. They feel strange. What about you?"

"Briefs. Definitely strange."

"Show me."

"I'm not going out there! Someone might see," David hissed.

"Just open your door and I'll open mine. On three. One, two—"

His pulse racing foolishly, David listened to the creak of Isaac's door and edged his open. Sure enough, he could see right into Isaac's dressing room. Isaac stood in nothing but the little shorts, which were decorated in squares of greens and blues.

Isaac's gaze raked over David, and he swallowed hard. "You look..."

"Silly?" David peered over his shoulder into the mirror. He could see the faint shadow of the crease in his backside through the cotton. "They're so tight! I know this is the way they're supposed to be, but..."

"You need to buy those."

"Huh? Aaron already bought them."

Isaac shook his head. "Right. I forgot." He peeked down the hallway before adding, "You look really, *really* good."

"Oh." David flushed as he looked down at himself. "You think so?"

Isaac nodded vigorously. "You look like the man in the picture."

Even though he was standing there practically naked—and practically in public, even though no one could see—confidence surged through David. "You should try them too. The boxers look good, but..." He could imagine how the tight cotton would hug Isaac's lean hips, and—

As the man at the counter began speaking, they both jumped and slammed their doors. David leaned against it, heart thumping. He stared into the mirror, suddenly feeling unbearably exposed and *wrong*.

Aaron's voice echoed from down the hallway. "Hey, man. My brother and his boyfriend are in there. They're new around here and need clothes, so we'll be here for a while. I practically filled the cart, so we'll start with the jeans."

As the man replied, David took a deep breath and blew it out. *Boyfriend.* Aaron had said it to a stranger like it was nothing at all. David couldn't imagine what it would be like if he and Isaac didn't have Aaron to help them. He'd thought he was so very worldly taking June's truck to the drive-in and wearing jeans. Reading a dirty gay magazine from the gas station. What a joke—he barely knew anything.

Then Aaron's voice was right outside the door. "You can only take eight items in at once, so I picked stuff for each of you. We'll start with the pants." He placed a few over the dressing room door. "I'll sit out here and wait for the fashion show. David, I went a size smaller than the jeans you already have. And there are skinny leg, boot cut, dark wash— actually, never mind that. Just try 'em on and see what you like."

David could barely get his feet through the bottom of the legs, so he hoped they were the skinny ones, as he couldn't imagine anything skinnier. The dark denim hugged his thighs, and he wasn't sure he'd be able to bend over. There were two mirrors in the stall, and he looked at himself from all the angles.

The shame evaporated, and energy pulsed through him as if the music in the air was singing inside him. It was frightening, but exhilarating. With his bare chest and the jeans clinging to his body, he could almost be an English rock star, or someone in a movie. He'd never looked so different in his life. So very *not* Amish. He ran his hand down his chest and belly, and then lightly over his fly. He still wore the briefs, and he tingled.

"How's it going, David?" Aaron asked.

With a deep breath, David opened the door. He grinned. "Not bad."

In front of the barber's mirror two hours later, David watched in fascination as the man snipped and sheared his hair with efficient movements—a far cry from Mother putting a bowl on his head and cutting around it.

"You want your bangs still?" the barber asked. He was an older man with graying hair and an accent David couldn't place.

"I'm not sure." The floor was littered with chunks of his hair, and when he reached behind his head, it was short all over, sheared well above his ears as well. "What do you think?"

The barber brushed David's hair over his forehead. "I'll shorten and thin them out. Too heavy right now. Yes?"

"Yes."

David couldn't see the mirror since the barber was in front of him now, and he concentrated on sitting still as the man snipped. He shifted his rear slightly, wondering how English men could wear briefs for hours a day. Although at least he didn't have to worry about getting anything caught in a zipper.

He tried to spot Isaac from the corner of his eye in the next chair. Isaac's barber was speaking to him in the same accent. David thought of the movies he'd seen. It was Italian, maybe?

"You see how it stands up now? Just use a little gel like I showed you. That's all. *Buono*," Isaac's barber said.

The man working on David stepped behind him again. "You like?"

His bangs were wispier now, only covering part of his forehead. It was shorter than he'd ever had it, and he felt lighter all over. "I like."

"So do I," Isaac said. "How about mine?"

Isaac had little sideburns, and his sandy hair was short at the back and over his ears, but it swept up a couple of inches at the front of his head. In his new jeans, sneakers and hoodie, he didn't look Amish at all.

For a peculiar moment, David was forlorn. What else would change as they made their way in the world? He shook the brief melancholy away and smiled. "You look great."

"You both do," Aaron called from his seat at the front of the shop where he flicked through a magazine. "Carlos and Tony are the best. Ready for lunch? There's a great tapas place in the Mission that isn't far. Tapas is little Spanish dishes. It's fun, and you can try a bunch of different things."

While Isaac went to the front, Carlos or Tony—David wasn't sure who was who—swiped at his face and neck, and David closed his eyes, trying not to fidget at the ticklish hairs of the brush.

"Thanks, Carlos," Aaron said. "We'll take a bottle of the gel too."

Ah, so that meant it was Tony who had cut David's hair. Tony swept off the large bib from around David's neck with a flourish. David smiled and thanked him and eyed the prices on a board, adding the cost to the running tally in his head.

At the till, Carlos asked, "Debit?"

Aaron handed him a plastic card. David realized he'd gone to the toilet at the store that morning when Aaron had bought the new clothing. Now he watched intently as Carlos ran the card through a little machine, and then handed it to Aaron.

Aaron tapped some buttons and gave it back. With a whirr, paper rolled out of the top, and Carlos ripped it off for Aaron with a smile. Somehow that was it, and everything was paid for without any actual money changing hands. The stores near Zebulon had these machines, but David had never given them any mind since he'd only used cash. Something else to learn.

"Ready?" Aaron asked.

No. But David nodded and followed Aaron and Isaac to the parking lot.

The streets were clogged with cars and trucks. From the back of Aaron's little blue Toyota, David stared at the bicycles weaving fearlessly between lanes. A siren wailed somewhere, but he couldn't see any flashing lights. Images of the accident loomed in his mind, always lurking. When Aaron spoke, David forced them back.

"David, Isaac mentioned that you know how to drive? If you want to get your license, Jen's cousin runs a driving school. You can both sign up. He'll give us a great deal."

As they came to a stop and a bike whizzed by, David winced. "Driving on the back roads in Minnesota is pretty different."

"Just throwing it out there. And I was thinking…" Aaron stepped on the gas and glanced over his shoulder as he changed lanes, smoothly fitting between two trucks.

"Was it the first time?" Isaac asked.

Laughing, Aaron punched his shoulder. "Har, har. You're funny now, huh? As I was saying, I was thinking about your business, David. The one with your friend June? I looked up the website, and your furniture looks amazing. I'm sure you could sell to people around here and keep up your online business as well. We could look for a work-space. Assuming you still want to be a carpenter, that is."

David blinked. "What else would I be?"

"Whatever you want."

Whatever I want. It sounded so easy when Aaron said it.

At a stoplight, Aaron glanced at Isaac beside him in the front seat. "I know you were working together, and there's no reason you can't keep doing that."

What else would they do? David watched the back of Isaac's head, trying to discern Isaac's reaction. *Of course we'll still work together.* It was the only thing they knew. When he thought of them in their own workshop again, he breathed easier.

"I know there's a lot to consider," Aaron said. "Like I said, there's no rush. One step at a time. I'm just excited." He took another turn, honking at a bike rider who zoomed in front of him. "Couriers," he grumbled. "They're crazy."

David wasn't sure what a courier was, but he definitely agreed they were crazy. Riding these streets on a bicycle alongside cars, trucks, buses and little trains seemed like a good way to die young.

"I was thinking after lunch we can do some sightseeing. Give you a feel for the city so it won't seem so overwhelming. San Francisco really isn't that big, although it seemed massive to me at first. And then do you want to see a movie tonight? Jen'll be at the hospital."

"I really liked the movie I saw with David." Isaac looked back with a hopeful smile. "It'll be fun, don't you think?"

"Yes." He'd always loved losing himself in the darkness, traveling to another world for a few hours.

Aaron braked for a red light and half turned. "And really, tell me if anything is too much. Like I said, I'm just excited you're here. There's a cool new superhero movie in 3D, which is going to blow your minds in the best possible way."

"Superheroes—like in the comic books you used to sneak into your trunk?"

"Yep. But bigger and better than ever." Aaron ran his palm over the back of Isaac's newly shorn head. "God, I missed you, little brother."

Isaac beamed. "I still can't believe we're here. Getting haircuts and seeing movies. It's scary, but..." He grinned and echoed Aaron. "In the best possible way."

David peered out at the city whirling by—the buildings and cars and people filling his senses in a constant hum. He jerked back from the window as another car roared past. It *was* scary, and he hadn't expected that. They'd left so quickly, he hadn't had time to think about it. He'd thought he was more prepared.

"Don't you think?" Isaac peered back, his face pinched in concern. "David?"

He hadn't been strong enough for his family, but he wouldn't let Isaac down. Ignoring the hammering of his heart as another horn blared, David smiled. "Absolutely."

CHAPTER Six

*D*ING!
    Beside David, Isaac was already holding his Clipper card and practically vibrating as the cable car appeared over the rise of a hill. With a grin, David fished his card from his jacket pocket. It wasn't a train, but it was close.

They'd spent the last few days going out on walks around Aaron and Jen's neighborhood and had ventured up to the top of the hill with the radio tower at Bernal Heights Park. From there they'd been able to see for miles in each direction. San Francisco was so vast compared to any place they'd ever been, and the bay and ocean were beautiful. From up there, it had all seemed so peaceful.

But today was their first day going into the heart of the city, and David didn't know where to look first. Near where they waited at the cable car turnaround there were dozens of fancy stores with big windows and fake ladies wearing skimpy clothes.

People bustled this way and that, and the noise was constant. When they were in their room at Aaron's house, David could imagine that everything would be okay. He could be confident, even. But beyond the safety of those walls, he was less sure.

The sun came and went behind clusters of clouds, but at least the morning fog had lifted. Still, David shivered as the wind gusted, and he was glad he'd worn a sweater beneath his new black raincoat.

There were a few women waiting by the turntable as well, one of them gushing about how cool it was to get the chance to ride a piece of history. As David watched the cable car approach, it sure looked modern enough compared to a horse and buggy.

"The wheels are metal," Isaac noted. "If not for the electricity, the Ordnung might approve it."

David chuckled. "But look at the yellow and red paint. Maybe if it were all black."

"True. But the car itself isn't electric. Aaron said it clamps onto the cable, right? That's how it moves? So it's the cables themselves that are breaking the rules."

"Hmm. I think Bishop Yoder would say the cable cars have succumbed to worldly temptation."

Isaac smiled sadly. "It's amazing, isn't it? How quickly we get used to breaking the Ordnung. Practically everything we do here is against the rules. But once you start, it's easy."

"Easy not to think about it, at least." For when he thought about it, David remembered how hard things were in Zebulon. His chest tightened as he imagined how Mother and the girls would be struggling without him. Who would break the ice in the well, or chop the wood for the stove? Or—

As the cable car dropped off its passengers and did a loop around the turntable to face the way it had come, David shook his head as if he could shake free his thoughts. He could never go back. Only forward with Isaac.

He and Isaac waited so the women could clamber on first. David looked for the machine to tap his Clipper card the way Aaron had showed them, but didn't see one by the driver. They sat on the bench in the front open-air part of the car.

Isaac glanced around. "I read in that book Aaron gave us that there's a conductor who comes around, and—oh."

A man in a bright yellow vest appeared, holding some kind of machine in his hand. He smiled widely and held it toward them. "Morning."

His skin was brown, and it looked like he had dark fuzzy hair beneath his cap. David thought he might be Hispanic. Aaron had shown them pictures of people on the internet and explained the differences. Some of the people working at the hospital near Zebulon hadn't been white, but in San Francisco he'd realized just how isolated they'd been.

"Good morning." David tapped his card on the machine, which made a *beep*. There were so many beeps and whirs and alarms in the English world. As if to punctuate his thought, a truck honked. As the cable car moved, David gripped the pole and looked around, but couldn't see anything amiss. Sometimes it seemed that English people simply liked the sound of their horns.

The conductor chuckled. "Where are you boys from?" He stood on the white wooden board that ran along the side.

David smiled ruefully. "Is it so obvious?"

"Well, your friend just pulled out a pocket map, and you look like you're expecting to get shot any second. But don't worry, folks hardly ever get shot. Not on the cable car, at least."

It took a moment for David to realize the man was joking, and he smiled. Isaac put the map back into the pocket of his dark green coat, which he'd picked because David had thought it brought out his eyes.

"We're from Minnesota. I just wanted to make sure we're going the right way. To Fisherman's Wharf?" Isaac asked.

"Absolutely. You can't miss it. This is the Powell-Hyde line, so you'll get off at the end near the water and walk down to your right. Got big plans?"

"We're going to eat hot dogs and crab cakes, and go to Alcatraz this afternoon," Isaac answered.

"Sounds like a good plan. Go see the sea lions too. Don't reckon you have many of those in Minnesota." As the bell rang and they slowed toward the bottom of a hill, the conductor tipped the brim of his hat. "Have fun, boys." He left to take more fares.

More people boarded as they made their way over the hills of Powell Street, and as a young woman climbed on and took hold of a pole, David shot to his feet. "Here you go, ma'am." He motioned to his seat and stepped onto the board.

Another woman got on, and Isaac stood as well. The younger one laughed. "If you insist." To the other woman, she noted, "Chivalry's not dead after all."

The older woman sat. "Your mothers certainly raised you right."

David and Isaac shared a glance, and David wondered if his own expression was as guilty as Isaac's. Then David was lurching right into him as the cable car accelerated. They both clutched the nearest pole.

"Hang on, Minnesota!" the conductor called out.

As the other passengers laughed, David tensed, his face flushing. But he realized it was good natured, and exhaled a long breath. The wooden board they stood on was covered in a rough gray material that reminded him of sandpaper, and wasn't much wider than his sneaker. As another cable car approached from the other direction, they had to lean in to avoid banging into the people hanging from it.

A laugh bubbled up in David's chest, and he returned Isaac's exuberant grin.

"This is amazing!" Isaac marveled.

It was so much *fun*, and they were going so fast. But then David wondered if anyone ever fell off. He held the pole with one hand and took Isaac's arm tightly with the other just in case. His ears tingled in the brisk wind as they sailed down another hill, but when he thought of the snow and ice in Zebulon, it didn't feel so bad.

He leaned closer to Isaac as they slowed for a traffic light. "I can't believe we've been here a week."

"Me either. The days seem to go by so fast. Nights too." Isaac ducked his head.

A rush of heat spread through David as he remembered the night before, on his hands and knees for Isaac in the middle of the bed, hoping the thumping of the headboard couldn't be heard upstairs. He pressed against Isaac with a little smile just for him.

To have hours together every night in a bedroom of their own was such unbelievable luxury. Not to mention the indoor plumbing and central heat. David wondered when he'd get used to it all.

"I can't remember the last time I went a week without working. Or chores. I don't think I ever have," Isaac mused. "Not even when I had the chicken pox."

David braced for the sinking sensation that hooked through him like a fishing lure whenever he thought about money and work. It must have shown on his face despite his best efforts, because after a glance around, Isaac gave his hand a quick squeeze.

"We deserve some time off, don't we?"

David nodded, but he wasn't sure. Why should he have time off? Mother and the girls wouldn't have a break—and would have even more to do now that he was gone. Why should he be able to sightsee and spend Aaron's money when he wasn't earning a penny of his own? Father had always said a day without work was a day without worth.

He inhaled deeply, the air growing saltier as they neared the wharf. There was no sense in worrying about it. They'd planned the day already, and nothing would change by stewing over it or ruining Isaac's fun. Besides, Aaron had said it was better to see the sights on a Thursday instead of the weekend. David couldn't imagine how thick the crowds would be then, and it was winter. The summer would be so much worse. But it was okay. He'd figure out work and money tomorrow.

"Look!" Isaac pointed as they rumbled across a street that dipped down. "The water."

Isaac *glowed*, and David found himself watching him more than the view. To see Isaac so filled with delight calmed his worries.

As they pulled up to the turntable at this end of the line, David smelled fish as well as the sea. The cable car stopped in a little park area that sloped down to the sandy beach. People milled around, and the sun poked out. Color was everywhere, and David could imagine the lights at night would glitter.

The conductor called out, "Don't forget the sea lions, Minnesota!"

David and Isaac waved to him and hopped down. "Can we see the water first?" Isaac asked.

"Of course."

Their sneakers sank into the sand, and they laughed as they approached the edge of the shore. Isaac darted forward and dipped in his hand.

"Oh my goodness!" He leapt back. "That's cold."

David stuck in his hand too. He yelped. "It sure is."

"We're actually here, David." Isaac surveyed the waves and white sails with bright eyes. "We just touched the ocean. Well, I guess it's still the bay here on this side of the bridge, but close enough."

"We did." All the uncertainty was worth the moments like this. David brushed a stray piece of dried weed that had caught on Isaac's jacket, and let his hand linger. "We can touch it every day if we want."

After a few quiet minutes, they walked to the right, ending up along a busy street lined with restaurants and businesses that must have been what the guidebook called tourist attractions. The signs were huge and all sorts of colors.

"What's an odditorium?" Isaac asked. He pointed to a sign that read *Ripley's Believe It or Not!*

"I'm not sure. Look at *that*." David gazed up at the depictions of four people that soared three stories high. "Madame Tussauds," he read.

Isaac stared. "I don't get it. Are those people in there?"

"I guess they're famous? I think the guy near the right is a singer who died. It was in a movie."

"Are they all dead?"

"I'm not sure. We could go in and find out if you want?"

Isaac shook his head. "It looks weird. I don't want to see dead people."

"Me either."

They walked on, and eventually stopped under an enormous round sign proclaiming the area: *Fisherman's Wharf of San Francisco.* Wooden spokes jutted out from it, and David realized it was meant to be like the wheel of a ship. He wasn't sure how he knew that.

"Spare some change?"

They turned to find an older man in rumpled clothing holding out his hand.

Isaac and David shared a glance. Jen had warned them about people she'd called panhandlers, and said to tell them sorry, but they couldn't help. *"Or else you'll be broke by noon."*

"I'm hungry," the man added. His face was wrinkled and fingers stained yellow.

David looked to Isaac again. He didn't doubt the man was telling the truth. It felt wrong not to help, and Isaac nodded after their silent conversation. They each pulled out a few dollars from their pockets and passed them over.

When the man smiled, a few of his teeth were missing. "God bless," he said, before walking away and asking the next people.

"Give, and it shall be given to you," Isaac recited. "Right?"

"Yes. Especially considering how much has been given to us lately." David smiled. "Now let's find those sea lions."

"But first a crab cake. I'm hungry."

David wasn't so certain about a cake made of crab, but he followed. There were tons of little booths selling food. He pointed. "That one's called the Crab Station." The little awning fluttered in the cold breeze and proclaimed:

*Fresh Crab * Clam Chowder * Fried Seafood * Seafood Cocktails*

"Seafood cocktail?" David asked. "You're supposed to drink it?"

They walked up and peered at the menu. Isaac frowned. "Let's skip that for now. How about crab cakes and—oh!—corn dogs! I had one once when I was a kid. It's a hot dog on a stick with something around it."

"Sounds good to me."

Once they had their hot food and sodas, they found a bench. Isaac took a bite of his corn dog and moaned. "So good," he mumbled. Then his eyes widened.

David froze with his crab cake to his mouth. "What?"

"I didn't pray," Isaac mumbled, and swallowed the rest of his bite. "It didn't even cross my mind."

"Mine either." David lowered his crab cake. "I've forgotten a few times now."

"Me too." Isaac shook his head. "We'd *never* forget at home. But here, everything's so different. So far away. It's like God is far away too. You know what I mean?"

He nodded. "You only had a bite. We can still pray."

"Okay."

They both stood and prayed silently with people chattering as they went by, salt and the cries of gulls filling the air. David closed his eyes as he recited the words in his head. *Lead me not into temptation.* He faltered. Could he really ask that?

When he opened his eyes, Isaac was watching him. "David, do you think it's okay if we skip the prayer if we're out? If we're at the table at home, we'll make sure we do it."

"Yeah. I think it's okay." There was so much to worry about already, and David figured it was the least of their offenses.

Soon his belly was wonderfully full. Hot dogs had been his favorite treat growing up, and the corn dog did not disappoint. It also turned out that not all cakes were sweet, and the hot crab patties had tasted of so many flavors he couldn't hope to guess them all. Like everything else out in the world, food in San Francisco was fancier and overwhelming.

They ambled along the boardwalk, peeking into stores selling all kinds of things from magnets to sports jerseys to sparkly jewelry. The Amish didn't even wear wedding rings, let alone proper jewels. David tried to imagine Mother with earrings and had to laugh.

"Look!" Isaac pointed to a sign.

Follow Salty to see the California Sea Lions.

David eyed the drawing of a smiling brown animal he assumed was a sea lion. It wore a blue and white vest and pointed with its arm, which wasn't really an arm at all. English people probably knew what the sea lions' little arms were called, and he felt embarrassed that he didn't, even though no one could guess his ignorance.

They followed to the side of the pier, where the sea lions laid together in heaps on about thirty small rectangular docks. Some docks were empty, yet the animals squeezed together on others. David shielded his eyes from the sun, wishing he had his hat and gloves in the biting wind.

A family moved away from the railing, and David and Isaac squeezed in with the other people. They watched the animals sunning themselves and making plaintive noises that were a mix of honks, barks and occasionally growls. David noted, "The conductor was right. There certainly aren't any animals like this in Minnesota."

"Look at those two. They're playing in the water." Isaac pointed.

"Maybe they're a couple."

Smiling, Isaac pressed his shoulder to David's. "Maybe."

David wanted to take Isaac's hand when they moved away and strolled the rest of the pier, but something still held him back. There were others around, and what if some of them didn't like gay people? Aaron and Jen said San Francisco was one of the most welcoming cities in the world for people like them, but it didn't seem possible for *everyone* to feel like that.

What if they held hands and it offended someone? What if they made someone angry? It didn't seem worth it. He tried to remember the term Jen had used. Ah yes—PDA. Public display of affection, she'd called it. The notion was absolutely foreign to him even if she said it was okay.

Isaac inhaled deeply. "I love being by the water. The way it smells and feels. It's so *dry* back home. And I love how no matter which way I look, there's something new."

It was true—Alcatraz rose from the bay to the right, and the Golden Gate Bridge soared to their left with the ocean beyond. Behind them was the city, its buildings seeming to go on forever. "Is the ocean like you'd dreamed it would be?"

Isaac's eyes shone as they reached the end of the pier and leaned against the thick wooden rail. He nodded to the left, where the bay gave way to the waves of the Pacific. "When I look out there, it's like how you said you feel when we're together. That anything is possible. And it is—look at us! Two Amish boys by the ocean. I wish I could jump in and swim."

A shudder of dread slithered through David as he imagined the depths of the water. *They'd have never found Joshua there.* He drew Isaac closer with his hand on his elbow, but kept his tone light. "I think it would be a little cold."

"Just a little, I suppose." Isaac reached into his coat pocket. "But here, stand with the water behind you. I want to take a photograph." He pulled out his new phone and tapped the screen. "Can you believe phones are cameras too? They've thought of everything."

David stood with the rail at his back. "I guess this will be my first picture." Isaac glanced up from the screen. "Is that okay? I like all the pictures Aaron and Jen have, and the ones hanging in June's house. It's nice to look at people. It doesn't seem wrong, does it?" He bit his lip. "But maybe we shouldn't."

"No. We should. It's forbidden by the Ordnung, but what isn't? We left that life. We can do what we want now." He wished he felt as confident as he sounded.

Isaac smiled softly. "I suppose it's no more wrong than everything else we're doing. Now I just need to remember what Aaron said about...hold on..."

David waited while Isaac tapped and slid his finger over the screen with his brows drawn together. Aaron had added them to his phone company account, and gotten them Apple phones for free since they were apparently older models. They were plenty new as far as David and Isaac were concerned.

David's was still in its box in their room since he and Isaac hadn't gone out without each other yet. The electric appliances in the house were enough for him to navigate at the moment. Even the stove was a mystery of buttons on a screen, and something called induction. Not that he'd used the stove in Zebulon. But at least he *could* have. He knew how to use electric tools, and the fridge at June's had just plugged in. Everything else seemed daunting.

"Ready." Isaac held up his phone, his tongue poking out between his lips in concentration.

With his head up straight, David stood motionless, his hands at his sides. He was wearing one of the new pairs of jeans that were "relaxed," although with his briefs on he was still rather constricted. Maybe he needed to try the boxers tomorrow.

"You're supposed to smile. You look as if Deacon Stoltzfus just showed up at your door."

David did smile at that, even though the pit of his stomach clenched like a fist at the thought of the deacon's beady eyes and stony face. After they'd pulled Deacon Stoltzfus's daughter from the river with Joshua, David couldn't remember ever seeing the man smile. But he vividly recalled his thunderous expression as David had said no to the church.

"Do you want one of the both of you?" an older woman asked.

Nodding shyly, Isaac handed her the phone and joined David. Their shoulders brushed together, and they stood still. Holding his breath, David lifted his lips in a smile and waited. *Does she think we're gay? Does she know we are? Does she care?*

The woman raised her eyebrows. "Come on now—try to look like you're having fun and not lining up for the firing squad. Should I make the faces I do for my grandson?" She stuck out her tongue and went cross-eyed.

They both laughed, and David breathed easily again.

"That's the ticket." She handed the phone to Isaac. "Got a good one there."

After thanking her, they peered at the picture on the screen. They weren't just smiling—their faces were alight with laughter. David stared at the image. "Wow," he whispered. "Look at us." In their English clothes and short haircuts, it was hard to believe it had only been ten days since they'd raced from Samuel Kauffman's house, past the benches filled with everyone they knew.

The people of Zebulon would hardly recognize them now. David brushed the pad of his finger over the screen, touching their faces. What would Mother say? He shuddered to think. *And I still haven't written.*

He couldn't change the past, so David shut away the thoughts as though he was sliding home the heavy bolt on the barn door. He smiled. "It's a good first picture. Maybe one day it'll be in a frame."

"Yes." Isaac nodded. "I'd like that." He put his phone away carefully in his pocket.

They started walking, but only got a few steps before Isaac jerked to a stop. "There's something I have to tell you," he blurted.

David stared, his pulse already starting to gallop. He could see the fear in Isaac's eyes, and in the way he gulped in a short breath. David waited as the possibilities tumbled through his mind. *He's not happy here. Not happy with me. He wants to go back. He thinks it was a mistake. He—*

"I want to go to school."

Blinking, David took this in. "Oh." He should have felt relieved, but tension still gripped his spine.

"I've been thinking a lot about it, and Aaron talked to the principal—that's the head teacher—of this school, and even though I don't have any identification, she said she could make an exception. This school's different. They make tailored education plans for each student so I can go at my own pace, and I could learn enough to get my GED. It's a school to help people who can't go to normal school. I can learn faster there, and—" He sucked in a breath. "Say something."

"Tailored education plans?" It was English, but sounded utterly foreign coming from Isaac.

"That's what it says on their page on the computer. I'm going to meet the principal next week, and take some tests."

"Already?" They'd barely arrived, and now everything was changing?

"I know—it's really fast. But it's February now, and the new semester is starting."

"Semester?" There were so many words here David didn't understand, even when he thought he should.

"It's what they call it. They split the school year in half. I don't know why. But if I don't go now I'll have to wait until September."

"Oh."

Isaac sighed. "Say something more than that. Please."

"I…" David stared down at the weathered wood of the pier, nudging a forgotten penny with his toe. Gulls squawked all around, and waves rolled as a boat steamed by, and he felt like the acid in his stomach was swelling like the tide. "Why didn't you tell me?"

"I wasn't sure what you'd say."

There had been times that week when David had napped or sat on the deck outside with a blanket around his shoulders, trying to find the stars. He'd wanted to give Isaac and his brother time alone to catch up and simply be together. Now a sense of betrayal pricked him, even though he knew Aaron was only trying to help. After all, why shouldn't Isaac go to school?

Because we're supposed to work together.

He cleared his throat. "I know Aaron mentioned school, but I didn't think you were really considering it."

"I didn't want to say anything until I knew if I could go or not. I'm sorry." Isaac sighed miserably. "I should have as soon as I realized it was a real possibility. But I thought you might be upset. And I can tell you are."

"I'm not upset," David replied automatically. He played with the zipper on his coat before stuffing his hands in his pockets. "It's fine. It's great! I just thought we'd work together again. I was looking forward to it."

"I know! I was too." Isaac's eyes were beseeching, and he stepped closer. "But I'll be nineteen this year, and if I wait…"

"You shouldn't wait." David tried to ignore the hollow sensation that carved through him. "I want you to be happy."

"You could go to school too. This place takes older students. If you wanted to, that is."

David thought of sitting in a classroom and reading textbooks. He'd always liked reading the books June lent him, even though he secretly hadn't always completely understood them. But to go back to school while his debts piled up by the day? "It's not that I don't want to learn. But I have to work, Isaac. More than that—I *want* to work."

The thought of having a workshop again—the scratch of pencil on pad as he sketched, the grind of sandpaper, and the resistance of the lumber as he sawed and shaped it to his will—it filled the spaces in him like water around rocks. Yet when he imagined it now, working alone somewhere in the maze of the city, he ached.

"I know. And I'll still help you. I can have a part-time job. That's what they call it."

David spoke before he could stop himself. "Don't you like carpentry anymore?" He'd driven Isaac away after the accident, and as the months passed, perhaps Isaac had found he didn't miss the work.

Isaac's face softened. "Of course I do, and I learned so much from you. Maybe it's what I'll end up doing anyway. But in Zebulon, it was all I *could* do. I was never going to make a good farmer, and I'd always liked carving. It made me so happy to work with you every day. It did. I love doing carpentry with you."

"You're not just saying that?" David winced, knowing he sounded pathetic.

Isaac looked around the thinning number of people on the pier before he tugged David's wrist, took his hand from his pocket, and thread their fingers together. "I'm not just saying that."

David exhaled a long breath. "I know. I'm sorry."

"It's just that now we're here in the world, I want to discover what else there is."

It made perfect sense, but David wished he could stop the slivers of hurt from burrowing into him. *Enough. Don't be selfish.* He nodded and squeezed Isaac's hand. "Of course." A gust of wind howled across the water, and he turned his back to it, shielding Isaac from the worst.

"Thank you for understanding. I knew you would."

"I want you to do whatever makes you happy. That's what's important. This is good." David smiled, trying to forget his fears. Isaac would be happy, and it really was the only thing that mattered. "This is great."

"In school we learned English and math, and not much else." Isaac smirked. "I guess obedience was our biggest subject. There's so much to learn here, and I want to face it head on. I don't want to be afraid." He shook his head. "I don't know if I'm making sense."

David couldn't imagine a life of not being afraid. But it was Isaac who'd already been planning to leave when they'd run. He was the brave one. David rubbed his thumb over the back of Isaac's hand. "It makes sense. I want you to do everything. See everything. You deserve it."

His eyes imploring, Isaac gripped his hand. "You deserve it too. You know that, don't you?"

David heard Mother's plaintive wail to the Lord in his mind. He wasn't sure what he deserved, but he didn't want to worry Isaac. He smiled. "Of course. And going to school is the right thing for you to do."

"You really think so?" Isaac's breath puffed out as he grinned. "I never imagined I'd get to do anything like this. We'll find you the perfect place to work, and get you the best tools. Everything's going to be okay."

Even if it wasn't what David had wished for, seeing Isaac so hopeful gave him a surge of confidence. "You're right. I'll find a workshop and set up my business on my own. I've done it before. I'm sure some of the customers I had with June will still be interested. I can do it by myself."

"Even if I don't see you all day, I get to be with you every night. I feel so blessed. I don't know if God listens to my prayers now after the things I've done, but sometimes I think He must."

Looking into Isaac's radiant eyes and holding his warm hand, David dreamed it was true.

CHAPTER Seven

"**D**AVID?"

He jerked up from where his chin had fallen to his chest, blinking at Isaac standing by the bed. "Uh-huh. I was just…" He looked at the pen and pad of paper abandoned on his lap.

Isaac smiled softly, reaching out to brush back a wisp of David's hair. "Sorry to wake you."

David rubbed his eyes. "I shouldn't be napping anyway. I've only been up a few hours." Granted he'd woken just after five, which somehow seemed early now. The wooden blinds were open, and the room was warm with morning sun.

"How's your letter coming?" Isaac asked as he climbed onto the other side of the bed near the mirrors. He leaned beside David against the padded headboard, and their shoulders rubbed. They were both wearing new T-shirts and what the English called sweatpants. Isaac hadn't put the gel in his hair, so it sat flat against his head, giving him tiny bangs again.

The only words on the page were *Dear Mother*. "Still working on it," David answered. An understatement if ever there was one. "I thought you and Aaron were having breakfast and spending some time together."

"We were. But you know you don't have to hide up here, right? Unless you want some time alone. Which is fine."

"I know." Truthfully David didn't want to be a…third wheel, as the English said. But he'd also been determined to finally get his letter written.

"I meant to ask—is that the side of the bed you like? I guess I'm used to sleeping on the left, but maybe you are too."

"I had my own bed at home, so I don't mind which side I take now. I hope you like sharing with me better than Nathan."

Isaac pursed his lips and tapped his chin. "Hmm. I *suppose* so. But if you start snoring all of a sudden the way he did, I'm pushing you to the sidewalk." He frowned. "No. The curb. I think that's how that goes."

David smiled. "I'll do my best." He nodded at the paper in Isaac's hand. "What do you have there?"

"It's what I wrote to my parents. I wanted to sleep on it before I mailed it. Can you…?" He held it out.

David unfolded the page. Isaac's script was tight and neat, as if he'd been concentrating on making every letter perfect.

Dear Mother and Father,

It is hard to know what to say. You all must be hurt and angry at my decision to leave. I need you to know that I did not make this choice lightly. I cannot live in Zebulon or any other Amish place. I prayed on it a lot, and I know in my heart that God has a different path for me.

I was not sure whether to tell you this or not, but I am with Aaron in San Francisco. That's in California. You should know that he cares about you all very much. He teaches math in what they call a high school, and he has a very nice wife. There are no children yet.

David is here with me. Neither of us wanted to hurt you or his family, but we realized we could not stay. David has been a loyal friend. He helped me see the truth in my own heart. I hope you can forgive us for going into the world. I will write more soon, and if you will write back to me, it would make me very happy. I hope Ephraim, Nathan, Joseph, and Katie are well. Please tell them I miss them. I have enclosed a note for each of them as well.

Your son,
Isaac

David refolded the paper and exhaled a long breath. "It's good. That was nice, what you said about me helping you see the truth. Thank you." Although he was sure Isaac's parents wouldn't thank him for it.

Isaac smiled. "I didn't even know I was gay." He shook his head. "It still feels odd to say that out loud. *Gay*. But without you I'd still be there, miserable and hopelessly confused about why I didn't want to date any of the girls, no matter how pretty they were."

They kissed softly, and David rubbed Isaac's nose with his own.

Isaac leaned his head on David's shoulder. "I'm sure the preachers would disagree, but I think it must have been God's plan for me to go and work for you. So we could find each other. I wish I could tell my parents the truth and try to make them understand that. But it's impossible."

David wasn't even sure he could truly believe it was God's plan. He *wanted* to believe it, but… "They're all at church right now. I think it's Atlee Yoder's house this time. I can't believe it's been two weeks since we ran out of the service. It feels like yesterday, but also a hundred years. You know what I mean?"

"I feel the same way. Like part of me is surprised we're not there, but the other part can't believe we ever were."

Glancing at the red glowing numbers on the clock beside him, David added two hours to the time. "They're probably in the middle of the long sermon. I bet it'll be Bishop Yoder doing it today. He'll probably have a lot to say after what we've done."

Straightening up, Isaac grimaced. "I can't say I miss the sermons at all." He rolled his head against the soft headboard. "Or sitting on those benches for hours on end until my back ached so bad I could almost cry. Sometimes Mervin would try to make me laugh." He sighed. "I guess he's glad I'm gone now."

"Do you think he might tell them the truth?"

Isaac's forehead creased, and he was quiet for a moment. "No. Even though he thinks it's wrong, he'll keep his promise." He picked up David's hand and played with his fingers. "Even though we could visit, I feel like I can't ever go back, David. That it would just make it all worse somehow. Everyone would try to convince us to stay."

"I know." The longing to see Mother and his sisters again swelled in him, and he turned on his side toward Isaac, tossing away the pad of paper and drawing him down onto the mattress. He slid his palm under Isaac's shirt to rest on his belly.

Isaac skimmed his fingertips up and down David's forearm. "Do you think it'll be better or worse to go to church here?"

David considered it. "This is the first time I've missed church aside from that winter the flu had half the town sick as dogs. I know it's a sin, but I can't say I'm sorry to be in bed with you now instead."

Isaac smiled tenderly. "Me either. Aaron said we could try other churches here, but I don't know what God would think. If we aren't plain, we're already not doing it right. I said my prayers this morning, but I forgot yesterday. I didn't think about it until hours later."

"I think it's because we don't have a routine. Once you start school and I'm working again, I'm sure we'll be better."

"I'm sure." Isaac jiggled not only his foot, but practically the entire bed.

"What is it? Nervous about school?" David was certainly nervous about going to look at potential workspaces. As eager as he was to get back to his carpentry, there was so much to consider and organize. He kept thinking *tomorrow*. He wished there was a magic wand like the ones in the movie they'd watched the night before.

"What if—" Isaac blew out a heavy breath. "What if no one likes me?"

"Impossible."

Smiling, Isaac rolled his eyes and nudged David with his foot. "Come on."

"I'm serious. Everyone will like you. You're smart, and kind, and you learn quickly. You're a good listener, and you see the possibilities in the world. An ideal student."

"Maybe you can come with me tomorrow and tell them that. You're very convincing."

"Your father asked once what I thought of you." David slowly circled his hand on Isaac's bare stomach under his shirt. "It was a Sunday, I'm sure. Out by the barn, waiting for church to begin."

In his mind, David could hear the clatter of buggies arriving in the damp morning. The whinnies of the horses, and the quiet rumble of the men talking. He'd been watching for Isaac, hoping to spot him before the service.

"When was this?" Isaac asked, a smile playing at his lips.

"A week or two after you came to work with me. I was already having such lustful thoughts for you, and I must have blushed as red as an apple when he asked. But that's what I told him—you were an ideal student. He seemed pleased—he even smiled. He was proud of you."

"I wonder what he thinks of me now," Isaac whispered. "Or if he's already forgetting me, like he did Aaron."

David continued his circles on Isaac's stomach, focusing on the warmth of Isaac's belly to keep the tension at bay. "Do you think it would ever cross their minds? That the reason we left together is because we're...together? I can't imagine my mother would even think of such a thing. No one ever talks about it—not even the preachers really. It's like being gay just doesn't exist."

Isaac tangled their feet together. "Like *we* don't exist. The real us, I mean." He sighed. "I don't think my parents would suspect it. Aside from Anna, I don't know if anyone has."

David bolted upright with a spike of adrenaline. "*Anna?* Anna doesn't know. She can't."

"Actually, I think she does." Isaac squeezed David's leg.

David leaned against the headboard and jerked his knees to his chest, wrapping his arms around himself. Every conversation with his sister from the past months reeled through his mind. "But..."

Isaac sat and folded his hands in his lap, fiddling with his fingernails. His foot jiggled again. "I'm sorry to upset you."

"I'm not...I..." He forced air into his lungs. "Why do you think she knows?"

"You said yourself nothing gets by her. The day we had church at my house, when I was helping your mother up the ramp? She asked if I could drive Mary and Anna home from the next singing since you'd be taking Grace." He swallowed hard, his gaze returning to his hands. "The way Anna looked at me... I just knew. She was so sad for me."

Nausea seethed in his gut, and David rested his forehead on his knees. "I can't imagine how you felt hearing that." He could, though. *Devastated. Heartbroken. Hollow.* "I hated pretending. I never should have. Not then, after everything between us." When Isaac's fingers brushed through his hair, David leaned into the touch.

"I felt like the time I got kicked by Abram Lapp's mule."

"Please forgive me." David lifted his head. "I never wanted to hurt you, but I knew I was hurting you all the same. I was weak."

Isaac's eyes glistened. "We're all weak sometimes."

"Never again. Not when it comes to you." David pulled Isaac into his arms, murmuring into his new short hair. "Never."

Isaac held on tightly. "Of course I forgive you. Always, my David."

Their lips met, and everything else was forgotten as David tasted Isaac, breathing him in with a familiar heady rush as they stretched out, bodies entwining and tongues seeking. Moving on top of him, David licked and kissed down the column of Isaac's neck as he rolled his hips.

He loved the sensation of Isaac beneath him, eager and responsive, making little noises in his throat that sent blood rushing straight to David's cock and left his head light.

"Do you think it's worse?" Isaac asked breathlessly, tugging at David's clothing. "To do this on a Sunday when we should be worshipping at church?"

David pushed himself up on one arm. He raked his eyes over Isaac—flushed cheeks and his wet lips parted, his eyes already dark with desire and his hair sticking up where he'd slid down the pillows. David shoved up the hem of Isaac's tee until it bunched around his neck.

He ran his fingers around Isaac's nipples and through the light hair scattered over his chest. Then down over his quivering stomach, drinking in the way Isaac's breath caught as David dipped into his bellybutton and teased the hair below his waistband. Isaac's cock tented his sweatpants, and David knew he wasn't wearing anything underneath.

"I want to worship *you*," he whispered. Isaac was beautiful and good, and David wanted him to know it.

Groaning, Isaac dragged David's head down for a hard kiss as he spread his legs and wrapped them around David's hips. Isaac gasped, "It doesn't feel wrong. Does it?"

David could only shake his head, desperate for them to be naked so he could experience the heat and sweat of Isaac's body against him. Since that first night among the trees with loyal Kaffi standing guard, touching Isaac—*loving* Isaac—had only ever felt right despite everything.

Not only because of how good it made David's body feel, but in the way it reached into his soul through every pore. In every shared moan and smile, in every tremble of limbs and press of lips, he was whole.

They tore off their clothes, and with Isaac on top of him now, David thrust into Isaac's hand, moaning at the friction that sent goose bumps over his skin. He ran his knuckles down Isaac's cheek. "There are so many things I want to do with you."

Isaac jerked his head in a nod, his voice already gone a little hoarse. "There's something I saw once in a magazine Mervin and Mark showed me. It was a man and a woman, but...I think it would work the same. And...I looked it up on the computer on my phone." He shuddered. "There were pictures, and descriptions."

"Yes. Anything." David was so hard in Isaac's grasp, and he slid his fingers between Isaac's ass cheeks, teasing his hole. He thought of the magazine he'd bought at the gas station near Zebulon, and how he'd pored over every word and picture, memorizing what the men did to each other before burning the glossy pages behind the barn one morning before the rooster woke.

"I want to..." Isaac licked his lips. "I..."

"Say it," David urged. "Tell me. You can say anything in here."

"I want to suck on your cock," Isaac blurted. "And I want you to suck mine at the same time. I want you to come in my mouth, and—" He inhaled sharply.

"*Yes!*" David could barely get the word out as he pushed at Isaac, urging him to turn.

As Isaac's thighs straddled David's neck and his beautiful ass filled David's vision, he felt the slick glide of Isaac's mouth swallowing him. He gasped, fighting the urge to buck up. It felt different to have Isaac above him this way, the sensations somehow new, as though Isaac was taking him deeper than before. For a moment, he could only revel in it, panting.

Then he guided Isaac's cock to his lips, nuzzling at his balls and teasing with his tongue. It was awkward trying to coordinate their movements, but soon they found a stuttering sort of rhythm. The sensations overwhelmed him—incredible pleasure as Isaac surrounded him with his mouth and body, and the salty flavor of Isaac throbbing between his lips, his musky scent filling David's nose.

It felt as though they were two parts of the same being, sucking wetly at each other's cocks, their grunts and moans loud in the morning stillness. The sunlight streamed into the room like a blessing.

David closed his eyes, his fingers tight on Isaac's thighs. Isaac was so thick and hot in his mouth, and David inhaled through his nose. Sweat dampened their skin everywhere they touched. His lips stretched over Isaac's shaft, the foreskin pushed down, and he felt so gloriously full.

When Isaac rolled David's balls with his hand, David didn't have time to bark a warning. His mouth was stuffed with Isaac's cock anyway, and he moaned around it as he came, his hips jerking up. His toes curled and he squeezed his eyes shut as the incredible intensity swelled through him. Isaac swallowed, coughing a bit, and David could feel some of it dripping back down. Isaac licked at it, and David whimpered around his cock.

Squirming, David found a better angle, and he urged Isaac to rock his hips. With harsh little pants, Isaac fucked into David's mouth. David took every thrust, relaxing his throat as much as he could, Isaac's pubic hair tickling his face. For a moment it felt like too much, and his mind screamed that he needed air. But he got in a breath, and his racing pulse calmed.

"David—oh, oh!" Isaac mumbled.

David wished he could see Isaac's face as Isaac fucked his mouth with abandon. David was filled with him—taste and sight and smell, and his jaw ached. When Isaac pulsed into his throat, David swallowed convulsively, milking him until Isaac pulled away and flopped to his side, chest heaving.

Isaac's feet were by David's head, and David nuzzled his ankles when he caught his breath. "If you have any other ideas, I'm all ears."

Laughing, Isaac shimmied and crawled up the right way around. Lying on their sides, they kissed messily, and David loved their taste mixed together on his tongue. Isaac idly stroked David's calf with his foot, and David felt boneless and at peace. He knew he didn't deserve it, but he thanked God all the same.

This must be what heaven's like.

David hadn't realized he'd spoken aloud until Isaac brushed their lips together and murmured, "We may never get there, but we'll always have this."

As David kissed the hollow of Isaac's throat, *this* felt like everything he'd ever need.

CHAPTER Eight

AT THE SOUND of his name, David almost fell off the couch.

Laughing, Aaron raised his hands. "Whoa, whoa. It's just me. I wasn't sure if I should wake you, but I want to get an order in for dinner. Don't feel like cooking anything tonight. Do you want to try Thai food, or stick to pizza?" He loosened his tie and undid the top button of his shirt.

David took a deep breath to slow the pounding of his heart. He'd napped *again*? He'd never slept so much in his life. *Idle. Lazy. Useless.* His stomach churned, and food was the last thing on his mind. "Whatever you want. Thank you."

"How did I know you'd say that? All right, let's do pizza. It's easy." Aaron perched on the arm at the other end of the couch with the cordless phone and pressed buttons.

After pushing himself up to sit properly, David blinked at the television. It was getting dark outside, and the blue light from the TV flickered through the room. The show about friends living in New York was on, laughter ringing out as a monkey pulled a woman's hair. He wondered if anyone in San Francisco had a pet monkey.

"I'm on hold," Aaron said. "They're always busy on a Friday. How was your day?"

"Fine. Good." David reached for the remote control and pressed the mute button as a commercial came on. The commercials seemed to be so much louder.

"Did you get your email address?"

He nodded. "I emailed June with it."

"Your first email! It's cool, huh? Any problems signing up?"

"No." Truthfully it had taken far longer than it should have. He'd wracked his brain for a password for almost an hour. It had taken almost as long again to peck out a simple message to June.

"Did you find the real estate site okay? See any spaces with potential?"

"A few maybe. I have to look more."

"If you want to bookmark the ones you like, we can—" Aaron held up his finger. "Yes, I'd like to place an order for delivery." He stood and paced idly around the living room as he spoke.

While Aaron rattled off his address and ordered dinner from a stranger, David glanced at the laptop computer on the ottoman guiltily. He'd found the website Aaron had written down for him, but then he'd stared at the pages of pictures and listings with no idea of where to start.

The information on the sites was supposed to be in English, but David could barely understand half of it. There were lists of words that seemed to be missing letters. *UTCL. Wtr pd. Sec dep. TRSH.* Then there were the prices, which made him feel positively sick.

As much as he wanted to find a place to work, there was so much to figure out first that when he tried, he felt completely overwhelmed and ended up watching TV or taking a nap. It was nonsense, and he woke each time with the familiar sinking sensation.

Naps! He'd only ever slept during the day the rare times he was sick in bed. Yet this week David realized with shame he'd napped every single afternoon. Isaac was at school, and here he was lounging about on the soft couch as if he hadn't a responsibility in the world.

Aaron yawned widely. "Sorry—long week," he said to the person on the other end of the phone.

A long week of work while David sat around uselessly, and Jen had worked even harder. She seemed to get very little sleep, and was saving people's *lives*. Yet she appeared to thrive on the pressure. He supposed it was like the way Mother had practically scrubbed off a layer of skin on her hands along with every speck of dirt from the house in the days before they hosted church. She'd never seemed happier.

Was she still in the wheelchair? Mary and Anna had already had so much extra work to do. There would be no napping or lying around for them.

"Thanks. Have a good night." Aaron pressed the big button on the phone and placed it on the glass table in the corner. "Hey, do you want a beer? I'm having one." He flicked on the overhead light.

"Sure." David rubbed his face blearily.

Almost a whole week gone by and nothing to show for it but an email address and the bank card that arrived in the mail. Although he'd had the account at the local branch near Zebulon for a few years, June had always dealt with the transactions and given him cash. Now he'd be doing it all himself.

He'd planned to walk to one of the bank machines, but every time he'd contemplated going out alone into the noise and commotion of the streets, he hesitated. Then the day had somehow disappeared, and he was still in his sweatpants.

Aaron handed him a beer and flopped down on the other end of the couch. He pulled off his red socks and put his feet on the ottoman as he took a long swallow from the bottle. "TGIF."

The bottle was cold in David's hand, the condensation soaking into his skin. He pondered the letters. Perhaps this was the same kind of slang the real estate website used. "Uh… T…"

Aaron laughed. "Sorry. That means 'thank God it's Friday.' It's what people say at the end of the week when they're looking forward to the weekend. My brain is fried. I love those kids, but they're exhausting." He groaned. "And I don't even want to think about how much grading I have to do. Not to mention organize the next PTA meeting and—no. It's Friday, and I'm going to enjoy it."

"Sounds like a good idea." David had no idea what a PTA was, but it all sounded…complicated. He sipped his beer, sighing as the cool liquid slid down his throat. He hadn't even realized he was thirsty. Beer was a little bitter, but he liked the bubbles.

"You feeling okay?"

Shifting under Aaron's gaze, David took another sip. "Yes. Of course."

"It's okay if you're not. I know it must be different now that Isaac's been at school all week."

"It's fine." The rebuttal came automatically.

"It's different, though, right? You're used to a house full of people. It's an adjustment. I know you must miss Isaac."

David shrugged as his cheeks heated. "I see him every night. He'll be home any minute."

"When he's here you're…lighter," Aaron mused. "You get this look, like he's the most amazing thing you've ever seen."

Looking everywhere but at Aaron, David tried to think of something to say.

"It's not a criticism." Aaron stretched out his leg and nudged David's knee with his foot. "It's great to see. You know he's crazy about you, right? He was telling me what a good teacher you are. How patient and understanding. I think he would have waxed poetic all day if he hadn't had classes. Oh, that means to talk glowingly about something."

David smiled, feeling looser in his shoulders and settling into the cushions. "He said that?"

"That, and a lot more. If you'd joined the church, it really would have broken his heart."

"Mine too," David replied quietly. "I knew it would never work. I knew it, but I didn't do anything about it." He grimaced. "Look at me now. There are all these things I need to get done, and instead I'm taking *naps*."

"Don't be so hard on yourself. If I had a nickel for every time I'd had a nap instead of just writing an essay and getting it done, I'd—well, I'd have at least a dollar. There's a word for it that you've probably never heard: procrastination."

"Procrastination," David repeated, rolling it on his tongue. He finished his beer, and his head buzzed pleasantly. His stomach growled, and he realized he hadn't eaten lunch.

"We all do it, believe me. Speaking of which, did you ever get that letter to your mom finished? It seemed like it was stressing you out. Understandably."

"I did." Of course it was still sitting upstairs on the dresser in an envelope. He needed to buy a stamp, a task which had felt somehow like a mountain to climb. "I said I was sorry, and that it wasn't anything they'd done. That I hoped they were well, and Mother's leg was healing. That I'd send more money when I could." He peeled down a strip of the damp label on the beer bottle. "I didn't know what else to say."

Aaron sighed. "Honestly, I don't think it matters what you say. There's only ever going to be one thing she wants to hear—that you're going home and joining the church. If you're not Amish, you'll never be good enough in their eyes."

David swallowed thickly. He knew it was the truth, but hearing it aloud made it more real. "Did you ever write your parents?"

"Dozens of times." Aaron leaned his head back on the cushions, his gaze on the window distant. "I never mailed them. I knew I was shunned for leaving after being baptized, and they'd just tell me I was going to hell if I didn't come back to the true path. There was nothing I could say that would ever convince them otherwise. But it made me feel better to write it all down anyway."

"Did you keep them?"

"I burned them." He huffed out a laugh. "It was all very dramatic. I was working on a dairy farm north of here up in Marin County. After I left Red Hills, I bounced around for a while, working odd jobs where I could. There was a couple who took me in, and they had a friend out here who needed a farmhand. That's how I ended up on the west coast." He drained his bottle. "One of the good things about being ex-Amish is that we have a great reputation for being hard workers. He sent me a bus ticket and took a chance on me."

When Aaron grew silent, David wasn't sure if he should prompt him to continue or not. He waited.

Aaron shook his head. "Sorry—I was lost in memories there for a minute. It's been a long time now since I've shoveled cow shit." He chuckled. "Can't say I miss it too much. Anyway, I had this stack of letters stuffed in the bottom of my backpack, and one night in the bunkhouse after a few beers, I took them out and read them all. Then I borrowed a lighter from a guy named Curly—a man who was completely bald, by the way—went outside, and torched them."

"Did it make you feel better?"

"You know what? It did. There was hardly any moon, but the stars were so bright. I breathed in the smoke and watched the paper curling into the orange flames. It was like a ritual. Not long after that I came to the city and got my GED. Started my new life. You'll do it too. Just take it one step at a time."

Tears pricked at David's eyes, a swell of hope and gratitude flowing through him. *One step at a time.* Before he could respond, a key turned in the front door, and surprisingly cold air blustered in.

"Hey, little brother," Aaron called out.

His cheeks ruddy, Isaac appeared from the entryway. His smile faltered as he looked at David. "Is everything okay?"

"Couldn't be better," Aaron replied. "We've got cold beer in the fridge, hot pizza's on the way, and you can tell us all about what you did at school today." He stood and took David's empty bottle along with his own. "Oh, and I was thinking we should go out to a bar tomorrow night and have some fun. Yes?"

Nervous excitement rippled through David, and as he watched the grin light up Isaac's face, he shook off his earlier doldrums. "Yes," he agreed.

As Aaron disappeared to the kitchen, Isaac sat close to David, kissing him quickly. "How was your day?"

"Great," David lied. He did feel better after talking to Aaron, and there was no sense in burdening Isaac with his stupid mess of feelings and sloth. Not when Isaac was clearly vibrating with happiness. "How about you?"

"I think I made a friend. More than one, even. I ate lunch with them, and we talked, and they were really nice. I think they actually like me."

David smiled for real. "Of course they do, unless they're dummies."

Soon he buzzed with more beer, and the three of them ate pizza in the living room right from the box. Isaac talked animatedly about an assignment he'd been given—*"It's a real book, and it's not about the Bible at all!"*—and David relaxed. It might be procrastination, but he'd enjoy tonight and figure everything out tomorrow.

THE RE SEEMED TO be just as much traffic on Saturday night as there was during the weekdays. David peered out from the back of Aaron's Toyota, taking in all the lights and movement. He wasn't sure where they were in the city, but the storefronts squeezed between cafes and restaurants were pretty to look at.

He realized his seatbelt was twisted across his chest, and he straightened it, smoothing a palm down the buttons on his new shirt beneath his open jacket. It was made from a synthetic material the color of red wine and was soft against his skin. He had it untucked over the skinny jeans that felt too tight to be worn in public. But Aaron said they were in fashion, and Isaac had nodded enthusiastically when David put them on.

As he fingered the strap of the seatbelt, he thought of the buggies back home, and how the only thing protecting them there was God's will. He closed his eyes briefly as the memories of blood and snow returned. If Mary had hit the tree, she would surely have died. He thanked God that she and Mother had survived, but if Zebulon allowed the safety triangles on buggies, it might have been avoided. Why did the accident have to happen at all?

You know why.

But if it had truly been to punish him for his sins, then what would become of his family now that he sinned openly? Would the Lord punish him again by hurting them, but worse this time? Or would Isaac be next? Concentrating on breathing, David forced his gaze back to the storefronts they passed, and watched the people on the sidewalks going about their lives.

"We're going to meet Clark and Dylan at the bar," Aaron said. "Clark was in the wedding pictures, remember? And Isaac, remember that you're not allowed to drink. You can get in since you're eighteen, but you can't drink until you're twenty-one."

"That's okay," Isaac said. "I don't think I like drinking much anyway."

Aaron chuckled. "Yeah, I hear you. It took a while to grow on me." He glanced in the rear view mirror. "David, you're twenty-two, so you can drink if you want to, even though you don't have ID yet. I can vouch for you to the owner. He's a friend of Clark's, so it'll be fine. You'd probably have a problem anywhere else, though."

"Okay." David tried to stop worrying about God and sinning. It was an endless circle and he knew there was no good answer. He shuffled his feet restlessly, the soles of his new leather shoes squeaking on the rubber mat. "Are you sure we'll fit in?" he asked.

"I'm sure." Aaron grinned. "I guess I should tell you it's a gay bar."

David stared, wondering if that possibly meant what he thought it did. He'd seen bars in movies, but a *gay* bar? His heart thumped.

Isaac whipped his head toward Aaron. "You mean...what do you mean?"

"I mean it's a bar for gay people. Mostly men, but lesbians go there too. Trans people too."

"What happens there?" Isaac glanced back at David with wide eyes.

Aaron laughed. "The same thing that happens at straight bars. People hang out. Have a few drinks, talk to their friends, maybe play some pool. Dance. It's low key, don't worry. We'll start you off slow."

"The gay people can dance with each other there?" David had never danced in his life, and the thought of doing it in front of other people made his hands clammy.

"Yep," Aaron answered. "In a gay bar you really don't need to worry at all that someone will get offended. You can be totally free."

Free. David smiled.

"But how can you go to a gay bar if you aren't gay?" Isaac asked his brother.

"It's a pretty mixed crowd at the Beacon. Jen and I have been a bunch of times. It's fun. Everyone's welcome." Aaron put on his blinker and slowed to turn down a narrow street. "I admit it was shocking the first time I saw two men kissing and holding hands. Hell, it was shocking seeing a man and woman kissing after I left Red Hills. Seeing how affectionate people are in the world took some getting used to."

"We saw two men on the street that first day when we went to the store for the bread. I couldn't believe my eyes," Isaac said. "I know you said it was common, but..."

"But knowing and actually seeing are two different things? I'm sure my eyes were bugging out of my head. I couldn't stop staring, and one of them winked at me." Aaron laughed. "I must have gone so red. But now it's just normal."

Normal. David would actually get to meet men who were like him and Isaac. Talk to them. He smoothed his palms over his jeans. What would this Dylan and Clark think about an Amish hick from the middle of nowhere? Would he and Isaac really be able to fit in? Even with their English haircuts and clothes, would people be able to tell they were different?

Aaron came to a stop at a red light. "There's something else I have to talk to you guys about, and there's no good time to say it, so..." He took a deep breath. "You probably don't use condoms, right?"

Isaac made a strangled noise that was mostly a squeak.

David's throat was suddenly dry, and he coughed. "Uh, no. We were both…we've never…not with anyone else."

"Right, and it's not like you could just run to the drugstore to pick some up." As Aaron accelerated, he glanced at Isaac. "How are you doing? Are you breathing? Do you know what a condom is?"

Isaac managed to nod. His voice was strained. "Mervin told me."

"So, generally speaking, the English go from one sexual partner to another, or from one relationship to another, until they settle down. If you have unprotected sex—that's without a condom—with someone else, you can catch sexually transmitted infections, including AIDS, which is a disease that can be fatal. This is something I learned after I left home, and so should you. I have no reason to think either of you are planning to have sex with someone else, but if you do, you need to use a condom. No ifs, ands, or buts."

"Why would we…with anyone else?" David asked. He tried to imagine it, and wasn't sure what he felt. Confused, mostly. "We're together." He knew what condoms were, but had never given them any thought. He knew a little about AIDS, but only that it was bad.

"I know. I'm traditional myself, and I'm certainly not expecting you to run out and fool around or have an open relationship. I…" Aaron blew out a long breath. "I'm probably doing this all wrong."

"Open relationship?" Isaac asked. "I don't understand."

"It's when you're committed to each other, but you still have sex with other people."

David couldn't believe his ears. "Then how are you committed to each other?" His gut twisted at the idea of doing the things he and Isaac did with someone else, and the thought of Isaac with another man. He clenched his fists. No. That would be so wrong.

"I realize it's confusing," Aaron said. "That's why it's important to be educated. I want to make sure you understand the risks when it comes to sex, and how to protect yourselves. You're not kids, but I know you haven't learned this stuff. At the bar you might meet men who'll hit on you, and are looking for a hook-up. Some people are in an exclusive relationship like you are. Some have open relationships, and others are looking for something casual. It's just very different here in the world than what you're used to."

"Apparently," Isaac mumbled.

Aaron ran a hand through his hair as he stopped at a red light. "So, like I said, I just want to make sure you know the facts. I don't want you to end up in an unexpected situation and not understand the risks. Does that make sense? I know this is a weird thing to talk about. But if you ever have questions, please ask me, okay? Even if you're embarrassed."

"Okay." David's ears were hot.

"When I came out into the world all I knew was bits of gossip I'd heard from my friends." Aaron grimaced. "After I picked up a nasty little disease from a girl at a party, I learned how important it is to be safe."

Isaac sat up straighter, his voice sharp with concern. "You got sick? Are you okay?"

"Totally. Luckily for me, it was cleared up with penicillin. But I realized how reckless I'd been. I don't want that to happen to either of you."

David exhaled, relieved that Aaron was okay. He thought of Joshua, and all the wild things he'd done; English parties he'd snuck out to. Had he known about condoms? In the end it hadn't mattered anyway.

Aaron laughed softly. "You know, I didn't even understand how babies are made for ages. I remember eavesdropping when Hannah talked to Mom about getting her period." He smirked. "Isaac, I wish you could see the look on your face right now."

"You talk about it like it's the weather!" Isaac paused and lowered his voice as if someone might overhear even though they were alone in the car. "It's the monthly thing girls get when they, you know…*bleed?* Mervin told me about that too."

"Right. It's part of the ovulation cycle."

David frowned, sounding out the strange word in his head. Isaac must have appeared equally puzzled, since Aaron waved his hand.

"We'll watch a video that'll explain it all. I'm sure there's something on YouTube. I think it'll be good for you to know basic biology even if you don't have to worry about getting anyone pregnant. Anyway, poor Hannah was so confused when she got hers. I had no clue what they were talking about, of course. Mom just told her it would happen every month, and *halt dich frei fuhn mansleit.*" He stepped on the gas and turned onto another street.

Keep yourself free from men. David wondered what mother had told his sisters. Anna had grumbled in her usual way from time to time about pain, but such things were never openly discussed. He couldn't remember when he'd worked it all out. Joshua had probably told him.

Aaron laughed. "I could not figure out what Mom meant for the life of me. Keep free from men? What about Dad? Eventually I pieced it together thanks to the horses and cows."

There was silence for a few moments before Isaac spoke. "I still don't understand about an open relationship."

As Aaron stopped and reversed the car into an impossibly narrow spot on the street, David pondered it. It was already a sin for two men to lie together, but to do it with more than two people? Jealousy burned in him as he again considered Isaac holding or kissing another man.

It would have been torture enough if they'd stayed in Zebulon to see Isaac with a wife, especially if it had been Mary. But at least David would have known Isaac didn't feel the same way for her as he did for him. David would have had to take a wife too—maybe Grace. He tried to imagine sleeping in the same bed with her. Touching her and sharing the kinds of things he and Isaac did, but it was unthinkable.

Aaron switched off the engine and turned in his seat so he was facing them both. "Okay, so some couples have an agreement where they still see other people sometimes. There are usually rules, and it's typically just sex with the outsiders."

Isaac gaped. "Do you and Jen…"

"No!" Aaron shook his head, laughing. "No way. That would just not work for us." He shrugged. "I admit that I look at pretty women on the street sometimes. It's only human, I think. But Jen's the only one I want."

David took a breath to say that he didn't want anyone but Isaac, but he hesitated as Isaac sat silently. David wished he could see his face. He was sure Isaac felt the same way—didn't he? Or was this one of the possibilities in the world he would want to explore? He was already going to school and making new friends. What else would change?

Maybe he'll meet someone he likes better and he won't want me at all. Why isn't he saying anything? Maybe—

"I don't want to be with anyone but David," Isaac said quietly.

The pressure that had been building in David's chest released. "Me either. I only want you."

Isaac turned in his seat, smiling. "For a minute I was afraid you were thinking about it."

David had to laugh. "Not even a little. I was afraid you were."

Aaron's cheeks puffed as he blew out a breath. "Okay. Glad we've got that out of the way." He smiled. "Let's go have some fun. The Beacon awaits."

CHAPTER Nine

"DO YOU WANT a beer?" Dylan asked, holding up a pitcher and a glass.

David nodded, reminding himself to breathe. It felt as though all eyes were on him and Isaac, although when he dared a glance around the bar, no one seemed to be watching.

The five of them sat at a dark wooden table midway through the room. As promised, there was a space David assumed was for dancing near the back—empty at the moment—and several big green tables off to the side. Pool tables, he was pretty sure they were called, with other small tables for sitting interspersed throughout.

The stools along the long bar were all occupied, and there was a hum of chatter in the air along with music featuring words he couldn't quite make out. No one really seemed to be listening to it, even though it was loud.

He chanced another glance at the framed picture on the closest wall, amazed to see the two men kissing each other. The art was definitely what set the Beacon apart from bars he'd seen in movies. Framed photographs of half naked—and sometimes completely naked—men. Men who were touching each other. There were a few women too, their bare breasts on display as they kissed.

Looking at the pictures, David's face went hot, which was silly considering the things he and Isaac had done. The things they'd said, and the dirty English words they'd used.

"You've got..." Isaac pointed to David's face.

He ducked his head, swiping his hand over his mouth. It was the white foam from the top of his beer. *Try not to look completely stupid.* Aaron was chatting with Clark and Dylan, and they hadn't seemed to notice, at least. He glanced back at Isaac beside him with a raised eyebrow to ask if he'd gotten it all.

Isaac nodded. His leg was jiggling a mile a minute, his knee bouncing. He sipped his glass of cola from a straw and looked around. "What do you think?"

Of course the other thing that set the Beacon apart, aside from the pornography, was the people. As Aaron had predicted it was mostly men, but some women as well. It wasn't as though everyone was kissing or groping each other, but there was something about the way they stood close, or leaned a shoulder or inclined their head. A brush of hands; an affectionate nudge. It was all so relaxed. All so *easy.*

David took another gulp of beer, making sure to wipe his mouth after. "It's good. Different."

"Yeah." Isaac leaned in. "Can you imagine what everyone back home would think?"

Swallowing hard over the bile that rose in his throat, David shook his head. As he peered around again, he sucked in a breath. Isaac followed his gaze, his eyes going wide. Two men across the room were kissing. One of them leaned against a pool table, and they both held long wooden sticks. They were laughing about something, interspersed with sweet kisses.

We really aren't the only ones.

David's throat tightened, and for a moment he thought he might actually cry right in the middle of the bar. He'd seen the gay couple in that movie back at the Sky-Vu, and of course had seen the men in the secret magazine he'd bought. There had been the men holding hands on the street, and Aaron and Jen had told them over and over that it was normal. That there were millions of gay people.

But here in the bar, surrounded by at least a *hundred* other people like him, David realized it was *really* true. "Do you think one day we'll get used to it?"

Isaac tore his eyes away from the men by the pool table. "One day, I guess."

A man walking by let his gaze linger on Isaac, who was wearing one of the tight T-shirts with long sleeves—a Henley, Aaron had called it. The dark green set off his eyes and sandy hair, which stood up a bit off his forehead with the gel. Even sitting down, Isaac's dark jeans showed off his lean thighs. His navy sneakers were something called suede, which was soft and fuzzy.

With a glare at the man, who was already looking at someone else, David rubbed his palm over Isaac's bouncing knee. "What do you think? Do you like it here?"

Isaac stopped jiggling, and he nodded. "It's nice to see other people like us." Tentatively, he covered David's hand with his own.

"Awww. Okay, so you two are *adorable*, and we want to hear all about your adventures in the big city," said Clark, turning his sharp, eager gaze on them.

Isaac whipped his hand back, and David took hold of his beer glass. He tried to think of something to say, but came up blank. "Um…"

Clark was tall and thin, with short dark waves of hair that looked stiff to the touch. His skin was pale, and David was pretty sure he could see Clark's nipples through his short-sleeved silver shirt, which was made of some kind of shimmery material. David wasn't sure how old he was, since his face seemed very smooth, although there were lines around his mouth.

"Clark, don't overwhelm them." Dylan clucked his tongue. "Down, boy."

Dylan had very dark skin, and his hair was knotted into dozens of short braids. He wore jeans and a regular T-shirt—nothing fancy like Clark—although the cotton did cling to his broad muscles. He looked to be in his thirties, but again David couldn't be sure. In Zebulon, he'd known everyone's ages, and no one wore makeup—certainly not *men*. Dylan didn't seem to, but Clark's lips were unnaturally glossy.

"I'm not overwhelming them!" Clark tilted his head. "Am I overwhelming you?"

"They've had a lot to take in the last couple of weeks," Aaron said. To David and Isaac he added, "Clark is just a little excitable sometimes."

"It's okay." Isaac smiled. "Um, it's really nice of you to invite us out."

Clark waved his hand with a flick of his wrist. "Of course! We need to welcome our new gays properly. Plus, you're Aaron's brother, and Aaron's brother's boyfriend." He raised an eyebrow. "Yes? Boyfriends?"

"Yes," they answered in unison.

Isaac added, "We don't have an open relationship if that's what you're asking."

"Duly noted," Clark replied with a chuckle.

Dylan held up the pitcher to David. "Refill?"

He was surprised to see his glass was empty. "It's almost gone, though." He didn't want to be greedy.

But Dylan was already pouring. "Plenty more where this came from."

"Aren't you polite!" Clark said, beaming at David. Then he grimaced. "And I promise I'll stop treating you like an exotic anthropological experiment now. My bad."

"Anthropology is the study of other cultures," Aaron clarified.

"My bad again." Clark leaned in. "Okay, let me just say that you have the cutest little accents."

"Accents?" Isaac asked.

"Yeah, but it's hard to place. It's because of the German you speak, right?" Dylan asked.

Clark piped up. "I thought it was Dutch?"

"It's German," David, Isaac, and Aaron answered in unison.

Everyone laughed, and Clark raised his hands, the bracelets on his wrist jangling. "My bad times three. Guess you get that a lot, huh?"

"The whole Pennsylvania Dutch thing makes it confusing for people," Aaron said. "It's a unique dialect of German. I didn't realize I had an accent at first either. I think it's gone now. The thing that's really hard is the English words we never heard growing up. Out here in the world it's different."

Dylan nodded. "That makes sense. Just ask us if we're not making sense to y'all, okay?"

"Speaking of accents, how much beer have you had?" Clark narrowed his eyes at Dylan. "Your Texas drawl doesn't usually come out until after midnight."

"What can I say? It's been a long week, and I might have started early tonight." He raised his hand as a waiter passed by and pointed to the empty pitcher. "Isaac, Aaron said you started at one of those alternative schools this week. How are you liking it?"

"It's great so far. The teachers are really nice, and no one's made fun of me. Not yet, anyway. But it's scary to realize how much I have to learn. All this history I didn't even know about. Wars, and how people used to have to drink from separate water fountains. I didn't realize just how ignorant they keep us back home."

"They have really small classes and mostly older students, right?" Clark asked. "Flexible schedules and that kind of thing?"

"Uh-huh. Some of us are youngies—I mean teenagers—but there are a lot of people in their twenties. It's set up differently than a regular high school. At least that's what they tell me. We come in and have classes, and meet with teachers in little groups. It's apparently a lot more flexible."

"My co-worker's kid went to one because he couldn't stay in regular school. He's got ADHD, but who doesn't these days?" Clark said.

David thought about AIDS and wondered if it was similar. "Is that serious?"

Clark rolled his eyes. "Nah, it just means the little bastard can't sit still and has the attention span of a goldfish."

"*Clark.*" Aaron gave him a look. "You know it's a genuine problem for some people."

"I know, I know. But everything is a disorder or a syndrome now.

Like SAD. Boys, that's Seasonal Affective Disorder, a.k.a. winter sucks. I mean, come on. In the winter the days are short and cold, and it's depressing compared to the summer. It's not a *disorder*."

Dylan added, "I've got to agree with him there. Everyone's happy with more sunlight."

"You have a point." Aaron picked up the pitcher and topped up glasses. "Although people in California shouldn't complain about the winter. Sure, it gets surprisingly cold here in San Fran, but it's still nothing compared to the snow and ice back east."

"It gets surprisingly cold here in *August*." Clark sipped his beer. "That's why they had to make this city so fabulous, or no one would live here. Weren't you boys living in Minnesota?"

David nodded. "It's very cold." Duh. They already know that.

"Colder than Ohio," Isaac added. He shuddered. "I do not miss going to the outhouse."

"Whoa—y'all used an outhouse? Seriously?" Dylan whistled. "That is hardcore. And in the winter? Yikes."

Clark held his hand to his throat. Dark nail polish gleamed. "I simply can't imagine. Nor do I want to. You poor things."

David thought of how the outhouse door handle froze in the coldest months, and wondered who was shoveling a path from the house. Meanwhile, here he sat in an English bar—a *gay* bar—amid the warmth and chatter of hundreds of people. It was too warm to wear his jacket—a jacket that was far lighter than anything he'd wear in Zebulon.

"Sometimes it feels like it was all a dream." It took a moment for David to realize he'd spoken aloud. He stared at his beer, conscious of all eyes on him. "That sounds dumb." *I should just shut up and not talk.*

Isaac nudged his arm. "I feel the same way."

"Doesn't sound dumb to me at all," Dylan said. "I'm from Nowhere, Texas. When I came here, it was a whole new world. It's a cliché, but it's true. My little town might as well be on the moon. That's the great thing about the city. You can come here and start all over again. Everyone at this table's done it."

David glanced around. "I suppose that's true." He made a note to look up what *cliché* meant.

"Aaron says you're a carpenter." Clark tapped his chin. "You know, I need a new dining set. I've looked in hundreds of stores, and I simply give up. Maybe you can build something custom for me."

"Of course." A tendril of excitement uncurled in David's belly. "I'm not sure if you'll like my style, or what you're looking for, but…"

"We can look at it right now." Aaron pulled out his phone and tapped. "He already has a website. Just wait until you see these pieces. Amazing."

While Clark and Dylan leaned over to look at the screen, David's heart pounded. Isaac gave him an encouraging smile. *They'll love it*, he mouthed.

Would they? Even with the English tools he'd used at June's, he didn't have the sophisticated machinery a furniture company would. His designs were simple and functional, and surely not fancy enough. His English clients seemed to like them, but maybe they wouldn't be good enough for San Francisco.

"So elegant!" Clark exclaimed. "Oh my God, I love that chair. Dylan, do you see this?"

Dylan grinned at David. "Wow, man. This is impressive work."

"Thank you." David tried not to feel too proud.

"Let me know as soon as you're set up, because I am hiring you. You do this all by hand?" Clark asked. "Isaac, you're a lucky boy. Those are some talented fingers on your man."

Blushing, David couldn't help but laugh. Isaac ducked his head.

"Sorry—I'm full of innuendo," Clark said, although he didn't seem sorry at all.

Aaron laughed. "You'll get used to it. Clark's…a force of nature."

"That's right." Clark took on a steely expression. "Paralegal by day. Purveyor of glitter and all things sparkly by night. A hundred and fifty-five pounds of fabulousness."

"A hundred and how many?" Dylan asked under his breath.

"Oh shut up. Fine, a hundred and fifty-seven."

"Math was never his strong suit," Aaron whispered loudly.

"What do you do? A para…?" Isaac asked.

"A paralegal," Clark answered. "Are you ready to be bored stiff? Although it's more interesting than what Dylan does. He works in tech—of course, this is San Francisco after all. He codes all day. Although his office does have a trampoline. I'll give them that."

While Clark and Dylan talked about their jobs, David's mind wandered to his own. He'd barely thought about it all day with Isaac, and now that he did the anxiety returned. Sweat gathered at the nape of his neck. Finding an affordable workspace was just the beginning. Where would he get his wood? How would the delivery work once he'd actually made the pieces?

June had handled all that stuff, and he didn't want to bother her. And he admitted to himself that he still didn't want to call her because he didn't want to know what Mother had said.

It could be months before the lawyer in Ohio managed to get their birth certificates, and David didn't know when he would be able to get his driver's license. Would he need it to go to one of the English lumber stores? Not that he had a vehicle anyway. When he imagined driving on the tangled city streets or the freeway where cars practically *flew*, acid bubbled in his stomach.

"Okay?" Isaac whispered.

Taking a breath, David nodded and gulped his beer. The others were talking about something he didn't understand.

Isaac frowned. "Are you sure?"

He wanted to spill out all his worries, but what good would that do? Isaac had enough of his own starting school—he didn't need David's as well. He smiled. "I'm sure."

As the conversation at the table quieted, Isaac motioned his hand between Dylan and Clark. "So, are you guys…"

They both laughed heartily, and Clark shook his head. "For a hot second back in the day. Let's see… I was a sophomore—that's the second year—at CCSF, and Dylan was a new college grad and fresh from the bus station. All wide eyed and vulnerable." He pinched Dylan's cheek.

Dylan slapped Clark's hand away with a laugh. "Yes, and I screwed up my courage and went to Angel Dust, a gay club that's been around since the name meant something."

David didn't know what it meant, but he didn't interrupt to ask.

Clark jumped back in. "There he met yours truly, an angel fallen from heaven to be his guide to the city and general fabulousness." He put his hand to the side of his mouth and hissed, "He actually wore a plaid flannel shirt to a dance club."

"As you can see, my fashion choices have improved," Dylan said. "Aaron, excellent sartorial work on our new friends here, by the way. You guys fit right in."

"Really?" Isaac asked hopefully.

"Absolutely." Clark drew a circle in the air with his finger. "It's all working for you. Both of you."

David wasn't sure whether to smile or run to the bathroom and look in the mirror to see for himself. He shifted on his chair. He was wearing the boxer briefs tonight, and he liked them better than the briefs so far. He took another swallow of cool beer, noticing that his head was buzzing pleasantly.

"Anyway, back to me. And Dylan, I guess." Clark flicked his wrist. "So, for a few days we went everywhere and did everything, and the sex was nice, but then we woke up and realized we're just friends."

"And the rest is history," Dylan added. "He and Jen were buddies from summer Bible camp, and when she came here for her residency, we clicked."

David stared at Clark. "You went to religious camp?"

"You bet." Clark pulled a tube from his pocket and swiped it over his lips, smacking them loudly. "What, I don't look like I grew up going to prayer circles and Jesus camp? Let's just say the Seventh-day Adventists and I parted ways as soon as I could get my tight ass out of

Stockton." He shuddered. "Ugh. Central California."

"He still sees his family, though," Dylan said. "They're pretty accepting, all things considered."

Clark snorted. "Not like they have a choice. What were they going to do, disown me?"

Awkward tension filled the air, and David drained his glass.

Clark inhaled sharply, reaching past Dylan to grasp Aaron's hand. "Sorry." In a blink, all his energy seemed to have evaporated, and his shoulders slumped. "I wasn't thinking."

"It's okay." Aaron patted Clark's hand. "Don't worry about it."

"Me not thinking?" Clark addressed David and Isaac. "That's a thing that happens sometimes. Okay, it happens a lot. So please know I don't mean to offend. You must be pretty stressed about your folks and leaving home."

Isaac smiled sadly. "Yeah. We're hoping they'll write to us."

"Do they know you're gay?" Dylan asked, reaching to pour more beer for everyone but Isaac.

David examined his hands. "No. If they find out they'll never accept it." He shrugged. "They can't."

Clark sighed. "Well, that's depressing. Sorry, gang—I'm the one who brought it up." He sat up straight and shook his head. "Enough of that, because this is your first time in a gay bar, and it will not be depressing if I have anything to say about it. Hey, is Ms. Jennifer going to get out of her scrubs for once and join us?" he asked Aaron.

Aaron pulled his phone from his pocket. "Her last text said she'd be here by ten-thirty."

Dylan laughed. "So that means she might squeak in for last call. She's dedicated, and that's why we love her."

"One of the many reasons!" Clark exclaimed. "She was the best friend a gay could have growing up. That girl made summers talking about Jesus bearable, and that is no mean feat." He gave Aaron a sly look. "I remember the day she brought this one around. He was still a baby, but we knew he was the one. Whenever she'd managed to give a guy more than five minutes of her time, they were somehow all douchebags. But Aaron was a keeper."

"What's a douchebag?" Isaac asked.

Smiling, Aaron, Dylan, and Clark shared a glance.

"Excellent question, and we're going to give you all the answers. Even the ones you don't want to hear because they involve vaginas," Clark said. He mimed rolling up his sleeves even though he wasn't wearing any. "Let's do this thing. So, there's something called a douche, and it's a feminine hygiene product. Wait—you probably don't know much about feminine hygiene."

Aaron laughed. "Funny you should mention that, because we were just talking about periods in the car."

"Whoa. Clearly we're going to have to back up right to the beginning. *Beep, beep, beep.*" Clark called to a passing waiter, "More beer!"

David found himself laughing, and then cringing, and then laughing again. And when he took a deep breath and wrapped his arm around Isaac's shoulders, no one even blinked.

CHAPTER Ten

"TIME FOR THIS old woman to hit the hay." Jen yawned widely. She was stretched out on one of the couches, her feet in Aaron's lap. She nudged him with her toes.

"Yeah, me too. I've got to get back to work tomorrow. We don't all have the day off." He tickled the soles of her feet.

"I know—I'm a real slacker. I'll think of your sacrifices next time I'm up to my elbows in some guy's intestines and I'm working a double."

"You were only at the hospital for, like, thirteen hours today." Aaron rolled his eyes. "Such a drama queen with your saving lives."

David smiled as he watched them get to their feet. He and Isaac were on the other couch, sitting close but not touching. Sound reverberated through the room from the TV, a fast song that played while the credits scrolled the screen. He kept turning his head during the movie, at one point certain a door was opening behind them. But of course there were speakers behind them in the walls and in the ceiling.

Jen put on her slippers. "You guys know how it works, yeah? Watch whatever you want."

The phone rang, and she frowned, checking her cell on the coffee table. "Hospital would try me on this first." The cordless house phone was sitting on the table as well, and she glanced at the little screen before saying hello. She was silent for a moment. "Oh, hi. Yes—Aaron's wife. Is everything okay? It must be midnight there." Her eyes met David's. "He is. Hold on."

David's heart sank. "Who is it?"

Jen held her hand over the bottom of the phone. "Your friend June."

For a moment he was terribly tempted to ask her to take a message, which was ridiculous. He should be excited to speak to June. *What's the matter with me?* He reached out, aware of the TV going silent. Isaac perched beside him, watching with concern.

David put the phone to his ear. "Hello?"

June's voice was so clear she could have been sitting right next to him. "Hi, David. Gosh it's good to hear your voice. Is this too late to call?"

"No. Is something wrong? It's late for you." He glanced at Aaron and Jen, who stood by the TV, waiting.

"Everything's okay. I couldn't sleep, and thought I'd take a chance that I could catch you. I'm sorry to worry you."

He exhaled in a rush. "Okay. I'm glad to hear it." He smiled at the others.

Jen and Aaron waved goodnight, and Isaac stood as well, pushing the big red button on the plastic remote control. The TV went dark.

David said to June, "I just need to…please wait for a moment." He whispered to Isaac, "You don't have to go."

"It's okay. Take your time. Tell her I said hello." Isaac pecked his cheek and disappeared up the stairs.

"Hello?" David put the phone to his ear again. "Are you still there?"

"Of course, hon. Give Isaac my best."

"I will." David sat back against the cushions. He had no idea what to say.

"How are you settling in?" June asked.

"Fine. Thank you."

She huffed. "Who do you think you're talking to? Come on—tell me what's going on. I've been very patient, but it's time for you to spill. How's Isaac?"

He smiled faintly. Same old June. "Isaac's good. He's going to school already, and he's happy to be with his brother again. Aaron and his wife have been very welcoming. They've done so much for us."

"Glad to hear it. And what about you? Must be pretty surreal to go from here to the big city."

Surreal. "That's a good word for it. It's...it's a lot." He paused. "I thought I'd be much more prepared than I am. It's different than I expected, actually being here in the city and living in an English house. I miss the smell of wood burning, but it's so warm upstairs at night."

"How's the weather? You're missing a whole lot of miserable snow here."

"It's warmer here. It can get cold, especially when it's windy, but not cold the way it is there. No snow or anything."

"Bet you don't miss it."

The sudden pressure on his throat choked him, and in that moment he ached to be near his family. "Have you seen them?" The question was barely a whisper.

"Yes. I took your money from the account like you asked and brought it to your mother. I could tell she didn't want to take it, but obviously she didn't have a choice."

He squeezed his eyes shut, gripping the plastic to his ear. "How is she?"

June sighed. "She's sad, David. Sad and angry. Not that she said much at all to me. I wish I could tell you she understands, but she doesn't. It was a very tense meeting. Mary and Anna were there too. Mary didn't look as though she'd been sleeping much. None of them did. Of course your mother wanted to know where the money had come from, and how I was involved."

"What did you say?" He hunched over, his elbows on his knees, staring at the pale floor between his bare feet.

"Well, I figured the truth was the easiest thing. I hope that was the right choice. I'm sorry if it wasn't."

David sucked in a breath as a chill ran through him. "You told her about the business? About...all of it?"

"The business, yes. You going to the drive-in, no. But she knows you were using electricity and whatnot at my place. I tried to explain that you'd only wanted to support them better."

Now Mother knew he'd lied to her. Not just for a few months, but for more than two years. He shuddered, imagining her face and wondering if she'd shown any emotion in front of June. She'd probably been a stone. "She'll never understand."

"Perhaps not, especially with you leaving the way you did. I'm not saying it was wrong, because I think you had to go. But it was a complete shock to her and your sisters. You hid your true feelings well, David. I hope that knowing it wasn't completely out of the blue will be a comfort to them. Eventually, perhaps. Knowing that it wasn't a flight of fancy, but that you'd been moving away from plain life for some time."

He swallowed thickly. There would be no comfort in that. The only comfort would be for him to return. Join the church, marry, and live a good Amish life. There was no in-between. "Maybe. Do you think the money was enough? Do they have food?"

"Of course they do. Sweetheart, they're fine. Mr. Helmuth came over while I was there, and he walked me out. He asked if I'd be speaking with you, and he wants you to know he'll take care of them. If you ask me, I think he's glad of the opportunity, and he seems a good sort."

"Yes." David breathed in and out deeply. "I still need to give them more money. What if something happens to Eli? It's my responsibility. When Father died—"

"When your father died, you were nineteen years old. Too young to have to take on so much. David, you've had to shoulder this burden for a long time. Relax. You deserve the chance to find your own way. To live your own life. I'm not saying your family isn't upset, because they are. But they're not going to starve. Okay?"

He nodded.

"*Okay?*"

"Oh. Yes. I forgot you couldn't see me." He laughed shakily. "Dumb, huh?"

"Not a bit, hon. Hey, once you're all set up online we'll start Skyping, and you can see me in all my glory."

"Is that where you can talk by video?" *Sweetheart. Hon.* He knew they were only words, and that his mother did love him, but the way June spoke to him made him feel warm and safe.

"That's the one! My sister Deb got me on it. It's easy. If I can figure it out, you can."

"It would be very good to see you again." He inhaled through a swell of affection. "I don't know how to thank you for everything you've done."

"I haven't done much, and that's what friends are for. By the way, since the bank account you have is our joint one, you should open your own as well."

"Okay."

"Now I haven't wanted to pester you because I know you've made a tough transition, but when you're ready, I've had a dozen emails from customers who want furniture. The site's still getting a lot of hits. After the buggy accident I put up a notice that there'd been a family emergency and the business was on hiatus. On hold, I mean. Got a bunch more emails of concern after that."

"People were concerned? That's very kind of them. I'm looking for a workshop here."

"Terrific! I'd sure love to tell them that you'll be back at work soon. I wasn't sure if you wanted to start handling the customers and shipping yourself? Now that you're out in the world you probably don't really need me."

David sat up straighter. "You mean you'd still be willing to help?"

"Of course! It keeps me out of trouble having a little something to do."

He blinked rapidly. Maybe it wouldn't be so much to handle if June was still going to help. "Okay. If you could still deal with the customers, then I'll make the furniture and figure out how shipping works. We'll still split the profit."

"I don't think so."

David slumped back. "I understand."

"Not so fast, young man. Absolutely you can do the work from there just like you did here, but we're not splitting the profits. I was buying materials, remember? You'll have to take care of that, and the shipping. But I'll maintain the website, communicate with the customers, and do the billing. I'll take ten percent, and not a penny more."

"But—"

"No arguments. It's a fair cut. I'm retired, and it gives me a little bit of work without taking too much time from my scrapbooking. Deal?"

He laughed softly. "Deal."

"Good. Now that we've settled that, there's something else I need to tell you."

David froze. "What?"

"Your sister Anna came by this afternoon. I'm not sure how she slipped away, and although your mother said she forgives me for leading you astray, she certainly made it clear she doesn't want me speaking to her children unless there's an emergency. But Anna doesn't seem like one to let rules stop her."

He had to smile. "No. Not our Anna."

"She told me she knew you weren't going fishing all those nights, and she thanked me for helping you leave. She wants to talk to you. I said I had to ask you first. What do you say? Is it all right if she calls you sometime when she can get over here again?"

His heart tripped. How wonderful it would be to hear her voice. "Of course. Yes. She wasn't... How was she? Angry?"

"A little bit. Mostly sad, and I think very frustrated with life right now."

He imagined Anna's mischievous smile, and Mary's exasperation. It was hard to think about one without the other. "Did she mention Mary?"

There was a pause, and then June sighed. "Yes. I think poor Mary's heartbroken. It seems she carried a torch for Isaac, yes?"

He nodded, and then remembered to say, "Yes." Shame settled over him like an old blanket. Then he recalled what Isaac had said. Before he could think twice, he asked, "Do you think Anna knows?"

With a start, he realized *June* might not know. When he and Isaac had arrived breathless at her door after fleeing church, she hadn't asked even a single question. His pulse raced. "I should tell you that Isaac and I... That we're..."

Amazingly, she laughed. "Oh, honey. I know."

"You do?" he whispered.

"I'd wondered about you, but the night you brought Isaac over for the first time I knew without a doubt. The way you looked at him? As if he'd hung the moon and half the stars to boot."

"You don't mind?" He wasn't sure whether to laugh or weep.

"Why should I mind? You're just the way God made you. You and Isaac love each other, and that makes my old heart glad."

He cast about for the right thing to say. "Thank you. I don't know what I would have done if I hadn't met you." Something she'd said bounced around in his mind. "If you could tell when you saw me with Isaac, do you think anyone else knows?" He got up to pace in front of the television.

"I don't know, David. She didn't say so, but I think it's a safe bet that Anna's figured it out. The way she asked about you and Isaac—there was just something in her expression."

"Not much gets past her. But if Mary finds out—if my *mother* finds out—" He struggled to breathe.

"Don't borrow trouble. There's no reason to think they will."

His lungs stuttered, and he felt light in the head for a moment, as if he'd had too much wine or beer. "They can't find out. I can't do that to them after everything else. After my brother—it would be too much."

"You know I won't tell them, hon. Try not to worry about it. You just get settled in your new life. That's more than enough for you to deal with right now. Remember, you can call me any time if it gets to be too much. If you need money, or advice, or just to talk." For a moment her voice tightened. "David, I was never able to have children of my own. It was a terrible loss that brought you to my doorstep, but I thank God every day for the blessing of having you in my life."

A sob choked him, and tears wet his cheeks. "I love you." Aside from Isaac, he wasn't sure he'd ever told someone that out loud. He'd said it to Mother in the hospital, but she'd been unconscious, a machine tapping out the beats of her heart.

June sniffed. "All right, that's enough mushy stuff, huh? I'd better get to bed. Stay in touch. I hope Anna can make it back soon to call you. Sleep well, kiddo."

"Goodnight. Thank you."

After a few moments a steady noise bleated from the phone, and he pressed buttons until it stopped. After turning off the lights, David stood by the window, watching the red and white lights of the odd car that passed by on the hill with a fleeting *whoosh*. For once the city seemed still.

In the little bathroom near the front door, he splashed his face with cold water and stared in the mirror. His eyes were a little red, but nothing that should worry Isaac. He was glad June called—in a good way it had made Zebulon feel a little closer. His family was all right, and he had to trust in the Lord to keep them that way. He closed his eyes and said a prayer.

When he was finished, David straightened up and looked at himself again. A new week was starting tomorrow, and enough was enough. It was time to stop letting himself falter and use excuses. He would find a workshop and figure out all the things he didn't understand.

"I can do this." His voice was timid, and he cleared his throat. "I can do this," he repeated, louder. *Better*. It would do for now.

Upstairs, Isaac was already curled under the covers. He raised his head. "Everything's all right?" he mumbled.

"Yes. Go to sleep."

"Mmm. I was going to tell you...that thing..." His eyes closed.

Laughing softly, David flicked off the lamp and tiptoed to the bathroom, closing the door gently. He smeared toothpaste on his new electric toothbrush. Aaron had bought a pack of two at a store called Costco that had big versions of everything in a huge warehouse. David and Isaac had followed him up and down the aisles in wonder.

He pressed the button and put the toothbrush in his mouth, still jumping a little at the whirling vibration. It was like using an electric sander on his teeth, but they'd never felt so smooth and clean.

When he'd spit out the last of the minty paste, he ran his hand over the stubble on his face. He hadn't shaved that morning, and the dark hair already growing in shadowed his cheeks and chin, and above his lip. Some English men did this on purpose—scruff, Jen had called it. David thought vainly that it didn't look bad. Maybe he'd keep it for a few days.

Back in the bedroom, he undressed in the dark and listened to Isaac's deep breathing. He'd always slept in a nightshirt before, but now he went naked, as did Isaac. David slipped between the sheets and rolled onto his side, pulling Isaac back against him. He rubbed his cheek against the short softness of Isaac's hair and kissed his neck.

When he woke, the night was still thick. The shadows of the room came into focus as David realized the noise was coming from Isaac, huddled in a ball on the edge of the bed with his back to David, his head buried in the pillow. Whimpers, sniffles—a sob.

"Isaac?" David was instantly awake, scooting across the space between them to hold Isaac close. "What is it?"

"I'm sorry," Isaac mumbled, choking on another sob.

"Shh." David stroked Isaac's arm and rubbed his hip, pulling him back against his body. "It's all right. Everything's all right." David's heart galloped. "I'm here. You're safe."

Isaac's head was still down, and his voice was muffled in the pillow. "It's nothing. Only a dream."

"A dream of what?" David caressed Isaac's head, pressing kisses to his shoulder.

Isaac shivered. "It seemed so real. I was home again, and…"

David swallowed thickly over the nausea that rose up. "What?"

"We were in church, and everyone was there." Isaac shuddered. "They knew the truth. Mother and Father were so angry. They hated me, David."

He eased Isaac over and cradled Isaac's head to his chest. "It was only a dream. I promise."

"I wish I could call them and hear their voices. Just to know they're okay." He trembled. "We're so far away. I miss them. I don't want to go home, but I want to see them. I wish…"

Isaac's tears were wet on David's chest, and he rubbed Isaac's back. "I know. I wish it too."

"I'm so glad you're here. If you'd stayed, I don't know what I'd do. I'd miss you so much I wouldn't be able to stand it."

"I'll never leave you, Eechel. I'm right here. Go back to sleep." He kissed Isaac's head.

David stared at the faint pattern of the street lamps through the blinds, shadows and light spreading over the walls and ceiling. His earlier resolve grew stronger with each little shuddering breath Isaac took.

No more procrastination and naps. He'd get his business up and running so he could take proper care of Isaac. He would keep him safe and happy. He wouldn't disappoint him. As Isaac burrowed close, David petted him and murmured a lullaby he hadn't heard in years.

"Schlof, bubeli, schlof…"

He wouldn't fail this time.

PART TWO

CHAPTER Eleven

"WELL, WELL, WELL." Clark whistled as he took off his mirrored sunglasses. "Looking good. The space isn't bad either."

David flushed, trying not to smile. He put down his saw and wiped his brow. He was down to just a T-shirt and jeans, the day warmer than any since they'd arrived in the city at the very end of January. It was almost April now, and spring was blooming. "Thanks. It's not much, but it'll do."

"Not much? Honey, this is San Francisco. This garage is a palace. You and Aaron done good finding this place. Not too far from home either."

"Just two bus rides." His least favorite part of the day, but unavoidable.

"Three from my office. I don't venture down to Excelsior for just anyone, I'll have you know." He winked. "But I make exceptions for hunky Amish men who are building me furniture."

David looked down and fiddled with a nick in the worktable he'd built. He was getting used to Clark's flirty ways, but it still put him off balance. He focused on the table. It was smaller than his was in Zebulon, but he was learning everything was smaller in the city. He was renting the concrete garage for more than he thought possible for a dusty rectangle behind a row of narrow houses, but it was his.

There was hardly any room to move with all the supplies packed in. It was a relief that the lumber store he'd found delivered. Eventually he'd get a pickup truck, but for now it would do. He shuffled over so Clark could walk around the table. "Sorry. It's a tight fit."

"That's what she said. Or he." Clark grinned.

He wasn't sure he completely understood the joke, but David laughed and motioned to the little couch along the back squeezed between the bathroom door and the wall. "Do you want to sit?" The garage had been used previously as a workshop, and the owner had fortunately built a tiny bathroom.

"You've even got a love seat in here. Why, David Lantz, are you trying to suggest something?" Clark batted his eyelashes.

David froze. "Uh, no. I just thought you might want to sit. It's from that store IKEA. It's Swedish? Not very well made, but it was cheap. It's comfortable enough, but you don't have to sit if you don't want to."

"Honey, it's okay. Breathe. Don't mind me. I'm a flirty bitch, and I just can't help myself." Clark peered at the collection of wood scattered on the table. "So this is where the magic happens, huh? Don't you get lonely being all cooped up in here by yourself?"

David thought of the cool dew of the grass beneath his bare feet when he'd walk to the barn on summer mornings, and the rough wet of Kaffi's tongue when he approached with sugar cubes nestled in his palm. Isaac's smile as he wiped sweat from beneath the brim of his hat, and the sweet warmth of fresh cookies.

"Not really," he lied, scuffing his sneaker through the sawdust covering the cement. "It was nice back home when Isaac was with me every day, and in the barn the roof was so high and the horses were there. I wish there was room here for animals, but I don't suppose I have any use for a horse in San Francisco."

"Nope—just bears." Clark waggled his eyebrows.

David had the feeling Clark was referencing something sexual as usual, but he couldn't imagine what. While he thought of something else to say, the music started from the next garage. He tensed, trying to tamp down the immediate irritation that gripped him whenever *the thump-thump-thump* reverberated down the alley. David could never hear the words—just the pounding rhythm.

"Someone enjoys his Jay-Z. Who's your neighbor?"

"Alan. He works on motorcycles, and he likes to listen to music. A lot."

"You should get your own sound system in here, baby. If you can't beat 'em, join 'em."

"Maybe." But David didn't want to listen to loud noise. He wanted to hear the scrape of his spokeshave and the music of the saw as the wood transformed into what he wanted it to be.

"I hear Isaac's loving school, huh?" Clark took off his leather bag from across his chest.

"He is." David smiled. "He's taken to it like a fish to water. He wanted to be a carpenter before, but there's so much more here for him." And if that hurt more than it should, David tried to ignore the sting. He was only being selfish in wanting Isaac with him every day the way it used to be. "But he still comes here a couple times a week to work with me."

Leaning a hip against the worktable, Clark unzipped his light coat and slung it over his shoulder before pointing to the stack of lumber on the floor. "Is that for the chairs? The color looks right." He grinned. "I'm getting excited!"

"Uh-huh." David found himself staring at Clark.

Clark frowned and patted his hair. "What is it?" He smoothed his palm down his shirt. "Don't tell me I have a wrinkle."

David tore his gaze away. "No. I've just never seen you dressed so…"

"Boringly?" Clark laughed. "My work uniform: slacks, dress shirt, tie, loafers. Rinse and repeat." He touched the purple fabric tucked into his shirt pocket. "I attempt to liven things up with color, but when I tried anything that sparkled, shimmered or had an ounce of fabulousness, my boss was not having it." He tapped his mouth. "No gloss either, although that bastard will take my Studio Fix from my cold, dead hands."

David mentally scrolled through the ever-growing list of new words he was learning, but couldn't think of what that could possibly be. "Your what?" He was trying to get better at asking when something didn't make sense.

"Only the greatest thing ever created." Clark opened his bag and pulled out a black plastic disc. He snapped it open and held it to David's face. "You lift from the bottom and the sponge is in there, but I use a brush. It's a mix of foundation and powder, so it evens out the skin tone and blots excess oil."

David peered at the round mirror. "It's makeup? For men?"

"Men, women, and those who have yet to decide. Here." He pulled out a tube from his bag, from which a wide brush emerged. "Close your eyes."

David did as he was told, and the hair of the brush wisped over his face, tickling his nose. It was similar to the barber's brush, but much finer.

"Open." Clark held up the mirror. "See how it just evens you out? Although you don't need much. And that Isaac! His skin is so creamy I could put it in my latte. Must be all that clean living."

David's nose was less shiny, and his cheeks a little less ruddy. He couldn't imagine wearing makeup every day, but it didn't look bad at least. "Thank you."

Clark snapped the Studio Fix shut and dropped it back in his bag. "Anytime. Even a strapping lad like you can blot. This is San Francisco, after all. Oh, and *mazel tov!* That's Jewish for congratulations, but the rest of the world has co-opted it." He pulled out a dark bottle with a golden label. "Champagne. Must be drunk cold, so put it in the fridge for a special occasion. Sorry it's late—I've been meaning to get down here for weeks."

"Thank you so much." David took the smooth bottle and ran his fingertips around the foil on top. "I haven't had champagne yet." He went to slide it into the back of the small fridge squeezed in by the couch.

"Aww, I'm popping your cherry." Clark waved his hand. "Never mind what that means. Anyway, just wanted to check in and see how you're doing. My table is amazing, and I can't wait to see the chairs. I can't believe how quickly you got it done. If I'd ordered a custom table from anywhere else, it would take months. Months! You're a miracle worker."

David shrugged, but couldn't help but smile. "I suppose I'm used to working quickly."

"It's that sexy Amish work ethic. Your parents taught you well."

His gut twisted. June hadn't had a visit from Anna again. *Maybe she doesn't want to talk to me after all. Maybe she thought on it more, and she's disgusted. If she knows the truth about me and Isaac, why would she ever want to speak to me again?*

There was a singsong beeping, and Clark pulled out his phone with a sigh. "*Der Führer*. I swear he can't go five minutes without me. Hold on a sec." He stepped through the open door of the garage.

David could hear the murmur of Clark speaking, and he turned back to his work. But instead of picking up his saw, he stared at the block of wood as his mind whirled. Alan's music thumped on, and David uncharitably wished Alan would just go away and shut up. His head whirled.

He found sometimes he could go for hours on end and not worry—especially when he was with Isaac. Then something would spark a memory, and the sinking sensation would return. He could tell himself a thousand times that he'd made the right decision, but with the guilt was a longing for his mother and sisters that bored into him like the distant, endless beat of Alan's songs.

Every day he hoped for a letter. He'd finally mailed his, but there had been nothing in return. David shook his head, scattering a pile of nails and then picking them each up again. What did he expect? He could have written pages, but he would never be able to tell them the whole truth.

The nails dug into his palm as he squeezed them. He could never share what was truly in his heart. Never. And Mother didn't even write to implore him to return home, and to the right path that would lead to heaven. Not that he could blame her after the way he ran like a criminal. Why should she care if he went to hell?

"How are you finding these new tools?"

The nails scattered as David jumped. "I didn't hear you come back in." He scooped them up one by one.

"My bad." Clark pointed to the wall. "That's smart with all the hooks. In the city we have to use every inch of space." He ran his fingers over the sander. "I can't imagine how you used to do everything by hand. No wonder you have all those muscles."

David tried to ignore the last part, but his cheeks heated anyway. "I actually used some electric tools before, but it was a secret. I had a workshop with my English friend."

"Do tell." Clark clapped his hands, waggling his fingers. "Was this secret friend tall, dark and handsome like you? What else did you get up to? No detail too small."

"Uh, we drank tea sometimes?"

"Before you manfully fucked each other's brains out over a sawhorse?"

David had to laugh. "She's a sixty-eight-year-old woman, so no."

Clark wrinkled his nose. "That's disappointing. But wait, wasn't Isaac your apprentice?" He raised his eyebrows. "I bet you taught him a thing or two, right?"

Keeping his gaze down, David lined all the heads of the nails in the same direction as memories found him. *On his knees in the stall with Isaac's cock throbbing in his mouth. Bending Isaac over the worktable. Shivering together in the makeshift shower, cleaning the sweat and seed off their skin.*

"Say no more! Your lack of eye contact says it all. I bet Isaac—" Clark broke off. "Speak of the devil."

His pulse spiking, David looked up to find Isaac in the doorway. He was wearing his new usual outfit—jeans, sneakers and a long-sleeved T-shirt. His light jacket was wrapped around his waist. As always, David's heart skipped a beat and desire stirred when he saw him. He waited for the smile that always lit up Isaac's face, but Isaac's expression was shuttered.

"Oh. Hi, Clark." Isaac nodded.

"Hey, munchkin! I was just checking out the new work digs. How's school going?"

"It's fine."

David blinked in surprise. It was the least enthusiastic he'd heard Isaac be about school since he'd started. "Did something happen? You're not usually out this early."

"My classes for the afternoon are canceled because of a teacher meeting. It's so nice that I thought we could go to the beach for a little while. But if I'm interrupting you…"

David frowned. "Why would you be interrupting?"

Isaac shrugged, jamming his hands in his pockets.

"You should absolutely take advantage of this weather. This is the first nice day in what, *months*? No fog, no damn wind, and the sun is shining? Get to the beach, stat. But bring a jacket. This is San Francisco, after all." Clark sighed dramatically and slung his bag back across his chest. "I, on the other hand, must return to my cubicle prison. David, I can't wait to get the chairs. You deposited the check no problem?"

"I did. Thank you again. You didn't have to pay for it all up front."

"Pish. All right, gentlemen. Don't do anything I wouldn't do. That leaves your options wide open." He winked and put on his sunglasses, whirling out the door.

David didn't wait to tug Isaac close and kiss him. He inhaled deeply, sighing as Isaac hugged him back. The familiar press of his body and the softness of his lips chased away any other thoughts as Isaac nuzzled David's neck. While David was only shaving every few days, Isaac's cheeks were smooth and soft. David ran his hands over Isaac's back and down to his rear. "Mmm. Maybe we should just stay here," he murmured.

Isaac laughed softly. "Very tempting."

David pulled back and examined Isaac's face. "Did something happen at school? You seem upset."

"No. It's just…" Isaac paused before shaking his head. "It's nothing. Forget about it. Come on—let's take advantage of the weather."

David glanced at his half-finished project. "I guess I can take a break. Do you know how to get to the beach? I only know the buses to come here."

Isaac pulled his phone from his pocket. "I have an appy thing that'll tell us. Jen showed me how it works."

"You're sure you don't need to be studying?"

"A few hours won't hurt. Tonight I'm meeting up with Chris, Derek, and Lola for a study group."

"Oh. Okay." It was still odd to think of Isaac spending time with people David didn't know. Also, he wasn't sure what kind of name *Lola* was, but Isaac seemed to like her. *Not that I should judge anyone.*

"Did I show you the video Derek sent me? It's another one on the YouTube. Did you know there are *millions* of videos there? This one was a dog playing basketball, and it was so funny."

David smiled. "You showed me. It was great." He'd learned how to text, email and talk on his phone, but that was it. He knew he should do more, but he didn't like asking Aaron and Jen for too much help considering how much they'd already done. "It's nice that your friends are showing you things."

"They've helped explain so much stuff. You really have to meet them. I know you're busy here, but I think they're starting to wonder if you're real."

David laughed uneasily. It was silly to be so nervous to meet Isaac's school friends, but what would he say to them? He spent his days in a garage making furniture. David doubted very much that they wanted to hear about wood grains. "I will. Soon."

"I'm glad I told them I'm Amish." Isaac ran his finger around the rim of his phone, eyes downcast and his smile disappearing. "Although I guess I'm not Amish anymore. Not properly English either. Something in-between."

"What's wrong?" He clenched his jaw. "Did someone say something to you?"

For a long moment, Isaac was silent. Then he whispered, "Mother and Father finally wrote back."

Dread hooked through David. He took Isaac's hand. "What did they say?"

"That I broke their hearts." Jaw tight, Isaac drew his shoulders up. "That because I disobeyed them and the Ordnung, now I'm on this dangerous path. That I have to come home and yield to the Lord instead of worldly temptation. Of course they didn't say a word about Aaron." He exhaled sharply. "Not a word! I don't know why I expected anything else. But I'd hoped…"

"I know." He held Isaac close, wishing he could do so much more.

"They said I'm keeping them awake worrying I'll go to hell. That I *will* if I don't come back." Isaac gripped David's shirt. "They think that already, that I'm going to hell, and they don't even know the truth about us."

All David could do was hold on. He pressed kisses to Isaac's head. "I'm sorry," he whispered. He wasn't sure how long they stood there trembling.

Swiping at his eyes, Isaac stepped back and smiled humorlessly. "They sent a clipping from *Die Botschaft* as well."

"Let me guess—it was a story about a person who'd gone into the world and died a horrible, miserable death."

Isaac snorted. "How did you know? I'm sure they're cutting out those stories every week now and saving them. I bet the kids are hearing them nightly." He sighed. "I wrote them as well, but Mother and Father might not have even given them the letters. Or maybe they did, and Katie and my brothers hate me too."

"They don't hate you. I know they don't." The thought of David's own sisters hating him was too much to bear.

Isaac twined their fingers together. "I don't know what I'd do if we weren't here together."

"You'd have Aaron. Even if you didn't, you're so strong. You could do it." He squeezed Isaac's hand. "It's me who'd be lost without you."

Isaac brushed their lips together. "Good thing we have each other then." He smiled tremulously. "Let's go see the ocean."

THE GOLDEN GATE Bridge soared to the heavens in the distance. They walked toward it along Baker Beach, the damp sand cold between David's toes despite the heat of the day. Inhaling the fresh air deeply, he listened to the gulls sing. Here, there was no honking traffic or thumping music.

The beach was dotted with other people enjoying the day, but none gave them a second look. The sun was still high in the cloudless sky, and David wrapped his hoodie around his waist. He held his sneakers in his right hand, and after a few moments of hesitation, Isaac's hand in the other.

The ocean was on their left, and Isaac stared as the waves crested and rolled over the shore. The rhythmic swells of the blue sea were something David didn't think he'd ever tire of, but he found his gaze returning again and again to Isaac's bright eyes and sunbeam of a smile.

"It suits you," David said.

Isaac turned to look at him. "What?" He was still smiling.

"All of this. Being here in San Francisco. Living the English way. The ocean."

A man and woman walking in the other direction neared, and for a moment David held his breath, waiting for them to sneer and whisper. But the couple only smiled when they noticed David's attention, and the man called out, "Beautiful day isn't it?"

Squeezing Isaac's fingers between his own, David nodded, exhaling.

Isaac bumped their shoulders together. He pecked David's cheek and laughed delightedly. "I love doing that where everyone can see. It still doesn't seem real."

"I wonder how long it'll take." Although David hoped he'd never take it for granted.

Isaac gazed out as they strolled. "That water goes all the way to the other side of the *world*. I can't believe we're really here. Sometimes I expect Deacon Stoltzfus to pound on the door and list off all the ways I've broken the Ordnung."

At the thought of the deacon, David shuddered. "He would look at me sometimes with such hate. Not that I blame him after what Joshua did. He lost his daughter because of my brother."

"It's no reason to blame you. Joshua made mistakes, but Martha and Rachel chose to do the drugs. It was an accident that they drowned. Besides, isn't it all God's will? The deacon can't pick and choose which things are and which aren't."

David smiled ruefully. "Sure he can. As long as everyone falls into line and does as they're told."

They walked in silence for a minute, watching a boat cruise by toward the bridge, its white sails billowing. It was Isaac's birthday in July, and David wondered how much it cost to go for a boat ride. The ferry to Alcatraz had been exciting, and he could imagine how glorious it would feel to really ride the waves.

"After the buggy accident you said God was punishing you for what we did. For us."

David jerked out of his fantasy. "Uh-huh."

Isaac stopped and peered at him closely. "I always knew what we were doing was wrong, but I couldn't stop myself. I didn't want to even try. But here in the world, so many people think it's okay. Even ones who used to think it was a sin. Do you still think it's wrong?"

David floundered at the unexpected question as though he'd been dropped into the waves. Looking into Isaac's amber eyes, the freckles across his nose, and his beautiful mouth that David wanted to kiss forever—how could he possibly say yes? Yet deep in the shadows, the seed of doubt still lurked.

He dropped his shoes in the sand and caressed Isaac's cheek. "I want to believe it isn't. That we're the way God made us, and this is right. From the moment we kissed that night outside June's, it's felt that way, even when I told myself it was wrong."

"You said once it didn't make sense that all the changes God made in the world before the eighteen hundreds were okay, and those after are vain and sinful. So if the Amish are wrong about that, why can't they be wrong about this too?"

David ran his thumb across Isaac's bottom lip. "Good question."

"I thought so." Isaac smiled softly. "Besides, I'd never want to be in heaven without you."

Their lips met, right there on the beach in the middle of the day, with the sun so warm on David's skin. Isaac explored with his tongue, his little breaths as they kissed going to David's head like wine. The sand squeezed between his toes, and Isaac leaned into him.

"We should come see the ocean more often." David rubbed their noses together.

"I'd like that."

David scooped up his shoes, and they ambled on. "We still need to take you on a train."

Isaac grinned, swinging their clasped hands. "Yes. I went on the BART, which wasn't quite the same as a real train that goes across the country. But it was really fun."

"When did you do that?" David couldn't help the disappointment that they hadn't shared the experience.

"After class one day. Chris took me."

Now a sharp sliver of jealousy burrowed home, even though David knew it was foolish. Isaac was learning so much more about the city, and he already felt like he couldn't catch up. "Your new friends have shown you a lot of things."

"They're so nice. They didn't even care—that we're...you know.

Gay." He laughed. "I wonder how long it'll take before it's easy to say that. Anyway, Lola thinks you work way too much."

David tensed. *And what does Lola know?* "I have to. You know we need money. I can't keep taking from Aaron and Jen." Besides, in his workshop he didn't need to ask endless questions about the simplest things. He understood exactly what he was doing. "It's fine for you to go to school and hardly work, but I don't have the luxury."

Isaac frowned as he dropped David's hand, along with his sneakers. "Aaron and Jen told us we can stay as long as we want without paying rent, and you said you wanted me to go to school. You thought it was a good idea."

"It is. I just don't like being criticized by some girl who doesn't even know me."

"Lola didn't mean anything bad. She wants to meet you, but you're always too busy. I asked you last week to come out to the museum, and you wouldn't. And the aquarium the week before."

David huffed and dropped his shoes too. "Because I had a table to finish for Clark, remember?"

Isaac gritted his teeth. "I remember. But an hour or two off wouldn't kill you."

"What do you think I'm doing right now?" David waved his arm around. "Here we are at the beach when I should be working."

"If you didn't want to come you shouldn't have." Isaac crossed his arms.

"I *did* want to come, but—"

"But if you're going to complain the whole time, what's the point?"

"I'm not! How was I complaining? I wanted to come, but that doesn't change the fact that I have work to do." David pressed his lips together. Minutes ago he'd been blissful, and now he and Isaac were practically shouting. "Just because you're not very interested in carpentry anymore doesn't mean I'm not." The words barreled out before he could stop them.

Isaac's nostrils flared. "Just because I want to go to school doesn't mean I'm not interested in carpentry. In Zebulon it was the only thing I could do, and here—"

"If you hated it so much—"

"I never said that! I didn't hate it. I *don't* hate it. I love working with wood, and you know that. I love working with *you*. But there's a whole world out here. A whole ocean!" He spun around to face the waves.

David closed his eyes and rubbed his face, trying to find his footing. Isaac was right—he was being unfair. "I'm sorry."

Isaac stared at the horizon. "I'm sorry too."

They stood in silence, watching the ebb and flow of the tide.

"I want to swim in the ocean, David."

"You will." David peered around. "We can come back in the summer. See that ledge up there? We can have a picnic. Do you think—" He turned back to see that Isaac was halfway to the water, dropping his clothes behind him as he went. David's stomach plummeted. "Isaac!"

If Isaac responded, it was lost in the crash of the waves. David's feet sank in the sand as he ran, and he pushed desperately. As he reached the shore an icy wave soaked him to the knees with the punch of a horse's kick. He gasped. Isaac was already diving under, and he vanished as the water rushed over him.

For two heartbeats Isaac was simply gone. David thought of Joshua, and a scream clawed at his throat. Then the tide drew back, and Isaac popped up, sputtering. He splashed toward David, wearing only his plaid boxer shorts, which stuck to him limply.

"Are you crazy?" David hauled Isaac against him and propelled him back to the beach. Sand caked their wet feet, and Isaac stumbled. David wrapped him in his arms, rubbing his freezing skin.

"It's c—cold." Isaac shivered.

"Of course it is!" He crushed Isaac against him.

"Y—you'll get wet too."

"I don't care." David yanked his hoodie from around his waist and ran it over Isaac's soaked hair vigorously. They were garnering stares now from the few people walking nearby, but he ignored them. "What were you thinking?"

Quivering, Isaac half smiled, his teeth chattering. "I don't know. I wanted to finally s—swim in the ocean after all these years. I didn't want to wait. What if something happens and this was my only chance?"

Gripping him, David could barely restrain himself from shouting. "Nothing's going to happen to you!"

With a trembling hand, Isaac brushed David's cheek. "Mother and Father may think I'm going t—to hell, but they can't stop me from living. They can't stop us, David. They're wrong. They're *wrong*."

"Of course they're wrong." David cursed himself. He should have known the letter from home wouldn't be so easy to shake off. His pulse was still flying, and he ran his hands over Isaac's arms and back, reassuring himself that Isaac was still whole and breathing. "You scared me."

Face creasing, Isaac shook his head. "I'm sorry. I didn't mean to."

"It's not like you to do something without thinking." David wrapped the hoodie around Isaac's shoulders, grateful the sun was still out. The icy shock of the water had evaporated his earlier anger, and he was left bewildered and worried.

"Yes it is. Just like when you kissed me for the first time. I dove right in." He splayed his shaking hands over David's chest. "I *love* carpentry. But there's so much out here in the world. Schools, and jobs, and oceans. I want to find out what else I love."

David swallowed hard. "I just want you to stay safe. Don't go too far from shore." *Don't leave me behind.*

"Oh, my David." Isaac kissed him softly with salty wet lips. "I won't. I promise."

He examined Isaac's face. Water still clung to his eyelashes, and his smile was wobbly. David took a breath, but couldn't seem to make a sound.

"You don't ever have to be afraid of that. Besides, you're here to bring me back." Isaac huddled close. "I want to discover the world, but I want to do it with you. Always you. Yes?"

David breathed deeply as his heart slowed, and the tension faded. Isaac was safe, and everything would be all right. Nothing else mattered. He rubbed warmth back into Isaac's skin, closing his eyes against the glare of the sun on the waves.

"Yes."

HIS HAIR DAMP with sweat, David woke gasping. Isaac stirred beside him, and he froze in place with his heart racing until Isaac settled.

After the dip in the ocean, Isaac had skipped his study group, and they'd curled up on the couch under a thick velvety blanket and lost themselves in a movie. It had been a good night, but it seemed a distant memory now.

David squinted at the electronic numbers glowing red on the table.

2:14

The nightmare was still vivid in his mind. Blood soaking the snow as always, but this time he heard poor old Nessie's screams along with his mother's as they both lay broken on the road. His sisters were there, and he tried to reach them, but they were in the snowbanks, out of his grasp.

Then he'd been at Baker Beach, his feet stuck in the sand as though it was cement. He gestured with his arms and shouted, but Isaac still ran into the waves. When he vanished under the surface he never came up, and David couldn't save him. Then they'd been back in the bloody snow, and Isaac's body was bloated and sodden just like Joshua's.

They'd left the blinds a bit open, and David could see Isaac's face clearly, his lips parted in peaceful sleep. David's chest heaved as he watched Isaac breathe for a full minute before he could convince himself that he was all right. He desperately wanted to pull him close again, but it would be selfish to wake him.

David wasn't sure if it was the moon or streetlights that streamed in, but he was thankful it was bright enough to go to the dresser and fish out a pair of boxers before creeping downstairs. For all he knew, Jen could get paged in the middle of the night, and it wouldn't be right to be wandering her home naked.

The white light from outside cast the downstairs in a pale glow, and he shuffled silently from room to room, the gleaming wood hardly even creaking beneath his feet. He had to clear his head and fully wake so he wouldn't return to the same terrible dreams. Yet as the minutes ticked by, the nightmare images refused to fade, and more thoughts tumbled into his mind.

Mother in her wheelchair with the heavy cast on her leg, not able to care for herself yet. Mary and her broken heart. Sarah and the little ones wondering where their brother had vanished to. Anna with his dark secrets brewing inside her, bubbling to the surface.

Isaac drowning because David couldn't keep him safe.

The helplessness and guilt burned through him like a match set to a hayloft. Suddenly the walls of the dining room tilted, and he braced his hand on the table as his muscles seized and his head spun. He swiped desperately at pinpricks on his face, and there was a crushing weight in his lungs.

He cried out—nothing more than a strangled moan—as cold sweat gathered over his body, his heart hammering so hard he thought his chest would break. His vision went fuzzy and black, and he cracked his knees on the floor as he crashed down.

I'm dying! God help me! Isaac!

He was powerless to stop it—he was going to die here on the floor and he couldn't save himself. Gasping, he felt as though he was watching from a far-off place. There wasn't enough air, and everything was spinning. His throat was closing and his heart was going to explode, and he'd never felt so alone.

Dying, dying, dying!

His hands scrabbling on the hardwood, David managed to suck in a frantic breath. Then another. And another. His vision cleared enough that he could make out the planks of wood, and he concentrated on breathing.

The dizziness began to fade, and the tingles that had pierced him lessened until they went away. His heart still pounded so hard he was sure it would burst, but he focused on expanding his lungs. In and out. In and out.

It's all right. I'm not dead. I'm still here.

David wasn't sure how long he was crumpled on the floor. He thought of his father in the field, and how he'd clutched his arm and toppled over in an instant. Was this a heart attack? Would David die the same way?

As the frenzy that had gripped him loosened inch by inch, David managed to haul himself to his feet. He trembled all over, and leaned against the table heavily, rubbing his eyes until his vision completely cleared.

The house was still silent. Isaac, Aaron, and Jen still slept upstairs. At first David wondered how they could have not heard him, but he realized he'd hardly made a sound. The screaming had all been in his head.

His heartbeat and breathing were normal enough again that he was able to examine himself. Aside from a tremor that he couldn't shake yet, he seemed to be fine. Not a heart attack after all. He'd see how he felt in the morning, but it must have just been some strange reaction to the nightmare. Yes, he was fine now. No need to wake Isaac.

David blinked at the cabinet on the other side of the table. Through a panel of glass there were bottles standing in a neat line, and a row of upside-down glasses on the shelf above. He thought of how wine and beer seemed to calm his nerves.

Before he knew what he was doing, the cabinet was open, and David held a bottle in his hands. Vodka from Russia, said the label. It was only a third full. Aaron and Jen had said to have anything, so surely they wouldn't mind. Just a little to help him sleep.

He upended one of the short glasses and unscrewed the cap on the bottle. The clear liquid poured faster than he expected, splashing onto the wood of the cabinet. He dabbed at it clumsily with his trembling hand and wiped his palm on his shorts before lifting the glass to his lips. The vodka didn't really taste like anything.

It burned wickedly as he swallowed, but he didn't mind it. He focused on the new sensation in his throat, and could feel it travel down to his chest as well. He imagined the iron ball that was lodged there melting as the vodka flowed.

Before he knew it, the glass was empty. He poured a bit more for good measure. He already felt better somehow, the nice buzz slowing the drumming of his pulse in his ears. Whatever had happened, it was over now.

He stole back upstairs. Ever so gently, David slipped under the covers. The remaining tremor finally withered away as Isaac mumbled and turned into his arms, warm and safe.

CHAPTER  *Twelve*

THE TOILET SEAT was already up when David shuffled into the bathroom, and he could see the outline of Isaac's body through the opaque blue shower curtain. He leaned over the sink and examined himself in the mirror.

His eyes were a little bloodshot, and there were dark smudges below them. He took a deep breath and blew it out. His heart seemed to be working normally, and he felt okay. A little unsteady and on edge, but fine. No need to worry Isaac with what had happened.

"Morning," Isaac called over the rush of the water.

"Morning," David mumbled. His mouth felt as though it was full of cotton, and his head was heavy. He shook out a few little brown pills from the bottle in the cabinet, and gulped down a glass of water. Then another, and another.

Yawning widely, he pissed. It had been strange at first, sharing a bathroom. Of course he'd shared an outhouse with his family, but that was a one-at-a-time proposition. Initially, he and Isaac had taken turns, always closing the door, until one morning when Isaac couldn't wait. Since then a barrier had been lifted.

As he flushed, Isaac's hand snaked out to tug him into the bathtub. David smiled, hoping the ibuprofen would kick in soon. The water he'd drunk was already helping at least. He pulled the curtain closed behind him as Isaac kissed him deeply, wasting no time in sweeping his tongue into David's mouth.

But then Isaac leaned back, his brow furrowed. "You taste different."

David's stomach dropped, and he forced a smile. "Sorry. I think they call it morning breath." It wasn't completely a lie. He turned Isaac around to face the shower spray and soaped his back.

"It's okay. Are you feeling all right? You look tired."

"Didn't sleep that well, but I'm fine." He smoothed his palms over Isaac's shoulders.

"Mmm." Isaac rolled his neck. "Remind me not to jump into the Pacific in spring again. It was so cold I think I pulled all my muscles."

A wave of nausea passed over David as he remembered Isaac disappearing beneath the waves. He concentrated on keeping his voice light. "I'm not surprised." He put the green soap on its little holder and gently rubbed Isaac's neck and shoulders.

Isaac swayed against him. "Feels nice."

"Good." David kissed down the knobs of Isaac's spine.

"I love indoor plumbing," Isaac murmured. "Although there was something to be said for the shower contraption you created in the barn."

David pushed his worries away and trailed his fingers over the globes of Isaac's ass. "I always dreamed I'd get you back there, wet and willing."

Isaac's shoulders shook, and he turned, biting his lip. "Did you?" He maneuvered David under the spray and lathered up.

"Uh-huh. You know that."

"Tell me again." Isaac spread his soapy hands over David's chest, rubbing his nipples.

The flickers of pleasure helped ease David's headache. "The first day you came to work for me, do you remember you had a shower? While you were back there I was so hard I thought I would embarrass myself."

Isaac grinned. Water dripped into his eyes, and he slicked his hair back, a soap bubble hovering on his forehead before popping. "You were?"

"Of course. You were naked and wet in my barn. I wanted to burst in and have you up against the wall." He was getting hard now, and he could feel Isaac's cock growing against his hip.

Isaac dipped his soapy fingers between David's ass cheeks. "You know what I remember most about that shower in the barn?"

"What?" David practically growled. He grabbed Isaac's hips and pulled him close, grinding against him.

Isaac pushed his finger into David's hole. He licked his lips. "When you put your mouth on me. Your tongue *in* me. I couldn't believe you were doing that. It felt so good." His gaze flicked to David's mouth and back up. "Can I...?"

David could only nod, and they jostled in the small space until he was braced against the wall at the foot of the tub with arms and legs spread. He shuddered as he felt hot breath on his skin. Isaac's gentle hands spread him open, and David craned his neck to see as Isaac kissed his hole tenderly.

He groaned. "Please, Isaac."

Then Isaac's mouth was sucking at him, his tongue pushing at the rim of David's ass. David's knees went weak. He hadn't known it could feel this good. He'd loved it when he'd done it to Isaac—had reveled in actually tasting *inside* him. It had felt so incredibly *dirty*, but in the best way.

And now he was opening for Isaac, trembling as Isaac's nose bumped him. Isaac's teeth caught, and his tongue—and now finger—pushed in. It burned, but Isaac spit into him, licking and kissing and making David's cock stand up red and straining, the glistening head pushing through his foreskin. David's fingers slid on the steam-slick tiles, and Isaac grabbed his hips.

"Don't stop. Please." David was begging, but with Isaac he felt no shame.

Isaac's thumbs spread him again, his tongue plunging back inside. He lapped at David's ass, mumbling something David couldn't understand.

Soon Isaac's tongue wasn't enough. "I need you to fuck me," David gritted out.

He heard Isaac get to his feet and squeeze open the bottle of lubricant they'd stashed in the shower. His motion was rough as he slicked David's hole, his exhales hot on the back of David's neck. David twisted his head this way and that before turning. "Need to see you, Eechel."

He tore open the shower curtain and they stumbled to the floor, Isaac sprawling on his back on the fluffy blue mat. David climbed on top of him, straddling his hips and reaching behind to line up Isaac's cock with his ass. When he sank down, they both moaned.

"Oh, David." Isaac watched where their bodies joined, his eyes dark and lips parted. "You feel so good."

Flexing his thighs, David sank onto Isaac's thick cock, the head stretching him. It hurt, and he reached up to pinch his nipples, the pain in his ass somehow lessening.

"I wish you could see how you look right now." Isaac stroked David's hips. "That's it. Almost there. I've got you."

David couldn't look away from Isaac as he lowered himself. *He's still here. He's real.* With a push and a cry, he took the rest of Isaac's cock. The sensation of being complete was so commanding that he could have been happy to just stay like that with Isaac throbbing inside him.

But he leaned forward, both of them groaning, and spread his hands on Isaac's chest. With needy thrusts of Isaac's hips, David rode him. The bathmat was a little rough beneath his knees as he fucked himself on Isaac's cock, but all he cared about was the sensation of being filled, of Isaac stretching him and making him whole.

Isaac touched him here and there, little rubs and pats that were uncoordinated. He murmured David's name, and David rode him harder and harder, rising up and slamming down, his bouncing cock leaking even though it hadn't been touched.

His gaze locked with Isaac's, and he brushed back the short wet hair from Isaac's forehead. Isaac was safe, and they were together. He felt the burn of Isaac deep inside him spread like electricity. What he felt for Isaac was always there, and when they flipped the switch the desire came alive and filled every pore.

Gasping, David circled his hips, throwing his head back as he rubbed the secret spot inside him. Again, and again, and again—until his balls drew up and he came, splattering Isaac, who reached up to milk him, stroking him just the way David liked it while he caressed David's thigh with his other hand.

"Give me more," Isaac urged.

David did—another rush of bliss flowing through him and dripping down Isaac's hand. He wanted to collapse, but Isaac was still like an iron poker inside him. David squeezed with his ass. "Your turn."

His chest heaving, Isaac bent his legs and fucked up into David, grunting with every thrust. His wet skin glistened with David's seed, and David wondered if next time he could take a picture, because Isaac was his most beautiful laid bare like this. "I want to see you like this forever," he murmured. "My Isaac. Come for me."

"Oh, oh, oh—" His head banging on the mat, Isaac shook with his release, his eyes closed and mouth wide open.

David reveled in the slick feel of it inside him. When Isaac slipped from his ass, he stretched over him and they kissed lazily. Even though they needed to jump back in the shower and get to work and school, David closed his eyes. The water was still running, and steam filled the air, wrapping them in a cocoon and keeping the world at bay.

"ID."

David blinked at the man behind the counter, who stared back flatly. David stuttered. "I, I…uh. I don't have any." He felt guilty for some reason.

The man chewed something with slow movements of his jaw. "Need ID."

David's palms got sweaty, and he glanced at the woman behind him at the little store. She narrowed her gaze, giving him a disdainful look. He turned back to the counter. "I'm twenty-two."

"Then show me your ID, and we can all get on with our lives." The man was around forty, and he wore a shirt featuring a big black ball on the front with a paw print and the words *Alley Cats* above. It stretched over his belly.

"I don't have any." Should he explain that he was Amish and some lawyer in Ohio was trying to get his birth certificate? Instead he blurted, "It was stolen."

The man shrugged. "Sucks to be you, kid. But I can't sell to you without it."

Anger sliced through David's embarrassment. "I'm a grown man! Just take the money!" He threw down a few bills and grabbed the vodka bottle. He had to bring it home to replace what he'd drunk. Alcohol was expensive, so it was only right.

The clerk whipped his hand out and wrapped it around the top of the bottle. "I said no ID, no sale. Am I going to have to call the cops?"

"Kid, give it up. Come on. There's a line," said a male voice.

David realized there were now two more people behind the woman, who huffed.

"Seriously—no one has time for this shit today. Come back when you have ID." The clerk yanked the bottle away and pushed the crumpled money across the counter. "Go on."

Face burning, David snatched the bills and shoved them in his jacket pocket as he stormed outside. It was raining and cold, and he bent his head as he stalked down the street. *Kid.* But they were right, weren't they? He didn't even have a wallet yet, just keys and cash stuffed in his pockets with his phone. Not one piece of identification to prove who he was.

And who am I?

Rain dripped into his eyes as he walked block after block. He'd had a good day, content in his workshop where everything made sense. There had been no thumping music today, and he'd lost himself in the rhythm of the work, smoothing wood and shaping it into the legs for Clark's chairs. Isaac had called in the afternoon, and David was happy listening to him talk excitedly about a report he was writing about the Civil War.

Now David's nerves jangled. *Kid.* Aaron had said he was just starting out in the English world—that he was young. But David couldn't be young. There was no time for that. He needed to be a man.

Cars zoomed, and people clogged the sidewalks. The air felt thick with exhaust fumes as a bus chugged by, and David turned down another street, and then another, trying to get away from the noise. As he came to a stop light and looked up, he realized it was almost dark. In the growing glow of the street lights, the rain was a mist.

Closing his eyes, he thought of a canopy of stars, and riding across the fields with Kaffi strong and sure under him. The warmth of his flanks and the roughness of his mane. He imagined Isaac's arms around him, his head resting against David's back as they made their way through the forest, alone in the night with the leaves whispering.

A horn blared, and David snapped open his eyes, jumping back as headlights flashed toward him, blinding. Somehow he'd stepped off the curb.

"Watch it!" someone shouted.

His heart pounding, David retreated from the sidewalk, pressing back against a nearby building. He was under a sign, and water dripped in fat plops on his head and shoulders. He focused on breathing until his hands stopped shaking. The fear that he'd have another incident like he had the night before had bile rising in his throat.

Please God. Help me.

He reeled off a prayer in his mind, and the dread receded. But when David glanced around, the back of his neck prickled. He squinted at the street signs, but the names were meaningless. He went back to the curb and peered in each direction.

There were shops, and what looked to be small apartment buildings. He realized with a shiver that he didn't even know which way he'd come from. A bus passed, but it was a different number and name than the *14*

Mission bus he took until he caught the *24 Divisadero* across.

It's okay. I'll call Isaac. He'll find me. It was pathetic how it took David three tries to press the right button, his fingers clumsy as his heart raced. He couldn't have gone that far. It was okay. He waited for the screen to light up.

Nothing.

He pressed the round button again. The phone stubbornly remained black. Muttering English curses, David wiped the screen with his sleeve and pressed the button over and over before trying the one on the top. "Come on!"

It was no good. He shook the phone violently, barely restraining himself from smashing it to the sidewalk. The urge to scream was overwhelming, and he blinked back tears. "Stop. It's fine. You're fine."

He was being ridiculous. If he truly was a grown man, surely he could find his way. Yet the alarm that curdled his stomach lingered as he walked the streets. Block after block, he only seemed to be making himself more lost.

David plowed on as a damp wind blew up. He stopped by a large window, peeking inside at the dark wood tables and televisions on the walls. This was what the English would call a pub, he thought. It looked warm and inviting, and he pulled open the door.

It was called Flanagan's, and inside he walked by banks of cozy booths, most empty. There were people here and there, but the bar wasn't crowded the way the Beacon had been, which was a relief.

He unzipped his jacket and hung it on a tall pole near the bar. Fortunately his purple Henley was only a little damp around the collar. The round stool squeaked as he sat. There was only one other customer at the bar, all the way at the other end, hunched over a beer and watching the basketball game on the TV behind the counter.

The bartender, a big, thick older man with bushy graying hair, nodded to him as he tossed down a hard paper coaster in front of David. "What'll it be?"

He thought of the night before. "Vodka."

"How do you want it?"

David blinked. "How do most people drink it?"

The man tilted his head. "Do you have ID?"

For an instant, David thought he might actually cry. He scrubbed a hand over his face. "No. I grew up Amish, and I left home a couple of months ago. I don't have any ID yet. I got lost, and I can't find the right bus to get back to Bernal Heights. I just want a drink."

The bartender's thick eyebrows shot up. "That's one you don't hear every day."

David worked to keep his voice steady. "I'm twenty-two, I swear."

"Okay. I believe you. Looks like you sure could use a drink. How about a vodka tonic?"

He had no idea what that was, but nodded. "Thank you."

The bartender returned a minute later with a short glass full of ice and a sparkling clear liquid. A slice of lime rested on the side, and there was a little white straw sticking out. "Here you go. Want to start a tab?"

"All right." David wasn't sure what that meant, but it probably wasn't bad. He peered at the lime. "Do I put that in the drink?"

"Sure. Give it a squeeze and a stir. What's your name?"

"David." He picked up the lime and squeezed, jumping as some of the juice hit his chin.

"I'm Gary." The bartender held out his hand. "Good to meet you."

David shook Gary's hand. "You too." He took a swallow of his vodka tonic. It was bitter, but he sighed in relief. If he drank this, he'd feel better. He wouldn't get sick like he did before.

"Tough day, huh?" Gary picked up a rag and began polishing glasses.

"Yes." David felt terribly foolish. "I'm not sure how I managed to get lost."

"Happens to the best of us. Don't worry—I'll give you directions so you can find the bus. It's only a few blocks away."

"Really?" David smiled for the first time in what felt like hours. "Thank you." He took another drink, the comforting burn and buzz already flowing through him.

Gary wore a simple black shirt and pants, and aside from the shiny buttons, David could almost imagine they were plain clothes. Which was stupid, since Gary didn't have a beard and obviously wasn't Amish. Still, there was something about him that put David at ease. "I've never been lost like that before."

Gary chuckled. "This city ain't exactly easy to navigate. Don't sweat it. Are you from back east? Pennsylvania?"

"Minnesota, actually."

"There are Amish people in Minnesota? Huh." Gary picked up the next glass from his tray and polished it thoroughly. "So what brings you to the coast?"

"My..." David hesitated. He didn't think this was a gay bar, so he should be cautious. "I left with someone else, and his brother lives here. We're staying with him and his wife."

"That's good that you have people to help. Must be quite an adjustment. Not that I know a lot about the Amish aside from what I've seen in movies and on TV. But I sure know that if you dropped me on a farm with no technology, I'd be toast. Total culture shock."

The ice cubes clinked in his glass as David finished his drink. *Culture shock.* "Yeah. I thought I knew a lot about the English world, but as it turns out, I don't know much at all."

"Another?" Gary pointed to David's empty glass, taking it away when David nodded and pulling out a fresh one. "English?"

"English is what we call anyone non-Amish."

"Gotcha. So how did you know anything about us?"

"I'd seen some movies and used electricity at my friend's house. I didn't think it would be this hard." As he said the words aloud, it was a strange relief to admit it. It was *hard*.

Gary placed the fresh drink on the coaster. "Seeing movies and stuff—did you do that during that...what do you call it? Rumspringa? I saw something on TV about Amish kids dealing meth. Crazy shit." He nodded to someone at the other end of the bar. "Hold on. Gotta get Joe a refill."

While Gary poured another beer from one of the shiny taps, memories flickered through David's mind. Joshua running wild in Red Hills, and their parents bemoaning it helplessly. The sharp rap on the door, and two policemen standing outside, their hats tucked under their arms. The terrible grief that led them to Zebulon and even more rules.

David swirled the straw around his glass, images of Isaac taking over his thoughts. The brightness of his smile, and the way his eyes went dark with passion. The sweetness of his kisses, and how his laughter and cries of pleasure had echoed in the rafters of the barn. All the rules in the world couldn't have stopped him and Isaac from loving each other. It was so much more than a rumspringa.

"Well, there's a happy face," Gary said as he took up his polishing again. "Penny for your thoughts."

"Just thinking about my friend. The one I came here with." David knew he was blushing, and he examined the polished surface of the bar, running his fingers over it.

"Good friend, huh?"

David took a deep breath. "More than that. We're…" He glanced up at Gary. The man was a perfect stranger, but somehow it felt right to talk about it. *Maybe the English and their PDAs are rubbing off.* "I love him." As soon as the words left his mouth, David braced.

But Gary only smiled as he put a glass on the shelf. "That's nice." He whistled softly. "Hoo boy, I don't imagine being gay is too popular with the folks at home. Being so religious and whatnot."

David smiled sadly. "No. Not at all."

"It's good you two found each other then. What's his name?"

"Isaac."

"Hey, that's my son's name." Gary pulled a leather wallet from his back pocket and flipped it open. "That's my wife Karen with Isaac and Julie. The kids are older now. So are we, of course. Should get a new picture done."

David peered at the photo of the happy family, which was in a plastic sleeve. Gary and his wife stood behind their children, who were teenagers. They all smiled brightly in front of some kind of background that had mottled blues. Isaac had Gary's wide nose and broad forehead. "You all look nice. I wish I had a picture of my family."

Gary returned his wallet to his pocket. "Do you just not have any with you, or are there no pictures allowed?"

"No pictures allowed." David sipped his drink. "Sometimes I feel like I'll forget what they look like." He forced a smile. "It's stupid." He reached for a bowl of nuts and popped a few into his mouth.

"Not stupid at all. So is that why you and Isaac left your town? Because you're gay?"

David nodded. "We could never be together there. But there were other reasons too. All the rules, and living plain…it's difficult. I questioned it sometimes." The words seemed to pour out with each sip of his drink.

"I think *difficult* is an understatement."

"I'd wonder if it's really the only right way. Maybe God cares more about what's in our hearts than whether or not we have electric lights, or how wide the brims of our hats are. Or even if we wear hats at all." He said the words, but he wished he could truly believe them. He ran a hand through his damp hair. "I'm sorry. I'm talking a lot. If you have work to do please don't let me stop you."

Gary held up his rag and a glass. "I'm doing it. Besides, I'm a bartender. It's my job to listen to my customers." He smiled. "And for the record, what you have to say is a whole lot more interesting than Joe bitching about the Warriors. Tell me, what is it you do? For work, I mean."

"I'm a carpenter."

"Is that so? I was never very handy, so my hat's off to you."

"Have you always been a bartender?" It didn't seem like a bad job.

"Yep. Since college. I managed to avoid the draft by the skin of my teeth, and I vowed I'd do something I enjoyed once I was done with the business degree my dad insisted on. So here I am. Have to admit the degree did come in handy when I decided to buy my own place."

"This is your bar?"

"It is indeed. Gary Flanagan at your service, just like the name on the window." He grinned. "Been twenty years, and it still makes me proud."

"Maybe I'll have my own store for my furniture one day." The thought made David warm inside.

"I bet you will. Just takes hard work, a bit of luck, and oh yeah, even more hard work." He pointed to David's empty glass with raised eyebrows.

David nodded. "I don't mind. I'm used to that." Something else Gary had said niggled at him. "This is probably a stupid question, but what did you mean about the draft?"

"For the war. Vietnam." Gary made David another drink, pouring the vodka with a high lift of his arm and not spilling a drop. "They drafted men—into the army, I mean—until the end of seventy-two, and I turned eighteen a couple months later. I hadn't really wanted to go to college, but I thought I'd better. We still didn't know if they'd extend the draft after all."

It rang a faint bell. "So if you were drafted, you had no choice but to go to war?"

"That's right." Gary wiped the counter with a cloth. "Maybe it was cowardly, but I had no desire to go kill in the jungle. Or die there, thank you very much."

"I don't blame you." David shuddered at the thought of war. "There's so much I don't know. We only go to school until the eighth grade, and we don't learn much at all about the outside world. I've read English books in the last few years, but I need to read more, apparently."

"No shame in that. Believe me, there are plenty of people who've had all the opportunities in the world to learn and can't find their ass with two hands. Let me tell you about a guy I used to know in college."

Laughing, David listened to Gary's stories. When he finished his drink, he thought about getting another. He felt so content. But then he noticed the clock behind the bar. "Is it almost nine?"

"It is."

David's stomach dropped. He must have wandered the streets for longer than he thought. "I'm usually home by six-thirty. Isaac will wonder where I am." He pulled money from his pocket. "How much do I owe you?"

"The first was on the house, so fifteen dollars for the others."

Should I argue? Would that be rude? "All right. Thank you very much." He peeled off a twenty dollar bill. "Is that enough of a tip? I honestly don't know."

Gary smiled. "It's more than enough. I'll give you some change."

"No! Please keep it all. Thank you."

"Okay then. It was a real pleasure meeting you, David. Come back again soon. Oh, let me get you those directions." He pulled out a pen and picked up a square paper napkin. "It's real simple."

"Thank you for your help, and for the drink. It was very good to meet you."

"Don't be a stranger." Gary extended his hand.

They shook, and when David navigated the few blocks to where he could catch the bus, he found himself smiling, his whole body tingling and flushed. He stopped in a little bodega to buy a plastic container of strong mints. He didn't want Isaac to know he'd been out drinking. English people did it all the time, but it might worry him. Still, David had needed directions, so it was a good thing he found the bar.

He sucked a mint as he waited for the bus. His earlier terror was distant now, and he hummed a nameless song. It was raining again, but it shimmered in the streetlights, and he didn't care that his feet were wet.

CHAPTER Thirteen

"**Y**OU'VE GOT THE charger, right?"

"I do." David drew his hand across Isaac's back and kissed his cheek as he got up from his stool at the counter. "I promise I won't let it happen again."

Isaac scooped his spoon into his bowl. "I don't mean to nag. It was just..." He crunched a mouthful of cereal and played idly with the zipper on his blue hoodie.

David knew Isaac had been worried sick by the time he'd come home. Isaac had even had Aaron drive him to the workshop to check for David. Guilt mingled with affection as he thought of how tightly Isaac had clung to him as they went to sleep.

The dishwasher was a contraption David hadn't tried to figure out yet, but he squeezed in his spoon and bowl. That much he could do. He came back around the counter and wrapped his arms around Isaac, tucking his chin over Isaac's shoulder. "I'm sorry."

Isaac leaned back, tracing his fingers over David's hands. "All these terrible thoughts went through my head. If you'd been hit by a car, they wouldn't even know who to call."

Imagining that happening to Isaac sent an icy shiver through David. "We should get wallets, and we can write our numbers down. For an emergency."

"That's a good idea. I suppose we should get wallets anyway. Hopefully we'll be able to get our ID soon."

David thought of the bottle of vodka he still needed to buy, and was glad Isaac couldn't see his face. Surely he'd find some place that would sell it to him, and he'd make sure he didn't drink anymore and wouldn't need to replace it again.

He ran his hands over Isaac's thighs and hips, feeling his empty pockets. "You never carry the knife now." Instead it sat on the little table beside their bed.

"I'm not allowed to bring it to school."

It made perfect sense, but it still saddened David for a reason he couldn't name.

"Hey, do you want to see a movie tonight?" Isaac asked.

"Sure." A memory of Isaac beside him in June's truck, staring rapt at the Sky-Vu screen made David smile. He wished San Francisco had a drive-in. Maybe there was one nearby in summer. Of course he'd have to get his driver's license, and the thought of city traffic made his palms sweat and pulse leap.

"Chris said he'll pick up tickets this afternoon, so we'll just give him the money tonight." Isaac scraped his spoon on the bottom of his bowl.

David's smile faded. "Chris?"

"Yeah. Lola's coming too. They really want to meet you. It'll be fun."

Fun. David knew it should be, but thoughts tripped through his mind uneasily. *What if they don't like me? What if I say something stupid? What if I embarrass Isaac?* With a kiss to Isaac's neck, he went to the fridge and poked around.

He hadn't really had friends in Zebulon. After he left school there was so much work to do at home, but more than that he'd started to realize that the unnatural urges that left him waking with shamefully sticky sheets were only getting stronger as time went on. What if his friends could tell? It was better to keep his distance.

Until Isaac changed everything. He was glad Isaac had made friends at school, but the idea of meeting them was daunting. He thought of something he'd seen on TV—making a good first impression, the English called it. He wanted to be at his best when he met Isaac's new friends. His smartest. He'd meet them after he'd had the chance to read some more books. When he had more to talk about. *Soon.* Next week, even. Yes, he'd meet them next week.

"Oh, wait." David opened one of the cupboards and took out a jar of peanut butter. He didn't look at Isaac as he went about making a sandwich. "I just remembered I have to work late tonight."

"You do? Why?"

David dragged his bare toe along the seam of one of the pieces of hardwood as he put two slices of bread on the counter by the sink. From the corner of his eye, he could see Isaac watching him, his spoon hovering in midair. "I have a new order I really need to work on. For one of Clark's friends." It was true that Clark's friend had asked about a desk.

"Clark?" Isaac asked, and then mumbled something.

"He told a bunch of people about the table. He's been really helpful." David spread the peanut butter over the bread, making sure it reached all four corners.

Isaac snorted. "Uh-huh."

"What?" David looked at him. "What's wrong?"

Eyes on his bowl, Isaac shrugged. "Nothing. He's just weird."

David frowned. It was so unlike Isaac to talk of someone that way. "Why? I know the makeup and the way he dresses to go out is…different. But he's nice. And he's a paying customer."

"I know." Isaac shook his head. "I'm just disappointed about the movie. Do you want me to skip it and help you work?"

Yes. "No, of course not. Go to the movie with your friends. Have fun."

"Are you sure?"

No. "Absolutely." It wasn't fair for Isaac to miss the movie because David was too nervous to meet new people.

"But I haven't been doing enough. You've been giving Aaron money for the things he bought *both* of us."

"Of course I have. You don't need to worry about money."

He pulled out the roll of foil from a drawer with a frown. Jen and Aaron had told him repeatedly to eat anything he wanted, but David knew he should be buying his own groceries. He was giving Aaron back as much money as he could as quickly as possible, but here he was eating their food.

Yet when he'd stopped at the grocery store on his way home one night, he'd only gone down one aisle before being completely overwhelmed. June had always stocked the little fridge in his workshop at her farm, and of course Mother had taken care of food at home.

Isaac huffed as he came around the end of the counter. "Yes, I do need to worry about money. I can't just expect you and my brother to pay for everything. It's not fair."

David waved a hand. "Isaac, it's fine. You should have fun."

"So should you! But all you do is *work.*" Isaac yanked open the dishwasher. "And this is full. Why didn't you put it on?"

"I don't know how."

"It's not hard." Isaac flung open the cabinet under the sink and pulled out the detergent. "Just fill up the little soap holder." He squeezed the bottle violently. "Then close the door and press this button. See? Easy. If I can learn how to do it, so can you."

As the sound of water flowing into the dishwasher hummed, David tried to keep his voice even. "Yes, I see. And we just went to the beach two days ago." Although that hadn't quite ended up being *fun.* "I have to make up the time."

"I know! But..." Isaac shook his head. "Forget it."

"Fine." David yanked out the foil and ripped it off on the jagged edge of the box, wincing as he caught his index finger. Grumbling, he shook his hand.

"Are you okay?"

"Yes," he muttered, swiping at the drop of blood on his finger.

"Let me see." Isaac snagged David's wrist and lifted his hand. He pressed his thumb to the cut.

"It's nothing." But David didn't pull away, enjoying the warmth of

Isaac being near. He wasn't sure how they'd gone from a peaceful breakfast to sniping at each other. He rubbed his other hand over Isaac's hip, drawing him closer.

A little smile flitted over Isaac's face before he brought David's finger to his mouth gently. "Kiss it better," he murmured. "I saw it on TV."

When David covered Isaac's mouth with his own, he tasted a hint of his blood. Aaron had gone to work, and Jen wouldn't be home from her night shift for a while since she was covering a few extra hours, so David gripped Isaac's hips and pushed him back against the edge of the counter.

As he licked into Isaac's mouth, loving the twist of Isaac's fingers in his hair, everything else faded away. Here, he was back on solid ground—just him and Isaac, with no worries about money, or how to buy groceries, or work dishwashers, or new friends to impress. Here, David knew what he was doing. He sank to his knees and pulled up Isaac's T-shirt and hoodie, kissing Isaac's belly and tugging at the button on his jeans.

With the hardwood beneath his knees, he could almost imagine they were back in the barn, hidden away in one of the stalls with Kaffi nickering nearby. Isaac caressed David's head and shoulders, his fingers dipping below the neck of David's T-shirt. After peeling Isaac's jeans down his thighs and nosing at his swelling cock through his underwear, David smiled up at him.

"Trying the briefs again?"

"Uh-huh." Isaac licked his lips. "They feel tight. Especially now."

"Mmm. I bet." David sucked at Isaac's cock through the gray cotton while he traced patterns on Isaac's hips. David had taken to boxers, although at home in his sweatpants or pajama bottoms he didn't wear anything at all. He mouthed at the wet head of Isaac's shaft while his fingers explored the familiar landscape of Isaac's thighs, connecting the dots of pale freckles and brushing through the sparse hair.

"*Please.*" Isaac groaned, thrusting his hips.

David teased him for another minute, inching the briefs down with more fleeting kisses and caresses. When he finally filled his mouth with Isaac's cock, he moaned at the familiar taste. He loved the feeling of it stretching his lips, spit leaking from the corners of his mouth as he sucked.

Twitching, Isaac palmed the back of David's head with one hand, the other clutching the counter behind him. "Yes, my David. It feels so good. Does it feel like this when I do it for you?" He gasped. "So perfect?"

Nodding, David sucked harder and reached for Isaac's balls, done with teasing and desperate to taste his release—needing to be the one who gave it to him. He touched the sensitive places he'd discovered over the months, each cry and shudder from Isaac's lips filling him with satisfaction and pride. This was something he wouldn't get wrong. This would always be the same no matter where they were.

When Isaac came in his mouth, David swallowed greedily, his nostrils flaring. He was hard in his jeans, but he didn't touch himself—concentrating only on Isaac and drawing out every last shiver of pleasure until Isaac pushed at his head.

"Okay, okay. Too much."

Then Isaac was on the floor with him, kissing him deeply and tugging at David's pants. They rolled around in the middle of the kitchen, laughing when Isaac swore at David's zipper. They tasted and touched until Isaac was on his back and David's jeans and boxers were around his shins. Isaac yanked David's hips toward him until David's knees were wide on either side of Isaac's neck.

"My mouth," Isaac insisted.

David didn't need to be asked twice. Bracing himself with one hand on the floor, he slipped the other beneath Isaac's head, cradling his skull as he rocked his hips. He watched his shaft fill Isaac's mouth, and Isaac moaned around him, sending vibrations through David's balls that ricocheted up his spine.

"Not long," David muttered.

Isaac stroked his hips and thighs, his fingers stealing around to tease at David's ass and urge him on. When Isaac choked a little, David pulled back. Isaac's eyes were watering, but he dug his fingers into David's hips.

"So close," David gasped as his balls tightened.

Pleasure filled him in a rush, a wave sweeping through him and stealing his breath. He shook with each pulse as Isaac swallowed. Some of it dripped from Isaac's lips, and the sight prompted another spurt. He trembled as Isaac licked him clean. "Oh, oh," he mumbled.

David rolled onto his back beside Isaac, and their chests rose and fell rapidly. Isaac's tongue darted out to catch the drops he'd missed, and David smiled. He knew they should probably talk about why they'd gotten annoyed with each other, but why dredge it up again? Everything was okay now.

"I should get cleaned up and go to school, and you should get to work."

"Uh-huh."

Isaac kissed David's cheek and pressed against him. "Thank you for everything you do. You're working so hard. What's that thing the English people say? Bringing home the bacon?"

David chuckled. "Yes."

"And the chocolate! I didn't say thank you for the little present you slipped in my backpack. How did you know Reese's was my favorite in Red Hills next to ice cream?"

He shrugged. "Aaron mentioned it. It was no big deal."

Isaac kissed him again. "It's a big deal to me."

Here with Isaac, anything seemed possible. David nuzzled his cheek. "Maybe I will come to the movie tonight." The thought made his palms sweat, but it was time to be brave.

"Really?" Isaac's face lit up. "It'll be so much fun. They'll love you. I know it."

David wasn't so sure, but he smiled. After a few moments he groaned. "We should move."

By the time they were organized and had their shoes on by the front door, Jen walked in. A chunk of her dark hair hung lank around her face, and her smile was halfhearted. "Hey, boys. Have a good day." She kicked off her shoes and put on her slippers, dropping a stack of mail on the side table.

"Are you okay?" Isaac watched her with concern.

Jen waved a hand. "Yeah. Just a long shift. There was a big accident early this morning with a tractor-trailer."

"A truck?" David asked.

"Right." She hung up her jacket in the closet and raised her arms over her head, yawning. Her green scrubs were stained and wrinkled. "I need a shower and sleep. Have a good one."

"Bye." Isaac opened the front door, and David followed, freezing when he glanced at the mail on the table. A letter stuck out from beneath a glossy flyer featuring pictures of diapers and toilet paper.

Mr. David Lantz

He'd know Mother's messy script anywhere. Isaac was already on the steps outside, and David couldn't get any words out. He watched his hand reaching to pick up the letter almost as if it was someone else's.

"David? We should get going."

Eyes glued to the stark white envelope with no return address, David nodded.

"David?"

"Coming," he said hoarsely. He snatched up the letter and shoved it in the pocket of his coat.

In the drizzle, they walked to the bus stop David used. Isaac said goodbye with a smile before turning toward the next street. The letter in his pocket felt so heavy David was barely able to wave. As he watched the bus approach in the gray morning, he realized his peanut butter sandwich was still on the counter. He didn't go back.

THE SINGLE SHEET of paper lay crumpled at his feet.

From his perch on the love seat, David could still see Mother's scratchy handwriting. It didn't matter that he couldn't see the full words—he felt as though every one was seared into his mind. He nudged the paper with his toe, watching it skitter across the concrete floor.

To David,

I had not thought it possible to be more disappointed in a son, but you have proved me wrong. I pray morning, noon, and night that you will return to us. Return to your family and community, and most of all to God, who will forgive your sins if you yield to him. You know this is the only way to go to heaven.

I don't know what has possibly come over you that you would be so disobedient. That you would give in to worldly pride and temptation. I am only glad your Father does not have to bear the shame that I do.

I beg you to find humility again, and return to Zebulon. You have broken my heart.

Your Mother

He'd closed the garage door to the damp morning, and the overhead light felt too bright. The *thump-thump-thump* of Alan's music pulsed through him, and David stared at the stacks of wood squeezed into the corners, and the tools hanging from the walls.

He wasn't sure what time it was. He knew that if he called, Isaac would rush over and hold him close. That he could lose himself in Isaac, and forget every one of his mother's words. At least for a little while.

No.

David had to be strong. Isaac had school. Isaac was fitting in. Isaac was turning on dishwashers, and making friends. He didn't need to be dragged down into this. He'd had his own letter already, and it had upset him enough. David pulled out his phone with shaky hands and carefully tapped out a message to Isaac saying he had to work after all and couldn't make the movie. He hated lying, but it was better for everyone. He didn't want Isaac to see him like this and worry. An image of Isaac disappearing beneath the waves haunted him.

Wishing he could stop hearing Mother's voice echo through his head, David scrubbed his hands over his face. "What did I expect?" He sounded hoarse and strange.

He'd known Mother would never understand why he'd left, and of course she didn't even really know the reason. He squeezed his eyes shut.

Bear the shame.

His breath coming short and fast, David commanded himself not to cry as thoughts crashed through his mind—his mother's horror if she ever discovered his true nature—Mary's heartbreak made all the more bitterly painful—his younger sisters' tears of confusion. They'd lost so much already.

If Mother knew just how much shame David could bring to her and their family, she would...he honestly couldn't imagine how she'd bear it. His love for Isaac would be unthinkable to her. She could never know the truth. None of them could. He'd hurt them enough by leaving, and there would never be the right words to make them understand his nature.

Return to your family and community, and most of all to God, who will forgive your sins if you yield to him.

"I'll never get to heaven." He had to accept it, but it still cut so deeply.

Maybe he could see Mother and the girls again in this world, but Father was already lost. He tried to remember Father talking to him about anything but farming or the Ordnung, but failed. That day,

Father had chastised him for letting a curse slip out when he'd bashed his thumb with a hammer. David could still hear Father's low voice booming out, although he wasn't sure if the years had distorted it and made it sound even harsher in his mind.

"You'll be on the path to hell if you talk like that! To curse is an affront to God. You know this, and yet still you sin."

It hadn't been more than an hour later when David had seen Father collapse amid the crops. His face had been gray already.

Maybe if I hadn't angered him with my sinning, he wouldn't have had a heart attack.

Father's death had brought David to June, and part of him had liked to believe it was God's will—a sign that the English world wasn't so bad after all. A sign that perhaps the Ordnung wasn't always right, even though Father's last words to him had been a warning.

Yet still I sin. Here he was thousands of miles away in a *city* with his lover. He'd broken his mother's heart and ignored his father's warnings.

Everything suddenly closed in on him as it had the other night, and it felt as though a flock of birds were trapped inside his chest, their wings battering him. Gasping, David leaned back on the love seat, the certainty that he was going to die choking him as his vision narrowed to a tunnel with only a pinprick of light.

Trembling, David prayed to God for mercy, caught in the grip of the sickness—or perhaps madness. It seemed to go on forever, and he thought the German words, unable to do more than gasp and gulp until the terror passed and he could breathe again, his vision clearing. He felt as though his whole body ached with unshed tears. He was so pathetic. He was going crazy here in the English world.

The little fridge hummed in the corner. Shaking, David crawled to it. The foil on the bottle of champagne tore easily, but it took minutes for his trembling fingers to unscrew the piece of wire. It took some doing to pop out the cork, and the sound echoed dully on the concrete as a few bubbles spilled over his fingers.

Collapsing on the love seat, David tipped the bottle to his lips. The champagne quickly went to his head as he gulped it down. He was fine. He wasn't going to die. He just needed to be stronger. That was the only thing the matter with him—his own weakness.

David breathed more evenly as the warm buzz filled him, blocking out everything else. He imagined it was how God's forgiveness might feel.

CHAPTER  *Fourteen*

"*E*IGHTH GRADE?"

David took another swig of beer. In the chair beside him, Isaac sipped on his soda, and nodded to a man whose name was…Liam, perhaps? Logan? There were three new people, and they'd rattled off their names, but David wasn't sure what they were now. He had to pay better attention, but it was so noisy.

"There's too much work to do on the farm to stay in school longer than that," Isaac explained.

Across the table, Liam/Logan whistled. "Wow. I can't even imagine. I've seen stuff on TV, and it always seemed so quaint. But to not even get a proper education? That's like child abuse."

David shifted in his seat, biting back the urge to defend Amish ways. Of course as time went on, he realized more and more how uneducated he was. But words like *child abuse* rankled. He wished Aaron was there. Aaron would know what to say, but he was arriving any minute with Jen.

"They didn't *abuse* us. It's just a different way of life," Isaac said sharply.

"Of course." Liam/Logan raised his hands. "I'm sorry. I shouldn't have said that. It's just hard for me to imagine. It was tough enough growing up gay in Sacramento. Gay and Chinese wasn't a fun combination. When I came here I thought I'd died and gone to queer heaven." He grinned. "So many men to explore; such little time."

"We're together." David wondered if it was strange that he and Isaac weren't touching. Glancing around the Beacon, there was certainly a lot of touching going on. He leaned closer and hung his arm around Isaac's shoulders.

"They're like high school sweethearts," Clark added. "Isn't it adorable?"

One of the other guys—Steve?—spoke up. "Aww. That's so sweet. I remember my high school bf. His name was Craig. He had the voice of an angel and the ass of a figure skater. We thought we'd be together forever, of course."

Everyone laughed but David and Isaac. David wasn't sure why it was so funny. He knew the English often didn't get married as young as the Amish did, but surely some younger couples stayed together?

His knee jiggling under the table, Isaac fiddled with the cuff of his shirt. He and David had both dressed in jeans and button-downs. Isaac's was a light blue, while David had stuck to black. After all the years wearing dark shades at home, he knew he should try some more colors, but he felt like he'd blend in better without color.

As a new song blasted on, an exclamation rippled through the Beacon. Clark danced in his seat. "I love this new Kylie! The diva from down under's still got it."

"That she does." Dylan tapped out the rhythm on the table.

David and Isaac shared a puzzled look. Sometimes it felt like people weren't even speaking English.

Liam/Logan's gaze slid to David. "Are you going to go back to school too?"

All eyes around the table focused on him, and it felt like everyone in the Beacon was watching and listening—and judging—even though he knew it wasn't true. He could feel his face getting red. "No."

David tightened his grip on his beer glass. Why had he agreed to come out? In the days since he'd gotten the letter from Mother, all he'd wanted to do was curl up and sleep. He told himself to relax and have fun, but it was easier said than done.

"David's a master carpenter." Clark raised his hands with a flourish.

He was wearing a sheer black shirt and glittery makeup on his eyes. "You remember my new dining set? This is its creator."

Liam/Logan and the other two men exclaimed, all of them praising David's work. David smiled and thanked them, and Isaac squeezed his knee under the table. It felt good to be praised, which in turn made him feel a little guilty. He snapped back to attention as Clark reached across the table and put his hand on his arm.

"I was telling Tyler you're the perfect man to have in the bedroom." He paused. "To make his new headboard," he added.

Everyone laughed, although Isaac only sucked on his straw, draining his soda. David smiled. "Um…thanks." He held out his glass eagerly as the waiter dropped off another pitcher of beer.

"Clark, you're making him blush!" The man who must have been Tyler rolled his eyes. "You're incorrigible."

Clark's nails gleamed with dark pink polish, and he squeezed David's arm through the thin material of the button-down. "Just calling it like I see it." He leaned back across the table with a wink. "Really though, if any of you need something involving wood, ask David."

There was more uproarious laughter, although David couldn't figure out why. Knowing Clark it was a sex joke. He glanced at Isaac, whose brow was creased. Isaac played with his straw, poking at the ice cubes in the bottom of his glass.

"I honestly didn't mean it to sound like that." Clark held up his hands. "I swear to God."

Dylan chuckled. "That's enough teasing." He sat on the other side of Isaac, and he leaned in to murmur something, the twists of his braided hair falling over his forehead. His shoulders relaxing, Isaac smiled and nodded.

"I really would like to talk to you about my bed," Tyler said to David. He laughed and brushed back his light hair. "Jesus—everything sounds dirty right now. Clark, you are a terrible influence, you know that? I mean about making a headboard. Do you have a card?"

"Uh…" David wished Aaron was there to look to. "No?"

Dylan spoke up. "He means a business card. Not sure if you've ever seen them? Anyone have one on them?"

Liam/Logan pulled out his slim wallet from his back pocket. "Here's mine." He handed a piece of paper to David. The card was made of thick glossy paper, and the words were printed in simple letters next to a symbol David recognized from one of the big banks.

Logan Lin, MBA
Financial Advisor

Logan's email address and phone number were there as well. David was pretty sure MBA was a degree from school. "I get it. I have a website that my friend does for me. I guess I could get cards and put that on it as well?" He handed it back.

Logan waved. "Keep it. If you guys ever need help with banking or investments, let me know. And yeah, you should get a card with your site and contact info. Any printing place will be able to do them. It doesn't cost much."

"Thanks." David slipped the card into his pocket.

"I still need to get a bank account," Isaac said.

"This must be so weird for you guys." Logan shook his head. "I can only imagine how fucked I'd be if I had to give up everything I know and go plow fields. Seriously, if you need any help figuring out money stuff, I'm happy to meet with you. No charge."

Isaac smiled. "Thanks. We appreciate it."

David smiled too. The beer was loosening the ever-present knot of tension, and he felt back on solid ground. Clark and Dylan and their friends were confusing, but they clearly meant well.

"D, are you going to Volume on Friday?" Clark asked.

Dylan shook his head. "Not this month. Maybe next time, though." To David and Isaac he added, "Volume's a gay club. We're too old to go every week like we used to, but one Friday a month they do a retro night. The music's the best."

"Retro?" Isaac asked.

"Oh, retro means…" Dylan smirked. "Well, it means *old*. They play music from the nineties and the early two thousands so we can relive our glory days."

"You boys should come with!" Clark pursed his lips. "Although not you, munchkin. Have to be twenty-one for Volume." He turned his gaze to David. "But you should check it out sometime."

"If Isaac can't go I don't want to."

After a moment, Isaac shrugged. "No, you should go. You can tell me all about it."

"Really?" David wasn't even sure he wanted to go to a club. The Beacon was loud and crowded enough. "But—"

"No buts. I don't want you to miss out because I'm not old enough."

"We'll see." David shrugged.

"I do declare—is that Dr. Paculba and her dashing husband I see coming this way?" Clark popped up from his chair and threw his arms around Jen, kissing her soundly. "You're actually early. For you." Then he kissed Aaron right on the mouth. "Hey, handsome."

David and Isaac shared a glance, their eyebrows raised. But Aaron was smiling and didn't seem bothered at all. "Hey, yourself." He stood behind Isaac and David, giving their shoulders a squeeze. "You guys having fun?"

"Uh-huh," Isaac answered.

Jen gave them both a kiss on the cheek. "Hey, boys!" She made a little exclamation as a new song came on. "Aaron! We are dancing right now! Do not pass go. Do not collect two hundred dollars." She yanked him toward the dance floor, which was packed with gyrating people. Clark, Logan, and Steve followed, leaving Dylan and Tyler talking and laughing about something.

As David puzzled over what two hundred dollars had to do with anything, Isaac grinned and nudged him.

"Hey! My friends from school just got here too."

David froze. "You didn't tell me they were coming."

Isaac was already pushing back his chair and waving across the room. "I wasn't sure if they'd be able to make it."

Nervous energy shot through David, curdling in his belly. "Why are they here? You see them almost every day."

Isaac frowned down at him. "They want to meet you. I thought you wanted to meet them too. Why wouldn't you?"

It was a good question—for which David had no good answer. He tried to smile. "Of course I do." He drained his glass and stood as three people approached. They all appeared to be around his age.

"Hey!" The girl threw her arms around Isaac.

The two guys held up their hands in turn, but instead of shaking with Isaac, they did a little slap-clasp thing with him.

Isaac turned to David, beaming. "Lola, Chris, and Derek, this is David."

One of the guys grinned. He was tall and looked Chinese like Logan, with close-cropped hair and a gleaming smile. "Hey, man." He held up his hand. "I'm Chris."

David clumsily tried to clasp Chris's hand the way Isaac had. "Hi."

Derek was blond and blue-eyed, and had faint red marks on his skin that looked like the scars Joseph Wagler had from pimples. He held up his hand, and David took it the same strange way. "Great to meet you," Derek said.

Lola extended her hand for a shake in the usual way. "The famous David. How's it going?" She was fairly tall, and had brown hair cut to her jaw with a streak of purple over her forehead. She was what David's mother would have called butter chubby, with wide hips and ample breasts. She wore a low-cut shirt that accentuated them.

He shook her hand. "Good, thank you. How are you?"

"Fan-*tas*-tic." She bounced, her short skirt swirling around her thighs. "Gay bars are the most fun."

Derek glanced around. "This place is cool." He shot Lola a look. "But you know you're not allowed to abandon us."

She rolled her eyes and squeezed between Derek and Chris, linking her arms through theirs. "Yes, I'll protect your straight-boy virtue."

Chris laughed. "Hey, you know it's all good, but I just don't swing that way."

"It's okay. My brother's here and he doesn't either," Isaac said. "You guys want to get drinks?"

"Is the Pope Catholic?" Derek asked. He lowered his voice. "You want us to snag you one?"

Isaac shook his head. "I don't want to get in trouble."

"We need to get you some fake ID," Chris said. "David, what'll it be?"

"Vodka tonic," he replied before he could think twice. Maybe it would help calm the anxious tension gripping him. He wished he could just leave and not have to embarrass himself.

Chris and Derek squeezed through the growing crowd and disappeared toward the bar. David shifted from foot to foot and gave Lola an awkward smile. Someone jostled him, and he inched closer to Isaac, glancing back at their table and blinking in surprise when he saw people he didn't know in their seats talking animatedly with Dylan.

"David, how's work going?" Lola was shouting over the music, which seemed to be getting louder and louder. "We saw your website, and your stuff looks *awesome*."

"Thanks. It's good." He cast about for something to say. "How's school?"

"Great! I'm almost ready to graduate and get my GED. And Isaac is doing *so* freaking well. He's like a little sponge."

David tried to think of something else to ask, but his mind was a void. He was jostled again, and sweat gathered on his brow. He felt like ants were crawling on his skin. Meanwhile, Isaac said something to Lola that he didn't catch, and they both laughed. As they chatted, David smiled and nodded, his mind turning uselessly like an upended buggy wheel.

Fortunately Derek and Chris returned soon, and David gulped his drink. The last thing he needed was to have an episode right here in front of everyone. "How much do I owe you?"

Chris waved a hand. "Just get the next round. It all evens out. So, how are you finding it here in the city?"

"Good." He cringed. He sounded so *stupid* and dull.

"Glad to hear it," Chris said.

David felt acutely aware of the seconds passing. He needed to think of something to say. *Anything.* "Why didn't you finish high school when you were supposed to?"

Chris hitched a shoulder and stared at his shoes. "You know how it is. Life happens."

David could sense Isaac's tension, and Lola was looking at him with her lips pressed into a tight smile. He realized he'd said something wrong. "I didn't mean that it was bad to finish now." His cheeks were hot. *This is why I shouldn't talk.*

"It's cool, man." Chris turned to Derek. "Hey, how'd your presentation go?"

As Isaac and his friends chattered about school, David nodded and tried to keep up. *Why is this so hard?* The music was like nails hammering into his skull, and sweat dripped down his spine. More and more people seemed to be crowding in. His drink was gone, and he needed another one.

"David, when did you first learn how to be a carpenter?" Lola asked.

"Do you guys want to dance?" he blurted. He didn't want to talk about work or Zebulon—or anything.

Lola grinned. "*Always.*"

Isaac's eyebrows flew up. "You really want to dance?"

Tugging him toward the dance floor, David nodded. *It's better than talking.* Squeezing through the writhing bodies to find an empty space, they waved to Aaron, Jen, Clark, and Logan. He and Isaac shuffled awkwardly, and David tried to concentrate on the beat. Aaron looked totally at home stepping and shaking to the music, so there was no reason David couldn't, but as he watched Isaac's school friends dance freely, he felt hopelessly out of place.

Isaac's breath hit his ear. "Maybe we should take lessons. I have no idea what I'm doing." He rested his hands on David's hips.

David hesitated for a moment before touching Isaac's shoulders. *It's a gay bar! You're allowed!* He felt better already with Isaac close to him. "I guess we just...go with the flow, I think they'd say."

Isaac bit his lip, and then launched himself at David, kissing him hard. "Go with the flow sounds good to me." He kissed David again.

Breathing him in, David held Isaac near, swaying and shuffling to the beat. The music was faster than they were going, but he didn't care. The rest of the people around them seemed to fade away as Isaac pressed their lips together. Holding him close, David didn't even need another drink to feel better than he had all night.

THE MUFFLED CHIRPING could barely be heard over the power saw, and David quickly shut it off and grabbed his phone from the corner of the worktable. June's name was on the screen, and he tapped it before remembering he had to swipe.

"Hello?" He paused. "June, are you there?"

"No. It's me."

Heart swooping, David steadied himself with a hand against the wall. "Anna?"

"Yes."

His breath was stuck in his throat, and his head felt light. He'd left the door open in the foggy morning to get some air inside, and he blinked at the wet pavement as rain splashed into a puddle.

"David? Are you there?" Her voice went distant. "June, am I doing this right?"

"Yes! Anna, I'm here." He inhaled deeply. "I'm here. It's so good to hear your voice. I'm so glad you called. Are you all right? Do you all have enough food? What about the hospital bills? Is there enough money? There's more coming, and—"

"David, stop. We're fine. You wouldn't believe how much money people from all over have mailed us after Mrs. Byler wrote the article in the paper. We're still getting checks and cash from Indiana and Ohio and even Canada. Besides, we're not helpless, you know."

Relief surged through him. "I know, but...you're not just saying that?"

"When have I ever just said something?"

He smiled. "Never."

"Money's always going to be hard here. We'll survive. You've already done more than most people would."

"Not enough. Are you sure you're all right? When I didn't hear from you..."

"I'm sorry it took so long. Eli caught me coming out of June's driveway when I visited before. Of course he told Mother. She's barely let me out of her sight since. Makes me read aloud from the Bible every night, or sometimes the stories in the dusty old copies of *Family Life* we still have."

"Let me guess—especially the ones about how Amish parents and the church are always right, and children who disobey learn this in the end and regret their misdeeds."

Anna laughed. "Those are the ones."

Closing his eyes, David leaned against the wall. To hear his sister's laughter again made his throat swell. "I miss you so much, Anna. How's Mary? What about the girls?" It was safer to ask about them first.

"The girls are fine. They're sad that you're gone, of course. Mary's...quiet. At first I tried to get her to talk about it, but she kept asking why Isaac would leave, and what she'd done to drive him away."

He ached to hear it, and tried to think of something to say. There was nothing. He'd helped break his sister's heart.

For a moment, Anna's voice was thick with emotion. "I hate seeing her so sad. She deserves to be happy. Jacob Miller is dying to drive her home from the singings, but she says no. I asked her why, and she gives excuses. I know it's because she's secretly hoping Isaac will come back."

"Oh, Mary."

"She's not like us, David. The plain life makes her happy. She'll be a good Amish woman. But right now when I talk to her about Jacob she only wants to know what was wrong with her that Isaac didn't love her."

David's stomach churned. He was afraid to ask. "What did you say?"

"Not the truth. Don't worry, David. I wouldn't tell her that."

Did Anna really know? His heart galloped. "Anna..." He opened and closed his mouth.

"I know you and Isaac love each other."

Blood rushed in his ears. Isaac and June had been right. "How? When?"

"I had a feeling, but I knew for sure one day when I came to refill the water pitcher and heard you two in one of the stalls."

No, no, no. Shame burned through him that his sister had heard such things. "I'm so sorry."

"I'm not. Everything *finally* made sense. I could never really understand you before. After that I started shouting when I came out."

He remembered her voice lilting toward the barn, calling their names as she made her way. "I don't know what to say."

"You don't have to say anything."

"You're not...you don't think it's a sin?" He gripped the phone.

"Do you?" she asked simply.

"I don't know. I mean, I *know* it is, but it doesn't feel that way." He shook his head, and then remembered she couldn't see him. "I hope it isn't."

"Everything's a sin anyway. You might as well be happy."

David had to laugh. Typical Anna in her blunt way. She made it sound so easy. "God, I miss you. Don't let Mother hear you talk like that."

"I won't, don't worry. And I keep my English magazines hidden.

Jeremiah's Sarah gets them from her older brother sometimes, and she passes them on to me. I've learned that English girls worry a lot about getting the right prom dress. Whatever that means. Someday I'd like to dress up in something fancy."

"Some day you will. I promise." The Amish life wouldn't be the one for Anna. He felt it so surely.

"You bet I will. How's Isaac?"

"He's good. Busy." Isaac was studying so much for tests that David had hardly seen him that week. "He's going to school. Do you know we're living with his brother Aaron and his wife?"

"June told me. Mother wouldn't let us see your letter. They sound really nice. I'm so happy you got out. So glad you said no to the church." She laughed. "At first I couldn't believe my ears when you said it. But after you and Isaac ran out, I really enjoyed the look on the preachers' faces. I thought Deacon Stoltzfus's head was going to actually burst into flames. His face was so red."

Goose bumps spread over David's arms. "I can imagine. He's never liked me. Not after…"

"Not after Joshua. You can say it. And yeah, he's not keen on any of our family right now I don't think. Ugh, I hate him and his beady eyes. He's always staring daggers at Ephraim too."

"Isaac's brother?"

"Uh-huh. He drives me home from the singings now that he's a youngie."

"Wait…you're *dating* Ephraim?" Protectiveness surged through him. Ephraim had better behave.

Anna chuckled. "Not really. We talk about you and Isaac, and about all the things we hate in Zebulon. I expected him to start dating Hannah Lambright, but she's almost going steady with David Raber. So Ephraim and I decided that he'll drive me, and we won't have to worry about dating anyone else since we're not staying much longer anyway."

"You're not?" His voice rose. "What are you planning? Where are you going?"

"We don't know yet. We have to wait until we're eighteen, and Ephraim just turned seventeen. If we go before then, the police could bring us back. It's better to wait."

"Whenever you're ready, we'll help you. You and Ephraim could come out here if you want. Just call, and we'll work it out. Anna—" His throat closed. "You know I only want you to be happy, right? All of you. Whatever you choose."

"I know. I don't want to leave Mary until she's settled. I'm hoping soon she'll be dating Jacob."

"That's Mervin's older brother, right?" He seemed a decent young man. David hadn't ever talked to him much, but hadn't heard anything bad.

"Yes. He's had his eye on her for ages. You probably didn't notice because you were too busy mooning over Isaac." She laughed. "Lucky for you people here don't seem to even think such a thing could exist in Zebulon."

A thought tugged at David's mind. "Did you tell Ephraim? About Isaac and me?" He wasn't sure how Isaac would take that.

"No. I can't promise that I won't at some point, but it hasn't occurred to him at all yet. I don't know how he'd react. He's very angry that Isaac hasn't written him."

"He did! More than once. Didn't Ephraim get the letters?"

She huffed. "I should have known. I'll tell him next Sunday, although things are already tense at home for him. The Bylers aren't too happy he's supposedly dating me. Not that Mother is any more pleased about it. This town can't decide which of you is more to blame for deserting Zebulon and all things holy. So many whispers. Mother is certain Isaac led you astray, and of course the Bylers are sure of the opposite. If they knew the truth I honestly think they might lose their minds."

"They can never find out. *Never*. Anna, you know how much it would hurt them. I can't do that to Mother. And if Mary knew about me and Isaac..." He started pacing.

"I know," Anna said softly. "I won't tell. I promise. I'll only tell Ephraim if I have to—and only if I know I can trust him completely."

"All right."

"About Mother...there's something else I need to tell you."

Panic gripped him. "Is she ill? Did something happen?" *What if her leg didn't heal right? What if there was something else wrong with her after the accident and the doctors missed it? What if—*

"It's nothing like that. She's much better now. Honestly, David. She's walking a bit more every day. She still gets really tired, but she's all right. I promise."

He breathed deeply, running his fingertips over the top of the worktable and through the sawdust scattered there. "Okay."

"It's about her and Eli. They published on Sunday. The wedding's next Thursday."

"Oh." It was what he'd hoped for, wasn't it? "I...is she happy? Is this what she wants?"

"It is. You remember before that she liked him? After you left he practically moved in. He's a good man, and she needs him. I think he needs her too. He was lonely on that farm all by himself, with his children grown and his wife long dead now. He was going to move into a *dawdy haus* attached to his son's place, but now he's staying put. We're moving to his house after the wedding. Mother's selling our farm to Joseph Yoder. He just married Josiah's Naomi, so they're moving out of his parents' house."

It was strange to think of another family living there and working in his barn. "Are you taking Kaffi?"

"Of course. He misses you, by the way. I make sure to give him plenty of treats."

David smiled softly. "Thank you. How do you feel about moving?"

"I don't really have a choice, so there's no point in being upset. His house is nice enough. Practically the same as ours. Mary and I will have our own room. No more sharing with the little ones at least."

"I thought after I left that Mary might take my room. She's the oldest."

Anna snorted. "Are you kidding? Mother's been keeping it as a shrine to you, along with setting your place at the table every day. She's convinced if she prays hard enough, you'll come back and tell her how right she was all along. We had to put up a fight to get the room at Eli's, but thankfully he was on our side. She wanted to keep one empty for you."

David choked down the swell of sick guilt. He whispered, "I wish I could make her understand. I wish…"

"Wishing won't change anything. You should still write her again. It makes her happy to know you're all right, even if her reply doesn't sound like it."

"I will."

"I'll try to call before too long. I should get back home. Tell Isaac I said hi, and so does Ephraim. Well, like I said, Ephraim's pretty mad at him, but don't tell Isaac that. I'll explain to Ephraim that Isaac did write him. That'll help."

"Thank you for calling." He hesitated. "I know we don't say these things often, but I love you. I love you all."

She sniffled. "Me too. Goodbye."

"Bye." He tapped the red button.

He wasn't sure how long he stood there staring at the dark screen before he called Isaac. He held his breath as it rang, willing Isaac to pick up.

"Hello—"

"Isaac! You won't believe who called."

"—I cannot answer the phone right now, so please leave me a message when it beeps. Thank you."

Beep. After a moment David realized he needed to say something. "It's only me. It's nothing—I'm sorry to bother you at school. I'll talk to you later." He turned off his phone.

It was nonsense to be upset that Isaac didn't answer. He was busy at school, and he'd told David before that he turned off the ringing during the day. They both had responsibilities, and David couldn't expect Isaac to always answer, even for him.

Shaking his head, David turned on the saw and went back to work, the saw's whine filling his ears. With each cut, the tension ebbed. As he picked up a new piece of wood to shape and coax into something new, he wished the rest of the world could be so easy to handle.

CHAPTER *Fifteen*

"JING-JING, WHY ISN'T the door locked? We could be anybody!"

At the kitchen counter, Jen sighed and called out, "Hi, Mom!" She glanced at David and Isaac. "Here we go. Remember what I said—be yourselves. Yes, my family is full of very religious Republicans, but they accept Clark, and they're going to accept you. Be prepared for hugs."

They followed Jen to the front door where her mother waited, carrying a large plastic container that smelled absolutely delicious. She thrust the container at Jen. "Is there rice?"

"Yes, Mom. Full pot. Jumbo. That much I can manage." She kissed her mother on the lips and tugged her out of the way as a man entered. "Mom, Dad, this is Aaron's brother Isaac, and his boyfriend David. Guys, this is Gloria and Estoy. Hi, Dad." She kissed him as well.

David had never seen someone kiss their parents like that, and he smiled quickly to cover his surprise as he and Isaac nodded to them. Jen's parents were both quite short, with almost matching cropped haircuts, silver gleaming in their dark hair. Gloria wore a floral shirt over pants and bright white sneakers. She examined Isaac. "Yes, yes, I see you are Aaron's brother! Such a pretty face." She threw her arms around him.

Estoy extended his hand to David. "Welcome to the family."

"Thank you, sir."

"Uncle Vic and Auntie Baby just pulled up," Jen said, peering out the window by the door. "Oh, and there's Aaron. He ran to the store."

Gloria hugged David, and he had to stoop. "Such a good husband.

Do you think my husband ever goes to the store? Let alone *cooks?*" She snorted. "He would be lost without me. But you boys today are different." She stepped back and eyed David and Isaac critically. "Which one of you is the wife?"

Estoy's bushy eyebrows shot up, and he glanced between Isaac and David.

"*Mom!*" Jen glared. "It doesn't work like that."

"What? It's a real question. I didn't mean anything bad. Was that bad?"

David smiled. "It's okay."

Isaac added, "We're not offended."

"See?" Gloria said to Jen before her brows drew sharply together. "What are you wearing?"

Jen looked down at her jeans, T-shirt and ever-present fuzzy blue slippers. "This is the house uniform." She winked at David and Isaac, who wore jeans and T-shirts but no slippers. Jen's purple tee read *San Dimas High School Football*. "I like to be comfortable, Mom."

"So do we! But at least our shirts have buttons," Gloria said. To David and Isaac, she added, "She wears scrubs all the time—you'd think she'd want to get a little dressed up once in a while!" She unlaced her running shoes. "Pacs, hand me my *tsinelas*."

Jen's father reached into the hall closet and pulled out two pairs of thin slippers from the collection in the back corner. David had wondered about the slippers before, but had forgotten to ask Aaron why they were there.

"I'm sorry…I thought your name was Estoy?" Isaac asked.

Jen laughed, still holding the huge container of food. "We Flips are very, very big on nicknames. Pacs is short for our last name. I know—it's weird."

Gloria said something to her husband in another language, and Jen clucked her tongue. "No Tagalog, remember? English so everyone understands."

"Yes, yes. Sorry!" Gloria sighed heavily. "I am always doing something wrong in my daughter's eyes."

Laughing, Jen went toward the kitchen. "Poor Mom—so hard done by!"

The next little while was a flurry of arriving family members, all bearing large dishes of food. There were introductions and many hugs, which David still wasn't quite comfortable with. Also a stream of questions.

"No electricity at all?"

"Tell us about this Amish mafia I see on TV. Do you know them?"

"Will you ever see your family again?"

"Why are Amish beards like that?"

David escaped outside to get a little fresh air on the narrow back patio. The sun peeked through the clouds, and he inhaled deeply. Since Jen's family didn't drink, there wasn't anything out at this party, and he wished he could have just a little something to calm his nerves. He hadn't had an episode again, but his chest felt tight.

Isaac seemed so much better at meeting new people and answering their questions. In Zebulon David had done okay with the staff working at the drive-in, but when there were big groups his tongue felt thick and he wanted to be anywhere else.

"There he is!" Clark slid the glass door shut behind him. "The Paculbas can be a little overwhelming, huh?"

David breathed a sigh that it was Clark, and he wouldn't have to answer any more questions. "They're all very kind. I don't think I've ever hugged that many people in a row in my life."

Clark chuckled. "Indeed. It's funny—all the white Adventists I knew growing up, including my family, were not exactly what you'd call demonstrative. But the Filipinos did not get that memo."

"The Amish aren't either. The adults especially. It's like as you get older, you get more and more...I don't know. Serious, I guess. It's not that they're unkind, or don't care. They're just..."

"Repressed?"

David had to laugh. "I suppose so." He motioned to the glass door and the people milling around the main floor. "It's nice, though. That Jen has such a big family. Her parents seem to really like Aaron."

"Do they ever. We weren't sure how it was going to go, to be honest. I mean, Jen already has a swishy gay BFF, and bringing home a white boyfriend could have been a bad scene. The key is that she waited so long to get serious about a guy. They were so relieved she's not a lesbian that they didn't care who he was. Plus, he's wonderful, so that's an added bonus." Clark straightened the collar on his silky red shirt.

"You're not quite as..." David waved a hand over Clark's outfit of shirt and slacks. "Sparkly."

Clark laughed. "I tone it down a bit for the family. Not that I'm anything but out and proud, but there's a time and a place for see-through mesh." He drew a little tube from his pocket and ran it over his lips before smacking them together. He held it out. "Gloss?"

"No thanks."

"You never know, you might like it."

David laughed. "It doesn't quite seem like me."

"True. You're very manly, with your tools and your strong silences. Tall, dark, and deliciously broody." He stood up straighter. "Oh! I almost forgot—I took a picture of the table in my condo." He pulled out his phone and tapped. "See how amazing it looks?"

The dining table did look good in the photo—big and proud, yet simple, with four chairs around it. "I'm sorry the rest of the chairs will be a few weeks at least."

"No worries. Not your fault the wood's on back order. I just have exquisite taste for the rare and wonderful, clearly. You should come over for dinner and experience your handiwork in its new home."

"Sure. That would be nice."

"What would?"

David turned to find Isaac in the doorway with a strange expression. "Clark was inviting us over for dinner."

"Yes, once I have all the chairs, I'll throw a lavish dinner party. With lots of wine, I promise." He glanced inside beyond Isaac and lowered his voice. "It's not that Jen's family doesn't know she and Aaron indulge, but she finds it easier to stick to soda when they're here."

Isaac shrugged. "I don't mind. I don't really like the taste of alcohol anyway."

Clark tilted his head. "Bless. I just want to put you in my pocket."

"Come and eat!" Gloria called out.

"Coming!" Clark shouted. "Make sure you try the chicken adobo." He held his fingers to his lips and kissed them. "Perfection." He brushed past Isaac and disappeared inside.

Isaac looked after him, and when he turned back to David, his mouth was a thin line.

"What's wrong?" David asked. He snagged Isaac's hand, worry rising.

Isaac opened and closed his mouth, and then sighed. "Nothing. It's stupid. Come on, we should go inside."

"Wait. Tell me." David squeezed Isaac's fingers.

"It's just..." Isaac glanced back inside. "Sometimes I feel like—"

Aaron appeared in the door. "You guys aren't hungry?"

"We're coming," Isaac said. He let go of David's hand. "It's nothing. Let's eat."

"Are you sure?"

"Absolutely." Isaac seemed to shake off whatever was bothering him. "My stomach's growling. Come on."

The food was spread over the dining table, pots and plates of exotic-looking meat and soups, and things David wasn't quite sure how to identify. Gloria shepherded them around the table, spooning generous portions onto their plates.

"This is chicken adobo, and this is *pancit*. You have to try the *kare-kare*. And the *lumpia* and the *caldereta*."

David's plate was getting so heavy he had to hold it with two hands. "I think I have enough to start. I'm afraid I'll spill it."

"I want to make sure you boys are eating enough. I know Jing-Jing certainly isn't feeding you."

From across the table where she scooped rice onto her plate, Jen rolled her eyes. "It's not like I'm busy at the hospital or anything."

Gloria spooned something else onto Isaac's plate. "I was a nurse, but of course my daughter has to do one better and be a doctor. So many brains. My grandchildren are going to cure cancer. If I ever have any, that is."

"I'm walking away, Mom," Jen said.

There were about a dozen people visiting, and they sat all over the main floor—in the living room, and by the kitchen counter, and anywhere there was a chair. Clark sat at one of the kitchen stools, but when David headed that way, Isaac tugged him toward the living room, and they squeezed next to Aaron and Estoy on the couch, balancing their plates on their knees.

David took a bite before remembering he hadn't prayed. Isaac was already eating as well. More and more they were forgetting, and David wondered if it even mattered. Just in case, he put down his fork and silently recited the words. He knew it wasn't nearly enough all things considered, but at least it was something.

Aaron swallowed a mouthful and pointed to one of the stews. "That might be a little spicy. Well, not *spicy*, exactly, but the flavors are strong. It takes some getting used to after the food we grew up on."

Jen's Aunt Erlinda spoke up from the arm chair nearby. "What kind of food did you eat?"

"A lot of chicken," Aaron answered. "Potatoes. Pie. Hearty kind of stuff. Pretty bland. Also a lot of sugar."

Jen came to perch on the arm of the couch by Aaron. "Oh my god, there's this pie made of molasses that Aaron made for me once. It was *amazing*."

Isaac laughed. "You made shoofly pie?"

"I did. I know—Mom would be horrified to see a man making pie." Aaron laughed.

"My sister Mary's pie is incredible," David said. He felt Isaac tense beside him, and wished he'd kept his big mouth shut.

"Aaron, why haven't you made this pie for us in all this time?" Gloria called from near the dining table, where she was still surveying the food.

"I wasn't sure you'd like it."

Jen said, "It's sugar. Who doesn't like sugar?"

"Well, you know your Uncle Junior is diabetic, Jing."

"Because he likes sugar way too much," Jen muttered.

"Perhaps you can bring it at Easter," Estoy said.

Aaron smiled. "Sure."

"You boys should bring all your favorite food. Then you'll feel right at home. How do you like the kare-kare, David?" Estoy asked.

He swallowed his bite, savoring the beef and sauce smothering his rice. "I like it very much. Thank you. It tastes like...peanuts?"

"Yes! Exactly. Good, good. You'll have much more of it in years to come." Estoy nodded, smiling kindly.

With his own smile, David scooped up another forkful. As they ate, Isaac talked to Estoy about what he was learning in history class, and David's thoughts drifted to Mary's shoofly pie and home.

The wave of longing might have knocked him over if he'd been standing. Surrounded here by Jen's family, he wondered what his own was doing. It was a church Sunday, and the singing would soon be starting.

He wondered whose house church was at. It would be the Lantz's turn about now. Perhaps the youngies were all taking their seats at the long table, Anna and Mary among them. Grace as well. He hoped she'd found someone new—someone so much better than him.

"What?" Isaac whispered.

There was a spirited conversation dominating the living room about something David didn't quite understand but was a sport of some kind. He shrugged. "Nothing. Just thinking."

A soft smile lifted Isaac's lips. "We all know that never ends well."

He nudged Isaac's shoulder. "Nope."

"Tell me."

David kept his voice low. "It's strange to think we haven't gone to church once since we left." They'd talked about trying different English churches once in a while, but each Sunday morning they wound up staying in bed.

"I know. We could go to another kind of church here, but it seems wrong for some reason. Disloyal. Which doesn't really make sense at all."

"It does to me." He glanced around the room at Jen's family. Raucous laughter filled the air, and people talked over each other in a mix of Tagalog and English. "It's like a barn raising, but with no work."

Isaac laughed. "It is."

"Jennifer tells us you're both carpenters," Estoy said.

David tried to ignore the pang for the days when that was true. With each passing week, Isaac was busier with school, and David insisted he not worry about coming to help at the workshop. It was better for Isaac to learn. Yet David missed him fiercely.

"David's amazing. He's taught me so much. I've always loved working with wood, but for now I'm going to school."

School made Isaac so very happy, and that was what mattered. *Even if he doesn't want to be a carpenter, he still wants me.*

"Okay, you guys have to settle this dispute since you're not invested in either team," Jen announced.

David focused on her. "Uh-huh. Okay."

"Here's the situation. There are the Oakland A's, and the San Francisco Giants. One of the bonehead players for the A's—"

"That's leading the witness!" someone called out.

"They're the judges, not witnesses," Gloria said.

"Then it's leading the judges."

Aaron leaned over. "Just go with it."

The food was heavy, and the room fairly vibrated with laughter and chatter. It was nice, but David felt a headache forming by his temple. He nodded and smiled, careful not to say the wrong thing.

IT WAS LATE when David returned to the patio. In the darkness, he listened to the murmur of cars and the city, wishing he could see the stars. So many nights in Zebulon he'd stared at the sky, imagining how vast the world was but having no idea.

The longing to be back in the country filled him like air in a rubber tire, stretching against his insides. Not Zebulon, but a new place. A peaceful place of his own and Isaac's where he could see the heavens and hear the crickets sing, inhaling oak and fresh grass.

The kitchen window over the sink was open, and voices drifted out—Jen and her mother.

"But how long will they stay?"

"As long as they want. Mom, I told you—I'm not getting pregnant yet. It has nothing to do with Isaac and David being here. The timing isn't right. So please drop it."

David was against the wall by the window, the bricks rough through his T-shirt. The hair on his bare arms stood up in the chilly night air. He knew he shouldn't listen, but he couldn't seem to make himself move.

"I just worry, Jing-Jing. You are no spring chicken."

Jen barked out a laugh. "I'm well aware."

After a few moments of silence, Gloria asked, "Do you think those boys are really...you know."

"*Gay?* Yes, Mom. They're gay."

"But maybe they're just confused."

Jen sighed loudly. "They're not confused. Neither is Clark, as you well know by now."

"It makes me sad, Jing-Jing. You know they won't go to heaven."

A clatter made David jump, and he held his breath, his heart lurching.

"I don't *know* that at all."

"Okay, okay. Don't throw things."

Gloria switched to Tagalog, and David stopped listening. Even after they'd gone, he shivered by the wall. He heard the words over and over,

Mother's voice joining in with Gloria's. Then Bishop Yoder and Deacon Stoltzfus's as well, until it was a cacophony in his head.

They won't go to heaven.

They won't go to heaven.

They won't go to heaven.

"David?" Isaac was there, taking David's face in his hands. "Are you sick?"

"No." David tried to smile. His heart raced, and he was dizzy. *God, please not now.* He forced a deep breath. He couldn't let Isaac see him come apart. "Just a little. I ate too much."

Isaac caressed his cheek. "Are you sure?"

Looking into Isaac's sweet face, pinched with concern, David wanted to collapse into his arms like a child and confess his terrible weakness.

No.

He couldn't burden Isaac with his muddled fears. It would only hurt him to hear what Gloria had said. "I'm sure."

"Everyone's gone home." Isaac brushed a hand over David's hair. "Come on. You should lie down."

"Okay. I'm right behind you. Get the bed warm." He kissed Isaac lightly.

Inside, David listened to Isaac's footsteps grow faint, and was careful to lock the sliding door. The main floor was quiet, with only a small light in the kitchen still on. For a moment, David could almost believe it was a lamp, and could smell the kerosene and imagine the heat of it if he touched his fingertips to the glass.

They won't go to heaven.

His bare feet only a whisper, David went to the liquor cabinet.

No.

"I don't need it," he said to himself. "I'm fine. Everything is fine."

David wasn't sure he believed it, but he made it upstairs and crawled under the covers Isaac held open.

CHAPTER Sixteen

THE POUNDING OF his hammer echoed off the concrete as David finished the final drawer of a kitchen hutch for a customer in New York. At least Alan and his music had been absent so far that day.

He hauled out his roll of bubble paper from beneath the worktable to wrap the drawers. It seemed strange to pay to ship something all the way across the country, but the customer obviously could afford it, and who was he to argue? It was good money, and David could pay off Aaron and Jen all the faster and then talk to them about room and board.

He swiped at his damp forehead. The week had been hot for late April. The bus was more crowded and sweaty than usual, and David still cringed as he remembered the crush of people—elbows and bags and breath as the vehicle lurched along, the bell dinging for every single stop. He was already dreading the ride home.

"Morning."

David jumped, his hand to his chest as he spun around to find Isaac in the doorway. There was a breeze outside that didn't make it in, but he'd left the door open in vain hope. Happiness bloomed in him. "Hi."

"Sorry to sneak up on you." Isaac dropped his backpack near the door. He hadn't put any gel in his hair, and it brushed a bit over his forehead like it used to.

"It's okay. It's a good surprise."

They moved into each other's arms, and Isaac inhaled loudly. "Mmm. I miss the scent of sawdust. I love that I can still smell it on you when you come home, but it's good to be here. I want to work together today like we used to. Time feels like it's passing really fast. You know what I mean?"

David nodded, his heart light. "But are you sure you don't need to be at school?"

"I'm sure. I went in and cleared it with my teachers. They're really flexible." Isaac leaned back and brushed at something on David's shoulder. "You were asleep when I got home last night, and you were gone this morning when I woke up. I feel like we keep missing each other lately."

It was true, and David wasn't sure how it had happened. "I know. How was the game?"

"It was fun. Baseball's kind of confusing, but Derek and Chris taught me the rules. I wish you could have come."

David smiled ruefully, holding up his hammer. "Me too, but..." He reached for another board. He'd barely finished a cabinet in time for a late pickup from the delivery company. Not that he'd been too upset to miss an opportunity to say more dumb things to Isaac's friends. He'd gone to Flanagan's again for a late supper and a couple of drinks. It was nice to talk to Gary every week or so. For some reason David didn't feel intimidated by him.

"Do you want to get started on the sanding there?" He jutted his chin toward a stack of rough wood.

"Sure." Isaac rolled up his sleeves and plugged in the electric sander before putting on eye goggles. "This thing makes it a lot easier than it used to be."

The whine of the sander was loud enough that they couldn't talk, but David felt peaceful with Isaac working beside him again.

"I missed this," Isaac flipped off the sander and reached for another piece of wood.

"Did you?" David smiled tentatively.

"Of course! School's great, but sometimes it's so much to take in. This is...I don't know. Comforting, I guess. And I miss being with you." He turned the switch on the sander.

David vaguely remembered Isaac's breath on his neck the night before, his lips tender as he slipped into bed and drew David against him. Watching Isaac now, bent to his work, affection and *want* washed over him. He put down his hammer and rounded the table, motioning to Isaac to turn off the sander.

Isaac took off the goggles. "What is it?" He squinted at the wood he was working on. "Am I doing it wrong?"

"No, no. You're doing it right." David tugged him close. "I just wanted to say hi."

He kissed Isaac softly, and Isaac melted against him, his arms stealing around David's waist. They deepened the kiss, their tongues exploring. With their hands and mouths, they said everything so perfectly. David slipped his fingers underneath the hem of Isaac's T-shirt and hoodie, caressing his skin and teasing the little mole near the base of his spine.

When they broke the kiss to breathe, a smile lit up Isaac's face. "Hi." He rubbed his nose against David's. "I miss you."

"I miss you too." David bit back a moan as Isaac kissed the sensitive spot behind his ear. He splayed his hands against Isaac's back.

Isaac nudged his thigh between David's and rolled his hips. His breath was hot against David's neck as he kissed and sucked. "Sometimes I wish we were back in your barn. Just the two of us for hours a day. It seems like here in the world there are so many other things to worry about." He huffed out a laugh, lifting his head. "Not that we didn't have worries in Zebulon."

David ran his thumb over Isaac's lips. "I want you so much my Isaac."

"Do you want to fuck me?" Isaac whispered, rolling his hips again.

They were both getting hard in their jeans, and David moaned. Tangling his hand in Isaac's hair, David kissed him fiercely. Isaac usually only used bad English words at times like this, and it made David's balls tingle to hear it. "Is that what you want?" He shoved his other hand down the back of Isaac's boxers and skimmed along the crack of his ass and over his hole.

Isaac groaned. "Yes. You in me."

David ran his fingertip around Isaac's hole, dipping just a tiny bit inside. "You want that?"

"*Duh.*" Isaac smacked David's shoulder. "Go close the door."

Laughing, David kissed him again. "So bossy." He scurried to the door and locked it. When he turned around, Isaac was peeling off his shirt and kicking off his shoes. David licked his lips. "Do you want to…on the couch?"

But Isaac shook his head as he unzipped his jeans by the table. "Here. Like we used to."

It was all David could do to not sweep the table clear with a stroke of his arm, but he managed to empty it without breaking anything. He unfurled a drop cloth. Isaac was naked now, and he bent over his backpack, fishing for something. When he straightened up he grinned.

"Like the view?"

His throat dry as if he'd swallowed sawdust, David nodded and tore at his own clothing. The cement was rough, and he snagged his jeans with his foot and stood on them as Isaac scooted onto the table with his ass at the edge. Isaac spread his legs, lifting his knees to his shoulders. His flushed cock curled up toward his belly.

"Like this? Just like the first time?"

"*Yes.*" David covered Isaac with his body, kissing him deeply. "You're beautiful." He bent and kissed the tip of Isaac's cock, working his tongue over and around the head. The salty taste of the drops there sent desire blazing through his veins, and he licked downward, lapping at Isaac's balls and nosing at the wiry hair. Isaac's thighs trembled, and he moaned loudly.

"Oh, *oh.* It feels so good. Oh, my David. Please…"

David loved the feel of Isaac's fingers moving through his hair, tightening when he licked a wide stripe along Isaac's ass and over his hole. He huffed a warm breath over it, and Isaac jolted.

"Please—I need you." Isaac grabbed at him. He shoved a tube of lube into David's hand.

Laughing, David popped the lid. "You came prepared."

"Yes," Isaac said boldly, although he blushed to the roots of his sandy hair. "I missed you. I want you."

David leaned over to kiss him soundly. He pressed his slick fingers against Isaac's hole, inching one in first. "What does it feel like?" He knew what it was like when Isaac was inside him—burning and full and *good*—but it made his blood sing even louder to hear it from Isaac. He pushed his index finger in to his second knuckle.

Isaac bit back a gasp, his eyes closing for a second. When he opened them, his gaze was dark, and he squeezed around David's finger. "It feels…tight. Like nothing else will fit, even though I know it will. It's not enough. It makes me want more." He squeezed again.

David obliged, inching in another finger and twisting his hand, feeling Isaac clench and then relax. "That's it, Eechel."

"I want more. It's burning like a hot poker, but it's nothing compared to your cock."

With jerky movements, David pulled his fingers free and slathered his shaft with the lube. He hauled Isaac right to the very edge of the table, pressing his thighs back. He nudged at Isaac's ass with the head of his cock. "Keep talking."

Isaac thunked his head on the table as he moaned. "It feels too big, and it's stretching me so far, but—" He cried out as David thrust into him.

With another push, David buried himself all the way. "Tell me."

Lips parted, Isaac panted softly. "It's like I can feel your heartbeat inside me. I was so empty, and now you're here." He ran a shaky hand over David's chest. "It hurts a little, but I love it. Love you."

Rocking his hips back and forth, David fucked him, their skin slapping together, the wet sounds loud in the small garage. "Love you so much. You feel incredible," he muttered. "So good."

He inhaled the smell of their sweat and sex, tasting it on his tongue as his lips parted. Watching Isaac spread and flushed beneath him, David wasn't sure why he worried so much. As long as he had Isaac, everything would be all right. Forget the city, and new people, and all the things David didn't understand. This was all that mattered.

His thrusts were erratic, and he was making low grunts that sounded strange and desperate. He wanted Isaac to come first, but as he stared into his warm eyes, the pleasure overcame him, twisting through like a tornado as he jerked and spilled into Isaac, bending him practically in half. He imagined he was shooting so deep that drops of him would be there forever.

"Yes," Isaac whispered, rubbing a hand over David's back. "Give me all of it. Let go."

Shuddering, David dropped his head to Isaac's collarbone, the tang of Isaac's sweat sweet on his tongue. They both groaned when David pulled out his softening cock, and David could feel Isaac hard and throbbing against his belly.

With his hands holding Isaac's thighs wide, David bent low and swallowed Isaac's shaft. He breathed like a horse as he sucked tight and deep. Isaac's hands were in his hair again, his fingers digging into David's scalp as David bobbed up and down. David's lips stretched over Isaac's leaking cock, and he hummed.

With a shout, Isaac came, pulling David's hair as his hips lifted. David choked a little as he tried to swallow it all, and when he pulled off, it dripped down his chin. Isaac gasped, and another spurt landed on David's cheek.

Isaac moaned, his chest heaving. "David." He pulled him close, his hands gentle in David's hair as he cradled him to his chest. "I miss you. Everything seems so fast lately. We need to slow down."

David's knees were weak, and if not for the table holding their weight he would have slid right to the floor. It was *wonderful*. He kissed Isaac's flushed skin, and said a prayer that life could always be this perfect.

"What?" David shouted.

"Give me your jacket!" Clark held out a hand and motioned to a sign that read *Coat Check*.

David unzipped his coat and passed it over. Clark wasn't even looking as he snatched it with one hand and texted with the other. A bored-looking young woman barely glanced up from her phone as she took custody of their jackets and ripped off a piece of red paper for Clark. Hands in his jean pockets, David glanced around. They were still in the entry area, and beyond thick curtains at the end of the hall he could glimpse flashing lights and movement.

He could certainly hear the music. He'd thought it was loud at the Beacon, but Volume was living up to its name. *Why did I come here?* He already wanted to go home. A hand clasped David's shoulder, and he spun around, relaxing when he saw Dylan. "Hi."

"Hey. David, this is Tim." Dylan's arm was wrapped around the narrow shoulders of a redheaded man, who nodded. They both wore tank tops and tight pants. "You got past the bouncer okay?" Dylan asked.

"Yes." He pulled out his new passport, which he'd tucked carefully in his deep back pocket. "We got our birth certificates, and Aaron figured it would be quicker to get our passports than waiting to get our licenses." That, and the idea of driving in the city still made him sweaty.

"So you grew up with, like, horses and buggies and all that stuff?" Tim asked.

"Uh-huh." David braced himself for a barrage of questions.

But Tim just smiled. "Cool."

"What's Isaac up to tonight?" Dylan asked. "Too bad he's too young to get in."

"He went to the movies with his friends from school. I was going to go with them, but Isaac insisted I come here so I can tell him all about it."

Clark appeared. "Hello, darlings." The metal bracelets lining his forearm clattered as he extended his hand to Tim. "This must be Tim. I've heard much. And you've met David?" He turned, and his eyes narrowed. "What are you wearing?"

David glanced down at himself. "The same thing I wore to the Beacon?" He flushed, glad of the low light as he ran a hand over the front of his dark button-down shirt. "Is it not right?"

Shaking his head, Clark took David's elbow and led him to the corner. Dylan and Tim followed. Dylan said, "He's fine, Clark. He looks great."

"Well of course he looks great—get a load of that face!" Clark grasped David's chin. "I'm liking the stubble, by the way." He made a little growling noise.

David was sure he was red all the way to the tips of his ears. Sometimes he shaved every day, but other times he let the stubble darken his face until it threatened to become a beard. Even though it would be different than Amish facial hair, the thought of having a beard at all seemed too close to what he would have worn if he'd joined the church.

"Honey, there are bar clothes, and there are club clothes."

David blinked at Clark, taking in Clark's pink mesh shirt that barely came to his midriff and really wasn't a shirt at all. His pants were golden and shiny, and so tight David wasn't sure how his blood was still circulating. His makeup was even more glittery than usual.

"It's okay—we'll fix you right up. I should have explained beforehand." Clark stepped back and looked him up and down. "Are you wearing an undershirt?"

David nodded, and before he knew it, Clark's fingers were flying over the buttons on David's shirt. He peeled it down David's arms and rolled it into a ball.

"We'll put it in your coat pocket. There we go. Simple and elegant, but sexy." He patted David's chest. "Wifebeaters are always in style."

"What?" He could feel the heat of Clark's hand through his thin white undershirt. "What do you mean?" He didn't even have a wife, let alone *beat* her.

"It's just a nickname for those kinds of shirts," Dylan explained. "Not PC at all, but when is Clark ever PC?"

"Oh. I...are you sure this looks okay?" David crossed his arms, shivering as the front door to the club opened with another group of men squeezing through.

"Am I sure?" Clark turned to Dylan and Tim. "Can I get some backup here?"

Tim whistled. "Seriously hot." He tugged on Dylan. "Come on, let's dance."

"I'll meet you there." Clark rolled David's shirt and hurried back to the coat check.

Following Dylan and Tim through the thick curtains, David could hardly believe his eyes. Everywhere he looked, there were men—most of them dressed in tight clothes that hardly covered anything, and some didn't have shirts on at all. There was a second level, and upstairs a balcony overlooked the dance floor on all sides, men leaning against it and watching the writhing bodies below. David felt as though the music was pulsating right *through* him and burrowing into his bones with each beat.

Despite the noise and the crowd, a thrill surged at the sight of so many men together. So many *gay* men. All in one place! It felt different than it had at the Beacon. Much more...he tried to think of the right word. *Sexual*, a voice from the back of his mind offered. Desire hummed low in his belly, and he wished Isaac was there.

Arms wound around his waist from behind, and for a moment the warm touch was nice, but of course it wasn't Isaac at all. He went rigid.

Clark gave him a squeeze before grabbing his hand. "Come on."

Dylan and Tim had already disappeared into the mass of dancers, and David followed Clark gratefully. The lights flashed colors everywhere—pinks and greens and blues. Everyone looked otherworldly, and David could hardly believe he was still awake and not dreaming this place. He watched as Clark spun around, his arms over his head. After a few moments, Clark frowned at him and leaned in.

"You okay?" he shouted.

"I don't really know how to dance."

With a smile, Clark gave David's hips a push. "Just move!"

Sure, he and Isaac had shuffled together at the Beacon, but here the men—and a few women—were dancing with wild abandon. *Hedonistic*, the preachers would say. David tried to relax, but men were bumping into him, and sweat beaded on his forehead. The air was thick, and he wondered if he could get a drink to keep him from freaking out.

Clark was suddenly pressed against him, his breath hot on David's ear. "If you want to relax, I could find us a bump."

"I don't...what?" David puzzled the words over in his head.

"A bump. A little chemical enhancement."

"You mean...drugs?" He blinked rapidly. *Drugs?*

"Yes, if you want to put it like that. I prefer to think of it as party favors." Clark grinned.

David didn't even have to think about it. "No." Joshua invaded his mind—climbing out the window that last night with his cocky smile. "I don't do that." His pulse zipped, his heartbeat jagged.

Clark raised his hands. "Okay. No pressure. You want a drink? I'm parched."

"Vodka tonic. Please," David added as he fished in his pocket for money.

But Clark was already sashaying away with a wave, swallowed by the crowd in seconds. David realized he had no idea where Dylan and Tim had gotten to, and he was suddenly very alone. As alone as one could be in a sweaty crowd of hundreds.

Fear prickled, and he sucked in air. *It's okay. I'm okay. Everything's fine. I can breathe.*

David met the unmistakably hungry gaze of a man who looked old enough to be his father, and he jerked his head away to stare at his dark sneakers. He tried to focus on the music and breathing in time with it. *In and out. In and out. Steady.*

When Clark returned, David gulped his drink gratefully. They danced on, but David felt adrift and conspicuous. He was certain everyone was staring at him. He couldn't hear any whispers above the pounding beat, but everywhere he looked, he was sure people were talking about him and how lame and weird he was. He wanted to go home.

It felt as though the crowd was getting thicker with every heartbeat, closing in on him. Even at the biggest barn raisings, he hadn't been with this many people in one place. And there he'd had fresh air to breathe, and he'd fit in without trying. Even once he'd known he was different, he'd been able to fake it.

Clark was oblivious, dancing with shakes of his hips that were graceful in a way David could never hope to be. Sweat dripped into David's eyes, and his undershirt clung to him. He bumped against people constantly, but at least after a few more drinks the calming burn in his chest helped.

Dylan and Tim appeared as if by magic from the throng. "You're a natural!" Dylan shouted, giving him a thumbs up.

Natural. David repeated the word in his head as he gazed around. He imagined what Bishop Yoder and Deacon Stoltzfus would say. Men groped and grinded against each other with complete abandon. Volume was about the vainest place David had seen yet in the English world, and that was saying something. A huge silver ball above the dance floor sent prisms of light over the slick, heaving mass of men.

Someone rubbed up against him, and David jerked away. He pulled at his damp undershirt. He'd need a shower when he got home. Thinking of Isaac waiting in their bed, he breathed a little easier. Maybe he could make an excuse soon and leave.

"Take it off."

He blinked at Clark. "Huh?"

"Live a little!" Clark grabbed the hem of David's undershirt and yanked.

Without thinking, David lifted his arms. The air did feel refreshing on his bare skin. He took the undershirt from Clark, who motioned for him to hook it through one of his belt loops.

"Isn't that better?"

He nodded. It did feel better. He was still hot, and maybe he'd had one vodka too many, because his head was so light.

Then Clark stepped right up against him, his breath puffing against David's face. "It can feel even better than that." His hands were on David's chest, fingertips teasing his nipples.

What? David stumbled back, but the dance floor was too crowded and he hit a wall of flesh. There was nowhere to go, and Clark was touching him again, his bracelets jangling.

"Let me show you how good you can feel, baby." Clark's makeup was smudged, his lip gloss still shining as his face swooped close. Then Clark's lips were *touching* him, and his other hand cupped him through his jeans.

Sensations flowed through David, his head spinning as he tried to make sense of what was happening. Clark tasted like cherries, and what he was doing with his hands felt good—

No!

David wrenched his head to the side, but there was still nowhere to move. He grabbed Clark's hands and squirmed away, shoving through the people on the dance floor, his lungs burning.

Clark caught one of his wrists, saying something David couldn't hear. David tried to squeeze faster through the mob of moving bodies with Clark still stubbornly holding on. He spotted the sign for the bathroom and pushed the door open. There were moans coming from the stalls, and someone was on his knees right by the sinks with another man's cock in his mouth.

David tore his hand out of Clark's surprisingly strong grasp. "Why did you do that?"

"Because you're gorgeous, and I want you. It's okay." Clark prowled toward him. "No one has to know. We can just have a little fun."

"No!" David slapped his palm against Clark's chest, holding him at arm's length. The pink mesh shirt was damp. "I'm with Isaac. I don't want anybody else."

Clark rolled his eyes. "Come *on*. That's really sweet and all, but time to grow up. It's not a big deal."

"It is to me. I thought we were friends."

"We are, sugar. I just want to be a *better* friend. I'll make you feel so good. Show you things you Amish boys have never even dreamed of. Come on, let me corrupt you." He smiled wickedly. "You know you want to."

David shook his head. "I don't want that. I don't want you. I love Isaac. Maybe we're stupid and naive, but he's the only one I want to be with."

Clark huffed. "Fine. It's your loss. Go home to your little boyfriend and your awkward fumbling. I'm bored now anyway." Sneering, he turned on his heel and stalked out.

Bile rose in his throat, and David stumbled to the far sink. He scrubbed at his hands and splashed cold water on his face. The mirror was streaked and spotted, and when he looked at himself through the mess—shirtless and sweaty, his eyes too bright—he was a stranger. His lungs constricted. *Air. Need air.* He somehow got his legs to run.

When he burst outside, he stumbled against the brick wall, gasping. It was happening again—needles stabbed him all over and everything went blurry. He was alone and he was dying. His heart was exploding, and there wasn't enough air. He scraped his hands across the brick.

"Hey now. It's okay, kiddo."

It was a woman's voice, and David felt strong hands rubbing his shoulders.

"Just breathe. That's it."

The woman kept talking, and David concentrated on her voice until the danger faded, and he was able to straighten up and turn. He shook.

"I…" His tongue couldn't seem to make words. *There's something wrong with me.* The fear swelled again as he finally allowed himself to consider going to a doctor to find out what it was. *What if I'm sick? What if I'm dying? What if I can't take care of Isaac anymore?*

He braced himself on the wall as he vomited on the cracked pavement, splashing the tips of his shoes. His stomach heaved, and he didn't fight it. When it was over, he spit and wiped his mouth with a shaky hand. Maybe he should talk to Jen about what was wrong with him, but the thought made him want to curl up and die. He had to be stronger. Better. He spit forcefully. *Father would be ashamed of how weak I've become.*

"That's it. Get it out." The woman wore a very short skirt, and was exceptionally tall with broad shoulders. Her curly blonde hair hung down her back, and she smiled with shiny red lips. "You're okay, hon. Rough night, huh?" She handed him a tissue. "You overdo it with booze?" She raised a narrow eyebrow. "Or something more?"

He shook his head and spit on the ground again. Cringing, he realized the man they called the bouncer was swaggering over. David wiped his mouth and blotted clumsily at his shoes.

"We're fine here, Ricardo." The woman made a motion with her hand. "Shoo."

Ricardo raised an eyebrow. "I don't want the cops here for an OD tonight, Shonda."

"It's all under control." She raised two fingers. "Scout's honor."

As Ricardo returned to the door, Shonda reached into her low-cut shirt and took out a pack of cigarettes that must have been tucked into her bra. She offered him one, but he shook his head. David tugged on his undershirt, realizing Clark had the ticket for his jacket and button-down. Quaking, he wrapped his arms around himself. The horrible aftertaste in his mouth made him queasy all over again.

"Have money to get home?"

David nodded. Thank the Lord he'd kept his money in his pocket. "Thank you," he croaked.

"Know where you're going?"

He nodded again. He'd memorized the bus route, and through the haze in his head the names and numbers were still there.

"Okay. Be safe, darlin'. Don't let the bastards get you down." Shonda inhaled deeply on her cigarette before grinding it beneath the toe of her huge boot. She disappeared back into Volume.

By the time David made it onto the bus, he was freezing, and he curled into himself. Again he felt like all eyes were on him in his undershirt, and shame seared his gut. *What did I do?* He dragged his hand over his mouth, wishing he could spit out the hint of cherry he swore he could somehow still taste amid the acidy remnants of his vomit. His skin crawled where Clark had touched him.

Maybe this was what some gay men did, but David didn't want it. He couldn't deny that for a moment it had felt good, and he'd never hated himself more—not even when he'd first realized he desired other men the way he should lay with a wife. That he wanted to rut with other men the way the animals in the barn did.

But being touched by Clark hadn't made his heart soar the way even a brush of Isaac's fingers could. Or the way seeing a glimpse of Isaac's smile could make David's worries vanish. The way his name sounded on Isaac's lips when they were inside each other. It was more than just bodies rutting together. It might feel good in the moment with other men, but what he had with Isaac was so much more. If that meant he wouldn't fit in with people in the city, he didn't care.

David ran from the bus stop, desperate to see Isaac. It was late, and he tiptoed inside the sleeping house, yanking off his shoes and hurrying up the stairs. But when he edged open the door to their room, the bed was empty. David dug his phone from his pocket, but there were no messages. The movie must have gone late, or maybe they'd gone out afterward to eat.

He wished fervently that he'd gone with them. He'd be with Isaac now, and Clark would never have touched him. He tugged at his clothes, shoving them into the bottom of the white wicker hamper in the bathroom. He brushed his teeth and gargled four times with minty mouthwash before climbing into the shower.

He wasn't sure how long he stood under the hot spray, but it must have been quite a while, because Isaac was in bed with the lights off when he emerged. David's shoulders relaxed at the sight of him. Isaac was home. Everything was all right.

Carefully, he slipped under the covers on his side. The blinds were closed, and he could only make out the outline of Isaac's body. He was turned on his side away from David, unmoving. For a long moment, David listened for his breathing.

"Isaac?" he whispered. He reached for him, but drew back his hand at the last second. There was no answer, so Isaac must have been asleep after all. As much as David ached to feel him near, he didn't want to wake him.

With a sigh, he looked at the outline of Isaac's body, wishing he could see Isaac's face—his lips inevitably parted in sleep, eyelashes sweeping over his cheeks, and freckles beautiful over his nose.

Tears filled David's eyes. Part of him wanted to wake Isaac and confess it all. Beg his forgiveness for letting Clark touch him, even for a moment. He shouldn't have had that many drinks. He shouldn't have gone to the club at all. What had he been thinking? It was all his fault.

In the end David crept downstairs and poured just a bit more vodka. A voice in his mind warned that it wasn't right—something in him was tipping out of control. He resolved to deal with it tomorrow. But tonight he needed to sleep, and he finished the glass. When he crawled back into bed, he was careful not to jostle Isaac, who was still curled away on his side in a tight knot, unmoving.

David listened, and a wave of certainty that Isaac wasn't actually sleeping washed over him. *Maybe I should tell him now.* The silence in the room felt unbearably heavy, and David listened to a car drive by, rattling into the distance. He opened and closed his mouth several times as he tried to think of the right words.

Finally, he rolled onto his side and let the vodka do its work.

CHAPTER Seventeen

"**K**NOCK, KNOCK."

David looked up to find the last person he wanted to see in the garage door. He'd opened it to keep from choking on sawdust, even though he was shivering in the foggy chill.

He regarded Clark with what he hoped was a stony expression, and didn't greet him. It was still early, although when he'd woken, Isaac had surprisingly been gone and the house empty. He'd thought about going back to bed, but had liked the idea of escaping to his wood and work. He and Isaac usually spent Saturdays together, but apparently Isaac had other plans—plans he hadn't shared.

Clark stepped inside. His hair was damp and flat, and raindrops clung to his long coat. His face was drawn, his cheeks blotchy, and he didn't appear to be wearing any of his makeup. David had never seen him look as old.

"I have your jacket, and I'm getting your shirt dry cleaned." Clark unfolded the jacket from over his arm and hung it on the hook by the door before holding up a cardboard tray. "Coffee?"

"No. If you've come about the chairs, I'm shipping them this afternoon." He nodded to the stack in the corner, carefully wrapped in the plastic bubble paper.

David glanced at his phone, which still sat silent and dark on the table. It wasn't like Isaac not to respond to his texts, which took too long to type with his clumsy thumbs. But he tried not to worry about it—not yet, anyway. Isaac and Aaron had probably gone out to spend some time together. Why should David mind? Still, he wished Isaac would reply.

With a sigh, Clark put the tray of coffee on the table, along with a paper bag that smelled of pastries. "I've come to apologize." He shoved his hands in his pockets. "I was a real ass last night. As you know."

David wasn't sure what to say, so he waited.

"I acted completely inappropriately, and I'm sorry. I know better than to pull something like that. I mean, shit—you're my best friend's little brother-in-law's boyfriend." He grimaced. "I love her, and Aaron. And you and Isaac are their family, and you're both great guys. I was so far out of bounds I couldn't even see the line. It won't happen again."

David needed to say something. "I thought you were my friend. I thought you were *our* friend."

Clark winced. "I know. I have no excuse. None."

"Why did you do that?"

"Why do I do half the things I do?" Clark snorted ruefully. "The truth is, as much as I flirt with almost everyone, I'm genuinely attracted to you."

David didn't know where to look or what to do. He crossed his arms over his chest and examined a pile of wood shavings. "I don't...I'm flattered, but..."

"It's okay. I know you don't feel the same way. I've always known that." He smiled sharply. "The problem is that I don't like not getting what I want. Especially after too many cocktails. I shouldn't have gone after you like that. You're just a kid, and I'm..." He curled his lip. "I'm old enough to know better."

David wasn't sure how to respond to this somber version of Clark. He hated what Clark had done, but he seemed genuinely contrite.

"When I was your age I was fucking every guy who looked at me twice. And it was fun, don't get me wrong. Still is." Clark picked up the paper bag and unrolled the top before rolling it again. "But you and Isaac are different. God, you're both *babies*, but anyone can see how much you care about each other. You both have hearts in your eyes, and I should never have tried to get between you. I just wanted sex, and it was unbearably selfish. You're such sweet kids, and you deserve better. I hope…well, I hope you'll give me another chance to be a better friend."

David took this in, and after a few more moments he nodded. "I will."

Clark's mouth opened and closed, and he gaped. "*Really?*"

"Yes. I forgive you."

Blinking, Clark stood up straighter. "Just like that?"

"Yes." He shrugged. "You're sorry for what you did, and you want to make it right. So I forgive you."

"Is this an Amish thing?"

David smiled softly. "I guess it is."

"Because if you never talked to me again I wouldn't blame you. Or Isaac. I should apologize to him too. Ugh, I've been a condescending prick to him more than once."

"No—don't. I mean, for that, yes. But don't tell him about last night." The thought of Isaac knowing Clark touched him made bile rise in his throat. "I don't want to upset him." He picked up his phone and pressed the button. There were no new messages, just the picture of he and Isaac laughing at the wharf the day they saw the sea lions. Isaac had somehow put it on David's screen.

"Whatever you want—it's your call. It really won't happen again. I promise." Clark thwacked his palm to his chest. "Hand on my heart. The way I acted was totally gross, and I've learned a very important lesson. NBC could make a One to Grow On about it. But don't worry. My lips are sealed."

David stared at their smiles in the picture on his phone. He had no idea what Clark meant about something to grow on, but it didn't matter. The knot in his chest ached, growing larger with every breath. "No. I have to tell him the truth. I have to tell him. I should never have gone to that club without Isaac. I should have known better."

Clark's brows drew together. "Don't be so hard on yourself. It was all me. You didn't do anything wrong."

"You don't understand. I didn't take care of my family when I was supposed to, and I promised myself I wouldn't let anything happen to Isaac. Now look what I've done."

Clark was still frowning. "David, no one's perfect. You're doing your best."

"It's not good enough!" he shouted. Taking a breath, David tried to calm his racing pulse. He couldn't lose control again. He lowered his voice and swallowed hard. "If I'd done something, my brother wouldn't have taken drugs and died, and we wouldn't have had to move to Zebulon. Everything was harder and stricter there. Then my father had a heart attack, and I couldn't save him. I was the man of the family, and it was my job to keep my mother and sisters safe. But I was selfish, and I ran away."

"David…" Clark shook his head. "I'm sure that's not true."

"It is! Mother and Mary almost died because I wanted to sneak away with Isaac and have sex. Then I abandoned them all. What kind of a man am I? Now I've let Isaac down too."

Clark reached out his hand, but let it fall. "You can't blame yourself for the shit that happens in this world. That's an awful lot of weight you're carrying around. I don't know exactly what happened with your brother, but I know you were not responsible for his choices. You're not responsible for accidents either, or your father's heart attack."

"But I should have done more."

"You did your best. You're doing your best now. And Isaac isn't a delicate flower you need to shelter from the storm. You can't be perfect for him. None of us are perfect. You're putting way too much pressure on yourself."

David wanted to believe Clark was right. But the doubts still clamored in his mind, whispering that Clark was English and could never understand.

"Sometimes I'm a selfish bitch and I can't stand myself. David, you're practically a saint. You're beating yourself up for being human."

Could he be right? David wanted to believe it desperately. "I'll tell him the truth, and maybe he'll understand."

"Well, this Amish forgiveness thing should work for you too, shouldn't it? He loves you. He'll probably be hella pissed, but he'll get over it." Clark opened the paper bag and popped a donut hole into his mouth. He held the bag out. "Come on, have some sugar. Don't let me eat all these calories alone."

David picked a chocolate ball from the bag. "Thanks."

"By the way, my friend Patrick saw my table and wants to meet with you. I gave him your number. He runs a gallery in the Castro, and he's doing an installation. Could be a really cool opportunity."

"Okay. Thank you."

"Of course, of course. Your work is stellar."

David ducked his head. He always tried his best, but it was still nice to hear. "And thanks for coming by. I was feeling pretty bad about it."

"Not that it helps, but I was feeling rather shit-tastic about it too. Don't let me or anyone else try to change you, okay?" He shook the bag. "Now eat! I can already feel my spare tire growing."

Trying to smile, David bit another donut and sipped the coffee Clark had brought him. He glanced at his dark phone, wishing Isaac would hurry up and call. He needed to tell Isaac what had happened, and the longer he waited, the sicker he felt.

"HELLO?" DAVID CALLED. He unlaced his sneakers and shook out his jacket on the mat before hanging it in the closet, making sure it wasn't touching any of the others while it dried.

"In here." Isaac's reply sounded far away.

David exhaled at the sound of Isaac's voice. He'd left the workshop a little past noon, anxious to find out where Isaac was and why he hadn't called. He hurried into the kitchen, which was practically dark given the gloomy day.

Isaac stood by the sink with his arms crossed. He was practically vibrating with tension, his gaze on the hardwood floor. David's heart skipped a beat. "Isaac?" He reached out.

But Isaac jolted back, bumping into the counter. "Don't."

Frozen in place, David swallowed thickly, dread uncoiling in his belly. "What is it?"

"You know what." Isaac spoke quietly. He still wasn't looking at David.

"I don't. What's wrong?" His mouth went dry.

"Don't lie to me." Isaac shook his head. "I know what you did."

Sick fear gripped David, and his pulse zoomed. Had Clark told Isaac after all? He must have. "I'm sorry. I can explain." Hot shame scorched his skin.

Isaac barked a bitter laugh as he flung out his hands. "Can you? Because I don't understand." He took a shuddering breath.

"Isaac…" David inched closer. "I'm so sorry."

"I don't understand this. I thought—" Isaac swiped at his eyes. "I thought you loved me. I told myself everyone was wrong. That we didn't need to see other people. That we already knew we were meant for each other." He sucked in a breath that became a sob.

"We do! We are." David reached out, but Isaac dodged him.

Sniffing, Isaac wiped roughly at his cheeks again. "You know, that first night when we went to the Beacon, I heard Clark talking to someone in the bathroom. I was in a stall, because I was shy about going in front of English people. Stupid, I know. He was on the phone, talking about how there was this hot Amish carpenter he was going to…" Isaac's nostrils flared. "That he was going to *fuck*. He said it was his new project."

David felt as though he was underwater, kicking for the surface. "I didn't know."

"I told myself not to be jealous because nothing would ever happen. Because I knew I could trust you." His voice went hoarse. "How could you do that?"

"Isaac, wait." David was sure he might vomit, this time right on the kitchen floor. "I don't know what Clark told you, but—"

"I *saw* you! He didn't have to tell me anything." Isaac clenched his hands into fists. "Chris got me a fake ID card. I didn't even think it would work, but they let me in. I was going to surprise you. I looked all over, and I went up on the stairs so I could see better. Then I spotted you."

David's heartbeat was so loud he imagined he could hear it like a drum. "Isaac, please. Let me explain."

"I saw you with him." Isaac's shoulders shook, and then he went very still, his face creased with pain. "You kissed him, and he was touching you all over."

God, no. "Isaac, he kissed *me*! I didn't want him to do that. I told him to stop!"

"You didn't even have a *shirt* on. In front of all those people! I saw you take him to the bathroom. I know what happens in there, David. I've seen it on TV in that queer whatever show. I wanted to go in there and scream at you, but...I couldn't. I ran away instead. I couldn't bear the thought of seeing anything else."

"He *followed* me! I was trying to get away from him, but he wouldn't let go. In the bathroom I told him no. I told him to stop. I'm with you, and I don't want anybody else. Nothing happened. I swear it. Please."

Isaac was silent for several heartbeats. "I want to believe you. I want to believe you so much, but..." He shook his head. "I guess we were fooling ourselves if we thought we'd never want anyone else."

It was like a punch to his throat. David croaked, "Do *you* want someone else? Is there...?" Derek and Chris flitted across his mind. Maybe they weren't straight after all, or maybe there was someone else at school, or maybe—

"No. I don't. I didn't think you did either."

The relief was short-lived. "Isaac, do you really think I cheated on you?" The hurt filled him like it was water in his lungs. "I didn't. I never wanted Clark to kiss me or touch me. I don't want him. Not him or anyone else. Nothing else happened in the bathroom."

"Really?" Isaac whispered.

Tears pricked David's eyes. "You *truly* think I would be with someone else? That I'm lying to you right now?"

Isaac wrapped his arms around himself, fresh tears rolling down his cheeks. "I don't want to think that. But Derek said—"

"*Derek?* What does Derek have to do with this?" Anger flashed through the shame and hurt.

"Nothing. He came to pick me up from the club, and we talked."

"You talked about me with him? Lola and Chris as well, I bet."

"They're my friends. They want to help."

David struggled not to shout. "They don't even know me. Who are they to—"

"You're right! They don't know you. Because every time I ask you to come out with us, you say no. You met them once only because you had no choice. Every other time you have an excuse."

"Work is not an excuse!" *Or maybe it is.* David shook his head. "Money is—"

"Money, money, money! It seems like that's all you think about now! There are other things, David. Yes, of course you need to make money. But you hide behind it."

"Maybe I do. But it's because I don't fit in here. It's so easy for you."

"Easy? *Easy?*" Isaac laughed incredulously. "None of this is easy, David. But I *try*. I learned how to use the internet. I spend time with English people, and sometimes I feel like I have no idea what I'm doing, but if you ask for help? People give it to you. But you hide yourself away in your workshop—except for where Clark's concerned, of course. Then you'll go out."

"Dylan was there too! You said to go! I didn't even want to. And I don't *hide*. I have responsibilities. I need to pay my way. And my family—"

"No. Stop using them as an excuse. Your mother's married to Eli

Helmuth now. She and the girls aren't your responsibility anymore."

It was true, but David shook his head. "I still owe them after the way I ran. And I can't just live here in your brother's house and not pay my way."

"I understand that. I'd feel the same way. I know I'm lucky that Aaron and Jen want me to go to school for a while before I worry about a job. But they want to help *both* of us." Isaac scrubbed a hand over his hair, which he'd cut again recently. It stuck up in short spikes. "I'm not saying you're wrong to work hard. But it shouldn't be some kind of penance! It's like you're not letting yourself enjoy the world because you don't think you deserve it."

"I..." He wanted to argue, but the words wouldn't come.

"I knew you were hiding something. I just never thought..." Isaac wiped his damp cheeks. "I can't get it out of my head—seeing you with him."

David closed his eyes for a moment, trying to calm the chaos in his mind. He swallowed hard. "That wasn't what I was hiding. I swear on the Bible that nothing ever happened with Clark until he kissed me last night. And that nothing else happened in the bathroom."

Isaac sniffed loudly. "What else is there?"

"Sometimes...sometimes I get really upset, and I drink." Sweat prickled his palms as his words hung in the air between them.

"Drink?" Isaac stared blankly. "But you're allowed to."

"I know." David had to drop his gaze. "But sometimes I sneak from the liquor cabinet." He motioned toward the dining room.

Isaac shook his head. "I don't understand."

"Sometimes it's like I can't stop worrying, and I feel like I'm dying."

"What?" Isaac stepped closer, his face pinched in concern. "*Dying?* What do you mean? What do you worry about?"

"Home. My family. Money. Taking care of you. Everything, I guess. When it gets too much I drink, and things go...quiet. It all fades away."

Isaac took this in. "That's what you did when you got up last night, isn't it? I wanted to yell and scream at you. I was lying there waiting, but

I...I don't know. I was scared. If I told you that I saw you, it would make it real. I was afraid of what you'd say."

"I wanted to tell you what happened. But I was afraid too. I drank instead."

"Why didn't you talk to me about this before now?" Isaac asked in a small voice.

"I didn't want to worry you. I want you to be happy. You're doing so well at school. It wasn't fair to burden you."

"*Burden* me?" Isaac's voice rose. "I'm not a child, David. I thought you trusted me the way I trusted you. I thought we trusted *each other*."

"I do trust you. Of course I do!" David grasped Isaac's hand. "Please—"

Isaac tore his hand away. "I can't."

It was like the icy waves of the Pacific crashed over him, and David swallowed hard over acrid bile.

"I want to believe you about Clark, but I keep seeing you with him in my head. I don't know what to think about any of this." Fresh tears shone in his eyes. "I think I need to be alone right now."

Isaac's words were blades. Backing away, David nodded dully. He put one foot in front of the other, and shoved them into his shoes. He shut the door behind him and walked into the city, hoping it would swallow him whole.

CHAPTER  Eighteen

T HE BOTTLE WAS empty.

Sprawled on the love seat, David stared at it in his hand. He'd had the whole thing, but it clearly wasn't enough because he was awake and thinking again. After leaving Isaac, he hadn't made it to the bus stop before the terror consumed him and he'd had to hide between two cars on a steep driveway, on his knees for a long time before his vision had cleared and he could stagger to the corner.

There was something terribly wrong with him. His father had died of a heart attack, and maybe he would too. But the thought had only led to more panic, so he'd forced it out of his mind.

Now his cheeks were tight with dried tears and his eyes puffy and probably red. He sniffed loudly and swiped his sleeve across his nose. It was dark in the garage, with only the light from the bathroom on, and he had no idea what time it was.

He tipped the bottle to his mouth, desperate for another drop, but there was nothing. With a strangled scream that tore at his throat, he threw it against the wall. Distantly, David noticed something, and he blinked at the drops of blood glistening on his hands and forearms.

With shaky fingers, he pulled the shards of glass free, barely feeling more than a pinch. Blood dripped from one of the cuts onto the couch cushion, and when he tried to clean it, he only succeeded in smearing the blood around.

I need to talk to Isaac. I need to explain. I need...

He closed his eyes, trembling. He'd ruined everything. He hadn't wanted to let Isaac down, but he had. The fact that Isaac had seen Clark kiss and touch him made David sick with shame.

Then he was just plain sick, stumbling to the bathroom so he could heave into the toilet. Blood dripped down his wrist as he cupped his palms under the tap to gulp some water. He knew he should go home, but the thought made his empty stomach clench.

David fished his phone out of his pocket and jabbed the button, but it stayed dark. Dead battery again. Guilt washed over him. Was Isaac worried about him? What time was it? Would Aaron and Jen be worried too? *I'm selfish and weak. Just like I've always been.* Or maybe Isaac didn't care that David hadn't come home. After all, he'd said he wanted to be alone. David wouldn't blame Isaac for never wanting to talk to him again.

Enough. Stop feeling sorry for yourself.

When David opened the garage door, he blinked at the sunlight. It looked like morning. He shuffled down to the main street, stretching his neck, which was sore after spending the night hunched on the love seat. He needed a shower and fresh clothes. He needed to talk to Isaac and make things right. But at the thought, panic surged in him. He had to collect himself before he went home.

It was Sunday, although he wasn't sure if it was a church Sunday in Zebulon or not. He'd lost track, and he realized he couldn't remember the last time he'd prayed. The last time he'd been so far from God.

He hadn't thought about where he was walking now, but he found himself outside Flanagan's. Inside was warm and welcoming, and the smell of onions wafted on the air. David plodded to the seat at the far end of the bar. There were several other customers in the booths, but it was a quiet morning. He checked the clock and saw it wasn't noon yet.

"Hey, David." Gary glanced over his shoulder. When he turned to drop a coaster, his smile faded. "You don't look so good, buddy."

David managed to sit without toppling over. "Vodka tonic. Please."

Gary watched him with a sympathetic gaze. "How about you have some water first, okay?" He filled a glass and placed it on the coaster.

"Drink this, and I'll be back in a minute." He clapped a big hand on David's shoulder.

The water was cool and refreshing, and David hadn't realized how thirsty he was. But it wasn't enough. If he wasn't careful, the terrible fear and pain would hit him again. He needed to fill the hollow in his chest before it could. He thought of the words he'd heard on the news. *A preemptive strike.*

"You look a little worse for wear," Gary said.

David blinked. He hadn't heard him return. "I'm fine."

Gary snorted. "Uh-huh." He had a damp cloth in his hand, and a First Aid kit sat on the bar. "Let's get you cleaned up." He took one of David's hands and dabbed at the cuts.

For a big man, Gary was surprisingly gentle as he tended to David's cuts. It felt nice to be cared for, and David didn't have the energy to fight. "I'm sorry," he mumbled.

"Don't be." Gary put a sticky bandage on the worst cut, and patted David's arm. "There you go. All patched. So what happened? Did you get in a fight? Your face looks okay."

"I broke a bottle. Speaking of which, I need a drink."

"Sure, in a minute. Just tell me what happened first." He refilled the water glass.

David automatically drank some more and wiped his mouth. "It was my fault."

"Okay. Did something happen between you and Isaac?"

David was taken aback. "You remember his name?"

"Of course. Same name as my son. Besides, the few times you've been in here you've mentioned him a lot."

"I have?"

Gary smiled. "Yep. You're pretty nuts about him. Just in case you didn't know."

For a moment, David smiled, but then he remembered. "I ruined it. He wants to be alone."

"Alone for good? Or temporarily?"

"I don't know."

Gary raised an eyebrow. "Sounds like you and Isaac have some talking to do. What did you fight about?"

His stomach roiled with the shame of it. David didn't think he could say it out loud. "I…" He shook his head.

"It's okay. Drink some more water. Did I tell you Julie made the dean's list at Stanford? And get a load of this project she did for her biology class. I have pictures." He fished his phone from his pocket.

David tried to focus on the photos, nodding as Gary talked. It was nice to just listen, and he breathed more easily. When Gary went to serve his other customers, David stared at his hands, tracing the edges of the bandage.

"Sorry about that," Gary said as he returned. "How are you doing?"

"Maybe they're right." David hadn't meant to say it out loud.

"Who?" Gary asked.

"I don't know. Everyone. People. They said we were like high school sweethearts. Even though we didn't go to high school. They said we're too young to be together. That we would never last."

"Hmm. *Everyone* said this?"

"Well, no. But some people, and they didn't say it exactly, but that's what they meant. But maybe they're right. Sometimes I feel so lost here. At least in Zebulon I knew all the rules, even if I was breaking them. In the world it's so different."

Gary seemed to ponder this. "It's true that this world can be a confusing place. Now about you and Isaac—what do *you* think? Because opinions are like assholes—we've all got one. Hell, I met Karen in our freshman year of college. We were babies, but I knew she was the one for me. And yeah, we broke up when we were seniors, and folks said we needed to explore and sow our wild oats. But you know what? I was miserable. I dated all the girls who would go out with me, and not one of them could compare to Karen. I begged her to take me back, and we've been together ever since."

David took this in. "You don't think it's bad for me and Isaac to only ever be with each other?"

"Hell no. And anyone who says otherwise is full of it. Do *you* want to date other men?"

David didn't have to think about it. "No."

"Then there's your answer. Who is anyone else to tell you what to do or how to feel?"

"But Isaac's not even nineteen. What if he... Shouldn't he get the chance to explore? Maybe he'll even go to college. I don't want him to be stuck with me. He deserves better than that."

Gary leaned his forearms on the bar. "Did he say he feels stuck with you?"

David played back Isaac's words. "No. But he could barely look at me." He rubbed his face. How had everything gotten so messed up?

"How about some food. Burger and fries sound good?"

"I'm not hungry." His belly clenched just at the thought.

"Humor me and have a few bites. It's on the house. I'll just put in the order. In the meantime..." He refilled David's water glass. "Down the hatch."

David swallowed obediently. "I'm sorry to be a bother. You must have work to do."

Gary swept his arm out. "And as you can see, the place isn't exactly hopping at the moment. The game doesn't start until two. Besides, I have an in with the boss. There's nothing else I need to do but stay right here and talk to my friend. Okay?"

"Am I really your friend?" David blurted. He winced at how pathetic he sounded.

"Of course you are. Hell, not many people will listen to me brag about my kids the way you do. Bartenders are supposed to be the listeners, but with you it goes both ways. I always look forward to seeing you."

He didn't know what to say. "Thank you." *Don't cry. Don't cry.*

"It's a big transition moving away from a place so different and coming to the city. It's a lot for anyone to handle, and it's okay if you're overwhelmed. It's okay to need help, David. You don't have to have all the answers."

As Gary brought menus to new customers, David let the words sink in. He thought of sitting on June's steps while she called for an ambulance, already knowing his life had changed. Knowing he was the only one left to take care of his family. Knowing he could never let them see who he really was. Knowing he could never *be* who he really was.

Yet he was here, thanks to Isaac. When Gary returned, David started talking. "I should have told him what I was thinking. I was afraid that if he knew how scared I am..." David peered deep inside the place he'd been trying to shut away. "He's fitting in so well, and I was afraid he'd leave me behind."

The words hung in the air with the low drone of the TV and the clatter of knives and forks at a table. Cars rumbled on the street as the door to Flanagan's opened and closed.

"A lot of people would feel that way, David. You want to be on the same page, and sometimes people get ahead or fall behind without meaning to. But it's still the same book."

Somehow David felt lighter, as if the words had been stuck inside him. "I need to talk to him."

"I think you're right."

A bell rang, and Gary disappeared. Staring straight ahead, David glimpsed himself in the mirror beyond the bottles. His eyes were bloodshot, his face pale and drawn, and his hair stood up. He probably smelled.

"Here you go. Get some lunch in you." Gary put down the burger and fries. "Ketchup?"

David nodded, breathing in the grease. Now that it was in front of him he was starving. He took a big bite of his burger.

"How is it?" Gary refilled the glass of water and plopped in a few more ice cubes with a little scoop.

"Good," he mumbled through his mouthful. For a minute, he just ate. Then he wiped his mouth with a napkin. "Thank you for everything."

"You still want that drink?"

David considered it before smiling. "No. I don't need it. I can do this."

Gary grinned. "Good answer. You're going to be just fine."

For the first time in too long, David believed it.

THE HOUSE WAS still. David closed the door behind him and toed off his sneakers. He may have looked awful, but he felt clear, like a fog had burned off in his mind the way it did in the city on summer days.

The not-so-little part of him that had been hoping Isaac would be waiting deflated. *What did I expect?* He gave his head a shake. Enough of feeling sorry for himself. It was time to talk to Isaac and fix things. Resolute, he turned and promptly knocked over the umbrella stand, sending it crashing to the tiles as umbrellas rolled toward the stairs. He righted the canister with a sigh. At least it wasn't broken.

"Clark?" Jen called distantly.

David jumped, and then cleared his throat. "It's David," he shouted up the stairs. He hoped he hadn't woken her with his clumsiness. He wondered why she was expecting Clark, and grimaced, hoping that if Clark was visiting it wouldn't make things with Isaac worse.

After a moment of silence, he could hear the thumping of her steps. When she rounded the corner on the lower flight of stairs, he was surprised to see she wasn't wearing her slippers. Her bare feet smacked on the wood, her bathrobe and long curls flying behind her. She launched at him when she reached the bottom.

"David! Thank God." She gripped him in a breathless hug.

He stood motionless for a moment, arms at his side, before tentatively hugging her back. It felt so good to be held, and he closed his eyes, stooping to drop his forehead on her shoulder.

She rubbed his back. "We were so worried. Are you okay?"

David lifted his head and stepped away. "I'm sorry. I didn't mean to make you worry." *Is Isaac worried too?*

"You didn't come home last night!" She held David's arms tightly and gave him a shake. "Why didn't you answer your phone?"

"The battery ran out." He winced. "I'm sorry. It was selfish to be gone all night without calling."

"Yeah, it was. Clark and Dylan and a bunch of their friends are out looking for you right now. Clark called a little while ago and said he found blood and broken glass at the workshop. The door was wide open. I've been checking all the ERs, and I was going to call the police soon."

Had he not locked the door? "I just cut myself. I'm fine." The thought that so many people were concerned warmed him despite his guilt.

"We've been worried sick. And then with everything else..." She rubbed her face. "Oh, David. When it rains, it pours. Isaac..."

A horrible tendril of dread spread through him into every pore. "What about Isaac? Is he all right?" It felt as though his heart was in a vise.

"He is, but David...he went back to Zebulon."

The words were like a physical blow, and his knees almost gave out. "No. He couldn't...he wouldn't. Not after everything." The thought of Isaac back home tore into him. David had only been gone a night. It wasn't possible.

Jen gripped his shoulders. "Breathe. It's okay. It's not what you think. Come on, sit down." She maneuvered him to the bottom of the stairs and knelt in front of him, her hands resting on his knees. "A nurse called late yesterday afternoon from the hospital near Zebulon. It's Nathan. He's sick."

David tried to understand what she was saying. "Nathan? Isaac's brother?"

"Yes. He has something called nasopharyngeal cancer."

He stared at her, his mind spinning like a children's wooden top. *This isn't happening. I'm going to wake up, and Isaac will be here, and this will all have been a terrible nightmare.* "Cancer?"

"Yes." Jen spoke calmly. "Cancer cells have grown in the nasal cavity and in his throat. He hadn't been to a doctor in years, and it was metastatic. It's rare, but when this type of cancer goes undetected, it can spread to the lymph nodes, and sometimes into the lungs and other organs. Into the bones."

He took this in. "How did they find out?"

"Nathan collapsed on his way home from school last week."

"Last week?" They hadn't even known. Why hadn't Anna called?

"He's stable, which is good. But he's on HDC—sorry, high-dose chemotherapy—and it's going to take a toll. The doctors don't think he'll make it without stem cell transplantation. Bone marrow."

This isn't happening. "Stem cell? Bone marrow?"

Jen gestured with her hands. "Basically they're cells that can grow into different other kinds of cells. They can help sick people get better. The chemotherapy is going to leave Nathan very, very weak. With the cancer this advanced, they have to be aggressive. They need to know if there's a matching donor in his family."

"You mean Isaac and Aaron's cells might match Nathan's?"

Jen squeezed his knees. "Exactly. I'll explain it more later."

"They went back to Zebulon already?"

"Isaac was beside himself. He left you a dozen messages and texts, but he and Aaron had to get to the airport or they'd miss the last flight. Their parents wouldn't come on the phone, and you can imagine how helpless Isaac and Aaron felt being so far away. They'll get tested there to see if their cells are a match. It's good that Nathan has so many siblings. Increases his chances."

"His chances," David repeated.

She brushed a hand over David's head. "You look like hell. I know you and Isaac had a fight, but is there anything else going on?"

No point in hiding it. "He thinks that Clark and I…that we…"

"That you what?" She eyed him sharply. "What happened?"

"When we were at that dance club place, Clark kissed me and tried to…" David waved his hand around awkwardly.

Jen pressed her lips together in a grim line, her nostrils flaring. "I'm going to kill him. Are you okay? How far over the line did he go? He's my best friend, but sometimes he's an idiot."

"I'm fine. He stopped when I told him to, and he came to apologize yesterday morning. He felt really bad."

"He'd better!"

"He really does. The thing is…Isaac came to the club to surprise me. He saw us, and I don't think he believed me when I told him I was trying to get away from Clark. That I didn't want to kiss him."

She swore under her breath. "I'm sorry that happened."

"It's not your fault."

"It's not yours either. Are you sure you're okay?"

The assurance was on his lips, but as she peered at him with so much warmth and concern, the truth tumbled out before he could stop it. "There's something wrong with me."

Jen frowned. "Okay. Wrong in what way?"

"Sometimes I get… It feels like I'm dying. I can't breathe, and it's like I'm having a heart attack. It passes after a little while, but I think there's something wrong."

"Any other symptoms? What about vision problems? Have you ever lost consciousness?"

As Jen rattled off a list of questions, David nodded or shook his head. She told him to stay where he was, and returned with the medical device she put in her ears to listen to heartbeats. A something-scope, he thought it was called. He lifted his shirt. The metal was cold against his chest, and he breathed in and out as she told him to. She put it against his back and listened there too before hanging the scope around her neck.

"Everything sounds just fine. I think you're experiencing panic attacks. It happens to more people than you might think, and for any number of reasons."

"You mean…I'm not dying? Or crazy?"

She smiled softly. "Not even a little, but we'll schedule some tests at the hospital just to be on the safe side."

"But that'll cost money, won't it?"

"Don't worry about that; I'll pull some strings. But we do need to get you and Isaac set up with insurance now that we've got your birth certificates." She sighed. "David, you should have said something."

"I know. I…I was ashamed. Especially because… Sometimes I've been drinking. It seems to help when I have the attacks."

"Oh, honey." Jen rubbed her face. "I should have realized you were self-medicating. I'm sorry I wasn't paying more attention."

"But you don't have anything to be sorry for."

"Sure I do. When someone you care about has a problem, sometimes they need it to be noticed. I know you feel like you're imposing here, and that we're Isaac's family and not yours. But we care about you very much. You're not alone. I want you to really know that. No matter what you're feeling you can talk about it."

He swallowed thickly. "Thank you. For everything. I don't deserve it. You've—"

"Hey." She took hold of his arms. "You *do* deserve it. So stop that talk, because I won't listen to it. You and Isaac had what we call a breakdown in communication. It happens to the best of us, believe me. Making a relationship work is hard, no matter how old you are, or where you're from. But you two love each other."

David nodded. "I love him more than anything. Have you talked to him today?"

"Not yet. I didn't call him or Aaron this morning when I realized you hadn't come home. I didn't want to worry them if it was nothing. They took a redeye last night, and it's a few hours to drive to Zebulon. They should be there now. I'll check in with Aaron."

The thought of Nathan being terribly sick and of Isaac being in

Zebulon made David ache. "I need to get back. He needs me. I have to be there."

"Are you sure you can handle it?"

"Yes." He inhaled deeply. He could handle it. He *would* handle it.

She stood and put her hands on her hips. "Okay. Next step is getting flights booked. We should be able to get you on a redeye tonight. Good thing your passports came through."

"What about you?"

"I need to work, and it'll probably take a few days before I can clear a leave with my chief." She blew out a long breath, her cheeks puffing. "Aaron doesn't even know if his parents will talk to him, but he has to try. It'll probably make it worse if I'm there, but I don't care if they don't like me. Aaron needs me." She smiled ruefully. "That's not true, by the way. I totally care if they like me."

"You're one of the best people I've ever met."

Her smile grew warm. "Right back at you." She held out her hands and pulled him to his feet, pressing a kiss to his cheek. "You go shower and pack, and I'll check flights."

Flush with purpose, David took the stairs two at a time. He almost didn't notice the piece of paper folded on his pillow. With trembling hands, he opened it, his pulse galloping.

David, you're not answering when I call. I wish you were here! Nathan is sick. I don't really understand it, but it sounds very bad, and I'm afraid that if I don't go right now he'll die before I see him again. They won't let him talk to me on the phone. I don't know what else to do.

Aaron's coming with me. I know I said a lot of things, and that we still need to talk. I love you. I hope you know that.

He carefully folded the letter and focused on the penknife sitting on the side table. David picked it up and ran his fingers over the worn handle, imagining he could feel the warmth of Isaac's touch there.

June's purple suitcase was open by the closet, and with trembling hands he looked. Isaac had taken his plain clothes, but David's were still crumpled inside. As he smoothed out the heavy fabric of his shirt, a lump rose in his throat.

He imagined he could smell the hay and horses in the barn. The sawdust and sweat. Echoes of the life he'd lived. He rubbed the heavy fabric against his cheek. For all his confusion here in the world, there was one certainty that consumed him now, growing steadier with each heartbeat.

Zebulon would never be his home again. But he was going back, and he wasn't leaving without his Isaac.

Join Isaac and David as they fight for their happy ending!

"DO I LOOK okay?"

As Isaac glanced at Aaron, he stepped in a pile of slush that soaked straight through his sneaker. It was the end of April, but the vestiges of winter still clung to northern Minnesota, and melting snowbanks dotted the hospital parking lot. Aaron stopped and smoothed a hand down his jacket. It was a nice raincoat—the color of red wine, fitted with buttons on the front—but they both knew it didn't matter.

Still, Isaac nodded. "You look great."

Aaron tried to smile. "Thanks." He pushed back a lock of blond hair that had crept over his forehead, and pressed a button to lock the doors on the sedan he'd rented at the airport.

The truth was that Aaron could be wearing his fanciest suit, but the only way to please their parents was if he donned plain clothes again—clothes that followed the rules of the *Ordnung* down to the very last detail. Isaac wasn't wearing Amish clothes either, and he realized it would be the first time his parents would see him in English jeans and a hoodie. His green raincoat was thin, and he shivered, wishing he had gloves.

Maybe he should have changed into his Amish clothes after all. Mother and Father would hate to see him like this, but he'd wanted to…what? Make a statement, he supposed. But what was he really saying? Was it brave to spit in his parents' faces and turn his back on his heritage? Or cruel?

Isaac tugged at his sleeves and scuffed his rubber toe across the wet concrete. Driving from Minneapolis to June's farm near Zebulon had taken longer than he'd expected, and it would be dark soon. If he asked Aaron to go back to June's now so he could change, the nurses might not even let him see Nathan by the time they returned.

They stood by the car, their breath clouding the damp, wintry air, and stared at the gray and beige concrete block that was the hospital. The glass doors of the emergency room split open as a nurse in blue scrubs came out. She lit a cigarette as she walked away from the door, joining a man in a wheelchair with a metal pole holding a plastic bag towering over him. The nurse exhaled a cloud of smoke and rubbed her arms.

"I guess we should go inside." Aaron stared at the doors with hunched shoulders.

"Yeah."

Neither of them moved. They'd been so desperate to get to Minnesota after the nurse had called. Mother and Father refused to come on the line, and she could only tell them so much. Nathan had cancer. He probably needed some kind of transplant. Could they be tested?

Now, standing in the slushy parking lot of the hospital under a gray slate sky, Isaac felt just as far away as he had in San Francisco. *Nathan has cancer.* The terror that his brother would die before Isaac could see him again had driven him here as though he were a horse kicked by a merciless rider. Not being able to speak to Nathan or their parents had been torture.

Yet now that he and Aaron had arrived, Isaac's stomach churned. A vision of blood soaking into the fresh white snow filled his mind, and David's voice echoed.

"I must repent or my mother will die. Everyone I love will pay for my sins. You need to stay far away from me."

Isaac swallowed hard over a swell of emotion. They'd come so far together, but somehow not far enough. David hadn't answered his calls and texts about Nathan. Why hadn't he? The ache to have David by his side burned hollowly in Isaac's chest. He itched to clutch David's hand and feel his warm, solid strength.

"David's coming tomorrow."

Isaac blinked at his brother, his pulse jumping. *Was I talking out loud?* "What?"

Aaron held up his phone. "Jen's taking him to the airport first thing. The redeye was booked, but he'll be in Minneapolis by early afternoon."

The surge of sweet relief was tempered by dark tendrils of disappointment and hurt. He wished he could scrub his brain and erase the image of David in that place. The image of Clark touching him. *Kissing* him. Kissing *his* David! Isaac's mind whirled uselessly. "Oh."

Aaron's eyebrows shot up. "*Oh*? That's it? Okay, tell me what happened. I know you don't want to, but before we go in there and deal with all...*that*, we need to deal with this. Spill it. What did you guys fight about?"

Sighing, Isaac jammed his hands in his coat pockets. His face flushed, and he wasn't sure if it was with anger or embarrassment. "He kissed someone else," Isaac mumbled. He hated even saying the ugly words.

"*What?*" Aaron's jaw opened and closed. "Are you serious? Of course you're serious—forget I said that. What happened?"

Isaac kept his gaze on a scattering of rock salt. "I saw them kissing at the dance club. David didn't think I'd be there, but I got a fake ID. I was going to surprise him." He laughed hollowly. "Didn't turn out how I expected."

"I... Wow. I really can't believe this. It doesn't seem like David at all. He's so in love with you. I mean, when he looks at you little cartoon hearts spring out of his eyes."

"Really? You think so?" Isaac blinked rapidly to fight impending tears, and breathed carefully. "Then why? I guess Clark has something I don't," he muttered.

"*Clark?*" Isaac nodded, and Aaron pressed his lips together. "I can't believe this. I'm going to kill him. Both of them! What did David say?"

"He said Clark kissed him like I saw, and that he tried to get away from him, but Clark followed. I saw them go into the bathroom together. David says nothing happened." Isaac inhaled through the wave of nausea. "But I know what people do in there."

Aaron's gaze narrowed. "Wait—David says nothing really happened?"

"I want to believe him, but...I can't get it out of my head, seeing them together. It makes me so angry and...sick. Sick to my stomach. I should have known. I heard Clark say that he was going to get David into bed the first night we met him."

Jaw clenched, Aaron shook his head. "Well, that I can certainly believe. I love Clark, but he can be a selfish ass sometimes. But David? I don't know. He's never struck me as a liar, Isaac."

"But we lied to our families and everyone we knew for months. We're *still* lying to them." He jabbed his finger toward the hospital. "I'm going to go in there and *lie*. Because it's bad enough I betrayed God and my community by leaving. But if they found out who I really am? It would be over for good. No visiting. No letters. Nothing."

Aaron sighed. "Isaac, when was the last time you got a letter? The only way they'll ever let you back in their lives is if you repent your evil, worldly ways, come home, and join the church. Whether or not they know you're gay won't really matter in the end. Yes, you're right—if they find out, they'll turn away from you. Right now you're not shunned like I am, but you'll never have a real relationship with them. Not unless you go back and do everything they want. Give up everything you have. Everything you *are*."

It was all true, but Isaac still shook his head. "I can't tell them the truth. They can't ever know."

"I'm not suggesting you should march in there and come out." Aaron took Isaac's shoulder gently. "Just that you should think about how far you're willing to go to keep that shred of hope alive. How much of yourself you're willing to give up, and for what? Maybe a letter or two a year if you're lucky?"

"It's better than nothing," Isaac whispered.

Aaron smiled sadly. "Maybe. And yes, you're right that you and David have lied about who you are, and the truth of your relationship. But don't hold that against him now. It's not fair. Hear him out. Has he ever lied to you before?"

"No. I don't know. I don't think so. How am I supposed to know?" That was what dug into him the most with sharp, angry edges—that he wasn't sure of anything now. Had David lied to him in the past? Isaac's heart said no, but maybe he was fooling himself?

"I know you're hurt and angry, and you have every right to be. Just don't make any big decisions right now. Whatever happens in the end, I support you, but don't give up on your relationship with David without really talking with him. He's a good person. You both are. You can work through this. I know you can."

He nodded. Part of him wanted to tell Aaron that David had apparently been lying about drinking as well, but the words wouldn't come. He didn't have a clue what to think about that. About any of it. He wanted so desperately to believe David had never wanted anything to happen with Clark, but he didn't want to be...what was the word Chris had used? *A chump.* It was as though Isaac's feelings were a big pot of stew inside him, stirring and stirring and stirring. It wouldn't be long until it all overflowed.

In his pocket, his phone buzzed. Heart in his throat, Isaac pulled it out and read the words on the screen.

I will be there soon. I love you.

He exhaled shakily, the jagged edge of his panic dulling as warmth flowed through him. As hurt as he was, he knew David truly did love him. If that made him a chump, so be it. There was so much he wanted to say, but it would have to wait until they were together.

"I guess we really should get in there." Aaron blew out a long breath. "It's easy to give you advice, but not so easy to take it myself. I know I shouldn't get my hopes up. They might not even look at me, let alone talk to me. God, it's been so long. Almost ten years now. Hard to believe, isn't it? Seeing them again, it's...terrifying. But exciting too."

Isaac squeezed Aaron's arm. "I'm here. We'll do it together."

On the other side of the lot, a large delivery truck rumbled away, revealing a horse and covered buggy hitched to a light post. Isaac's heart skipped a beat as he recognized old Roy right away. He thought of dear Silver, and hoped he'd see her again soon. Looking at the buggy, it hit home—Mother and Father were really inside, and so was Nathan. His little brother was in there, lying in a bed not knowing if he'd live or die, and here Isaac was worrying about himself.

Without another word, they hurried across the lot, almost in a run by the time the glass doors *swooshed* open to admit them to whatever might wait inside...

Keep reading *A Way Home*

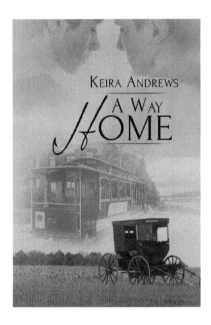

Will returning to their Amish roots renew their faith in each other?

Isaac and David never thought they'd go back to the Amish world. But when Isaac's younger brother is stricken with cancer, they don't hesitate to return. Their relationship is on the rocks after insecurity and fear drove a wedge between them in San Francisco, and David is determined to make things right. Yet if they thought navigating "English" life was confusing, being back in Zebulon is even more complicated.

Their families are desperate to bring them back into the fold, and pressure from the community builds. Isaac and David yearn for a future together, but each day it becomes harder to hide the truth about who they really are. They're caught between two worlds, and if they're not careful it could tear them further apart.

Can Isaac and David make their way back to each other—and find a place to call home?

This gay romance is the third chapter in a series of forbidden Amish love from Keira Andrews. It features explicit sex, graphic language, family drama, and of course a happy ending.

Read now!

Join the free gay romance newsletter!

My (mostly) monthly newsletter will keep you up to date on my latest releases and news from the world of LGBTQ romance. You'll also get access to exclusive giveaways, free reads, and much more. Join the mailing list today and you're automatically entered into my monthly giveaway. Go here to sign up: subscribepage.com/KAnewsletter

Here's where you can find me online:
Website
www.keiraandrews.com
Facebook
facebook.com/keira.andrews.author
Facebook Reader Group
bit.ly/2gpTQpc
Instagram
instagram.com/keiraandrewsauthor
Goodreads
bit.ly/2k7kMj0
Amazon Author Page
amzn.to/2jWUfCL
Twitter
twitter.com/keiraandrews
BookBub
bookbub.com/authors/keira-andrews

About the Author

After writing for years yet never really finding the right inspiration, Keira discovered her voice in gay romance, which has become a passion. She writes contemporary, historical, paranormal, and fantasy fiction, and—although she loves delicious angst along the way—Keira firmly believes in happy endings. For as Oscar Wilde once said, "The good ended happily, and the bad unhappily. That is what fiction means."

Made in the USA
Middletown, DE
18 January 2021